EXTENSION
SERVICES

DANGEROUS PRACTICE

A Selection of Recent Titles by Clare Curzon

ALL UNWARY
CLOSE QUARTERS
COLD HANDS*
THE COLOUR OF BLOOD*
DON'T LEAVE ME*
GUILTY KNOWLEDGE
NICE PEOPLE
PAST MISCHIEF

* available from Severn House

DANGEROUS PRACTICE

Clare Curzon

This first world edition published in Great Britain 2002 by
SEVERN HOUSE PUBLISHERS LTD of
9–15 High Street, Sutton, Surrey SM1 1DF.
This first world edition published in the USA 2002 by
SEVERN HOUSE PUBLISHERS INC of
595 Madison Avenue, New York, N.Y. 10022.

British Library Cataloguing in Publication Data

Curzon, Clare
  Dangerous practice
  1. Detective and mystery stories
  I. Title
  823.9′14 [F]

ISBN 0-7278-5815-7

Typeset by Palimpsest Book Production Ltd.,
Polmont, Stirlingshire, Scotland.
Printed and bound in Great Britain by
MPG Books Ltd., Bodmin, Cornwall.

One

September, 1921

Anyone with a history like mine might not consider re-marriage a safe option, but I had no doubts at all. The last thing I expected was any sinister outcome.

It was not even leap year, so I hadn't that excuse; but before I leapt I'd done what Clive required of me: I'd set out to discover exactly who I was. After Julian's attempt on my life,* and the more recent clash with my natural mother, my brief visit to Ireland had completed the quest. With a clearer idea of myself and of what we could expect of each other, I felt ready when Clive inspected me at arms' length and asked, 'So, Lucy, what next?'

I smiled into his squirrel-bright eyes. 'Perhaps you would ask me to marry you?'

'If you're quite certain.'

That was the sum of our discussion, because each had such a patent need for the other. So neither actually asked, and neither formally said yes.

It was pointless to wait. The bishop was consulted, my family informed, strings were pulled. We were to be married within three weeks, in the family chapel at Stakerleys, before Papa sailed for India with David, Prince of Wales. I spent the intervening days consulting house agents and, when a charming house became available in Swan Walk, Chelsea, put its purchase in the hands of our London solicitor.

Familiarising myself with my future husband's occupation – half academic, half clinical – I attended some extramural lectures at University College in Bloomsbury and visited the

---

* *The Colour of Blood*

1

experimental centre where Clive was the capital's youngest practitioner in psychotherapy. There I met his junior partner, Dr Stanley Atkinson, some eight or nine years his senior but only lately transferred from general medicine. He seemed quiet and kindly, a little hesitant, reclusive behind thick-pebbled lenses and a neatly trimmed, greying beard. Besides Matron, whom I didn't meet at that time, there were just four nurses and a stocky, surly-looking porter called Jefferson, an ex-Artillery gunner whose face was deeply scarred by shrapnel from brow to opposite jaw, with an empty eye-socket filled by an unconvincing glass ball.

Clive was to give the third lecture of the university's present extramural series, and I attended, eager to discover a further facet of the man I loved. His introduction was informal and unexpected.

'Picture, if you will, a chessboard.' His hands flew out to describe a flat, square surface.

From my seventh-row seat in the steeply stepped lecture theatre I recognised the jaunty mischief in his animated face. The tautness of the private moments before had dissolved; he was at home with his subject and his audience.

'Observe its pieces on the board, in their appointed starting places.'

He seemed to pick on a single face among his listeners and raised a warning finger. 'But wait. Already I see a look of protest above – can it be? – a clerical collar.'

I heard random titters. *Oh no, Clive. Not cheap laughs at the Church. Not treachery to your good guardian and your formative years spent in the bishop's palace.*

'It is right to question my equating a human creature with a carved piece on a chequered game-board. But consider: static at one point of time, yet the chessman is capable of movement to any relevant position. And relevance is defined by the piece's predetermined function.

'So am I claiming that we humans are equally restricted? To some extent we are, because our genes set basic limits on our powers before ever society moulds our behaviour; on which in turn we may superimpose the exercise of an individual will. As we develop and learn, specific attitudes become typical for each of us. We establish habits of action, habits of mind,

2

with which we feel secure. These govern the relevant moves we make on the chessboard of life.'

The lecture continued, absorbing to me as to the other non-specialists who made up the main part of the audience, because he constantly had us look in one direction and then consider the opposite view. Accustomed to the quiet of my studio, uninterrupted by outside concerns, I felt challenged now by words instead of by form and colour. I followed the vertigo of the chessboard as he described it balanced precariously on a light table with one overhanging corner jarred by the passing of a large dog. Some pieces fell, to roll helplessly; others were jolted from their own square on to one of its opposing colour and so could proceed no further.

We were hauled back to consider the human parallel. For many of us, Clive said, our major cataclysm had been the Great War with its appalling loss of life and suffering, both physical and mental. But the individual's personal balance could equally be overthrown by less earth-shaking events such as occurred in everyday life, at work, or even within the apparent security of the closest family.

Until now our attitude in viewing the mentally injured had too often been one of repugnance. We had turned away, ashamed for them, murmuring hollow words about 'a stiff upper lip' and 'not letting the side down'. We had failed to admit that we all had different levels of resistance to pain and to the expectation of disaster. Our fabric was not universally robust, nor were experiences the same for all. Like the chessmen, some of us were unmoved when the blow struck, some were jolted into an alien situation, some fell.

Confronting such an aftermath of battle, actual or figurative, we must preserve an open mind, accepting mental illnesses as equally worthy of our sympathetic care with those of the body – and no more repugnant. Those unfortunates who suffered were not to be shut away but drawn out. We must listen and watch and question until we came to some understanding of what caused the wound under the scarring. Only then could we be of any help.

'Presented with mental illness we have no aetiology to define its cause. There are no physical tests as for urine

3

or blood, so our systems of classification depend on a collection of symptoms and our own fallible grasp of semantics . . .'

So the lecture wound on, leading inevitably to the name of Sigmund Freud. At this point an undercurrent of excitement ran through Clive's listeners like a wind through a cornfield. Would he declare himself positively for psychoanalysis or for one of the new breakaway schools? He never satisfied us on this, stating the case for recognised systems as differing but not necessarily exclusive.

This first presentation of anonymous case studies from his clinical work promised to have a good following. He won a standing ovation, and why not? It was precisely what the lecture's title promised: 'An Introduction to the Understanding and Treatment of Mental Disturbance in the 1920s'. I had sat through a number of extramural lectures in this theatre but none so plain-spoken and free from polysyllabic gobbledegook. Doubtless later in the course I should be finding myself tangled in technicalities.

In the atrium afterwards I came on Clive surrounded by a group from the audience. Not all were congratulating him. A distinguished silver-haired gentleman in immaculate evening dress stood tapping his gloves against a thumbnail as he delivered his patronising verdict:

'Nothing quite new there, of course. One hears much the same enthusiasm from several younger faculty members who are dazzled by this "psychiatry" business. It may be a current vogue in Austrian-Jewish society and in North America, but it is not for us more stable-minded British, I assure you.' One couldn't miss the quotation marks he applied to the despised word.

'Not such a young science in itself, sir,' Clive replied, not at all put out. 'Since before Plato the subject of the mind has exercised the mind.'

The great man raised a superior eyebrow. 'A science? At very best a pseudo-science. At worst, dangerous mysticism.' He consulted a gold half-hunter from an inner pocket and declared he must be off to inspect the wards at St Thomas's. Then he went his impressive way with a vee of followers trailing behind like ducklings after their mother. This was

4

Professor Sir Digby Parker-Ellington, consultant surgeon and scourge of the university's Senior Common Room.

'Well, how's that for a stuffed shirt?' demanded a wizened monkey-face appearing beyond Clive's elbow. 'And by "stable-minded" does he imply our national passion is confined to horses?'

I looked down to see why the man was bent over and discovered he was undersized, little more than four and a half feet tall, yet regularly formed. Clive hadn't mentioned any pygmy friend, but of course he would never have referred to anyone in that way.

'Poor old Park Railings,' the small man went on. 'There's nothing gives him such a lift as putting others down. He lives in fear we'll find a way to make organ-invasion obsolete.'

Clive turned and seized my hand. 'Lucy, may I present my good friend and our future best man, Jeremy Owen. Jerry, this angel is my fiancée, Lucy Sedgwick.'

'So happy to meet you at last, Miss Sedgwick,' he said. His voice had a Welsh lilt, and the palm of the hand that took mine was rough as though from hard work. The name was familiar.

'I've heard a lot about you,' I said truthfully, 'and all of it most complimentary.'

I knew that every wedding produces at least one organis-ational hiccup. Here, it seemed, was to be mine, because it was understood that my half-brother Edwin should support Clive on the day. However, this was not a convenient moment to question any change.

Perhaps, I thought wryly, it was fortunate to have only the best man's identity in doubt. Last time, appallingly, I had chosen the wrong groom.

I looked again at Jeremy Owen and pictured him in my handsome half-brother's place. 'We're dining with my guard-ian,' Clive was explaining, 'if ever we find him in this crush.' Then I recognised the white thatch and eyebrows of the bishop weaving towards us among the other heads.

He kissed my cheek and we moved off, with Jeremy close behind, clearly included by previous invitation. Crushed together in a taxi, Bishop Malcolm leaned forward to tap Clive's knee as he perched opposite on one of the pull-down seats. 'Good sermon, my boy.' His eyes were twinkling with humour and I realised then how alike the two were.

I considered my fiancé, compact of figure, with sun-tanned face, curly brown hair and merry eyes. There was no visible way in which Clive resembled his dead father, the stooped beanpole of a travelling tailor who used to visit us in my childhood. I remembered how I'd shrunk from his touch, seeing his wicked shears as a mechanical extension of the long, angular fingers. I had behaved abominably at my fittings, trying the man to the limits of his considerable patience.

That was perhaps one trait that Clive actually had inherited; and God knew, he'd need all that tolerance with me, once the knot was tied.

Our cab arrived at Pall Mall and we clambered out at the doors of the bishop's club. As his goddaughter, I'd accompanied him there before, but now, as the only lady with three gentlemen, I found perverse amusement in the glances of disapproval shot from above certain half-spectacles as we were ushered through to a zone where entertaining females was less taboo. My passing was the signal for a crackling of raised newspapers and the occasional muted *hrrrmp*.

Dinner was delightful – less the meal itself than the sprightly conversation. I hoped fervently that when we were married Clive would continue to talk with me at this level. That other time, with Julian, we had seemed never to hold a proper discussion but fought verbally, he to dominate and I to rebel. Now this trio, so disparate, stimulated each other good-humouredly to a sort of tennis-match dialogue, with myself as a less able partner – or even the dividing net. When the ball flew too high over my head I was reduced to private musing.

Jeremy Owen, I'd noticed, had addressed me as Miss Sedgwick. Was that diplomacy, or was he truly ignorant of my scandalous past? Naturally I'd preferred to use my maiden name since discovering that Julian had married me bigamously, and in any case, who would care to stay linked to an infamous criminal? Forget it – that was all past. But *done with*? I felt a little inner shiver. There was still that old cause-and-effect business. The most that I could hope for was to carry on *pretending* it was all wiped away. Which might make my life a distortion.

Hadn't Clive said we should have full knowledge of the wound below the scars? Such probing sounded painful. Dear God! it struck me then: was Clive accepting me as more than a bride? – as an intriguing case study as well? Did he see me as one of his fallen chessmen?

My godfather laid a hand on mine as I crumbled bread on my side plate. 'Lucy, convention demands I offer a penny for your thoughts, although I'm sure they'll prove of greater value.'

'I'm sorry, Bishop. My mind was back in Clive's lecture.' I searched desperately for a quotable topic. 'I felt he was once on the brink of condemning the War Office for its policy of shooting deserters.'

'That is bound to follow, as something of a bombshell.'

'To raise the ire of the choleric colonels,' Owen said with glee.

'I'm not political. I'd rather provoke discussion than anger,' Clive claimed. 'What right has anyone to take the life of a man because he obeys the natural instinct of flight when faced with danger?' All humour was gone from his eyes. 'These men were destroyed in action as surely as those cut down in acts of heroism. My own short service at sea as naval surgeon taught me a lot about fear. Now my present care is for unfortunates who survived while damaged, whether they lost limbs or their reason.'

'But you will have a real fight on your hands if you ever hope to mend public shame concerning those who deserted, leaving their comrades to be slaughtered,' the bishop said feelingly. 'We can only pray that a more charitable attitude will eventually prevail.'

'War itself is a madness,' I said. 'How can you expect an enlightened public conscience only three years after the Armistice?'

'Perhaps,' said my godfather, 'the new League of Nations will have some stabilising effect on Europe, to cool the hotheads. It has been too much a bully's world until now. And one hopes that the women's vote will ultimately serve to moderate tempers, at least in our House of Commons.'

'The *mature women*'s vote,' I reminded him. 'When will our male legislators see a female as anything but a brain-less flapper until magic transformation at the age of thirty?

7

While men, with their superior intellects, get the franchise at twenty-one!'

Jeremy Owen laughed. 'You must be content that men are at least able to select women to be Members of the House, although I hardly think that packing the Commons with suffragettes will set the world to rights. We are all fallible, even the ladies.'

'Don't you really mean "especially the ladies"?' the bishop enquired wickedly. 'I've heard you maintain they'll merely do as their husbands say, and so double the mistakes of before.'

'Well, that's my experience of the Valleys,' said the Welshman, colouring. He turned on me abruptly. 'How about you, Miss Sedgwick? When eventually enfranchised, how are you likely to vote?'

'Secretly,' I said in protest. 'By one's legal right.'

The other two laughed, but the small man looked put out and threw the argument back to an earlier slant. 'War,' he said dogmatically, 'is a universal human function – an inescapable fact of life. We all war with someone in much that we say and do – men and women alike in this. And across the sexes. In fact I'd say that conflict between man and woman is one of the most natural and deadliest kinds of warfare known.'

'Thank you,' I said sharply, 'for this encouragement to the married state. I was hoping for something better this time round.' Which slightly embarrassed everyone, myself included, when my godfather caught my eye and slowly shook his head.

We hadn't hit it off, this little man and I, which shouldn't have troubled me; but it was early days for us both to have shown how exposed we were to each other's taunts.

Clive's cab dropped me off at the Sedgwick town house in Belgravia, but as Jeremy was still with us I had no opportunity to ask why arrangements for the wedding had been altered. No doubt my brother would be able to fill in the details himself, but I found he was not at home, and Chilvers could only say that he had been suddenly called away.

'He's not indisposed?' I asked anxiously.

'No, miss. There was a telephone call from her ladyship, and soon after that Mr Edwin ordered a cab for one thirty. He seemed in some haste.' The butler's prim little mouth puckered with disapproval. 'He insisted on packing a bag for himself.' Chilvers was not at all happy with the self-sufficient ways of the younger generation.

'Only one bag?'

'Yes, Miss Lucy. A small handgrip.'

So it appeared that he'd not be gone for long. There was yet hope that he'd return in time to serve as best man, since the wedding was now only two days off. It was strange, though, that he had left no message for me – unless Clive had been meant to deliver one verbally and, preoccupied with his lecture, had forgotten to pass it on. Yet he had thought to warn me that his little Welsh friend was to stand in for Edwin.

Perhaps to dwell on the substitution would have seemed slighting to the little man. Jeremy Owen would certainly prefer to see himself as a first choice, even at such short notice. So rather than bruise his friend's self-regard my fiancé had chosen to leave me in suspense without explanation. Surely a trifle cavalier, even though I had claimed to be indifferent about the final arrangements, provided that the entire family supported me in the Stakerleys chapel.

Edwin's absence irked me less than the fear that some family disaster had called him away. I immediately rang Mama and enquired generally if all was well at home. She was delighted to hear me and answered all my questions. Edwin was not there. They expected him back tonight. Yes, everyone was well, including my darling baby. Grandpapa, in his wheelchair, was at present in the orchard to oversee the fruit-picking. Grandmama Fellowes had arrived from St Leonards, so Forbes was available now to collect me from London at whatever time I wished tomorrow.

It wasn't necessary. I was quite capable of travelling down by train, but she wouldn't hear of it, perhaps imagining I had a load of last-minute purchases for my trousseau. I must have seemed a graceless kind of bride to her. Perhaps I should make an effort to raid Knightsbridge that afternoon to dispel the impression of casualness.

The truth, of course, was somewhat different. Having made such a disastrous marriage before, I quite detested all the trappings of the ceremony and wanted only the departure scene, with the confetti and rice, and everyone waving wildly; then to find myself alone with dear Clive, safe from the past and with a quite new future opening ahead.

I should not be seeing him again until we met at the altar, but as soon as I arrived at Stakerleys I would ring him to discover the exact situation regarding Edwin and Jeremy.

Chilvers told me at breakfast next morning that Forbes had arrived at a little past eight o'clock and was prepared to make a return journey at any time of my choosing. I found him in the housekeeper's sitting-room and explained I should prefer to leave at eleven, which would give us ample time to arrive before luncheon, which was served at Stakerleys at a quarter past one. We would set off southward and go along beside the river by way of Chelsea. It was a roundabout route designed so that we'd pass the new home where Clive and I would start our life together. Our street hadn't quite the cachet of Cheyne Walk, with its recall of Thomas Carlyle and later literary notables, but it was only a minute's walk away and still central to the quarter of artists and writers. From the river end of Swan Walk I could imagine a ghostly impression of Whistler's frock-coated figure fading into the grey and silver of the misted Thames.

As we approached our house, a van was unloading my easels and a number of sacking-covered objects that must be canvases. A man in overalls stood by, checking the number of each on a notepad. I had wanted to oversee the removals myself but had not been able to face the Fulham house again with its horrific memories. Nothing else was to come from there but the contents of my cramped attic studio.

Now I should have space aplenty with almost the entire top floor of our new home. As Clive had said, there I'd be able to swing not a cat but a whole cageful of tigers. The other two levels would be for family use, since he needed no surgery or waiting room, because all his consultations would be held at the clinic.

I sat back to enjoy the rest of the journey via Heston, Datchet and Eton Village. In the narrow High Street I was reminded of the many visits to Edwin at school there; and to poor little Rupert, who had died of pneumonia in his second year at the College.

Burnham, as we drove through the silent beech woods, was the first hint of true homecoming. There can surely be no county more lovely than leafy Bucks with its gently swelling Chilterns, nor any house more generously welcoming than dear Stakerleys. In less than another twenty minutes we were there, bowling up the long drive to face its many windows, giving back the sunlight as though gold-plated.

Mama came out to welcome me. 'Lucy, at last!' she exclaimed. 'I've hardly known how to wait for you. There are so many last-minute decisions to make. I am determined that everything shall be exactly as you wish, absolutely perfect. But first, of course, you will want to see little Eugenie. She is in the rose garden in her baby-carriage, with Mabel and your grandfather. Shall we go?'

My baby was asleep, her soft, pink cheeks aglow like the inner surface of a conch shell. In the fortnight that I had been absent she had plumped out and must have grown an inch or so. I kissed her tiny folded fingers and then Grandpapa's brow as he held my hands and murmured my name. He had never spoken a great deal since the second stroke. It was an effort for him, but I knew that, parked in his wheelchair in the gardens, he would sometimes whisper to his favourite plants.

'Mama,' I announced, 'before the wedding I should like to have my little one christened.'

She was delighted. It gave her yet more to organise, and she was in her natural element, disappointed as she must have been at my paring all the wedding rituals to a minimum. Now she would modify the decorating of the chapel with a design more suited to a baby, and with symbolic herbs such as rosemary, thyme and lavender strewn on the tiles about the font.

'And the godparents?' she asked.

I hadn't given it a thought. My main concern, perhaps the only one, was to change the name by which my baby was to be called. She must officially remain Mama's namesake, but for daily use I had another in mind that echoed my lover's, her murdered father.

'I could take your advice on that,' I said. 'Someone who will not be too old when she's of an age to need advice most. Edwin as a godfather, do you think? We'll defy convention and have two, because I believe I once promised

11

poor Geoffrey, since that marriage is likely to stay child-less.'

I saw Mama's eyebrows lift at the mention of my natural mother's husband, but she made no comment. Isabelle's infertility after my botched birth was an accepted tragedy in the family.

'And for godmother someone from the village,' I rushed on. 'Perhaps the vicar's daughter, Charlotte. Then the reverend's nose'll not be out of joint that I'm asking the bishop to officiate.'

We were summoned just then to the dining-room, and immediately after luncheon, at which I was warmly welcomed by the family, the ladies joined me in my bedroom to help open the trunks sent on in advance.

'I've found the bridesmaid's dress,' called Lady Isabelle, burrowing feverishly through layers of tissue paper, 'but where is the bridal gown?'

'There isn't to be a bridesmaid, Isabelle. That's the dress I intend wearing.'

'But it's short! And you cannot possibly be married in green. It's most unlucky for a wedding.'

'It isn't green at all. It's aquamarine, my favourite colour for crêpe de Chine.'

Grandmama Fellowes brought her expertise to bear and approved the pointed hemline sewn with tiny aquamarine bugles and pearls. 'Look,' I invited, 'here's the matching cloche hat with curly feathers to tickle me under the chin. You can scarcely expect me to parade myself in virgin white, with a history like mine.'

Nobody argued, but Mama glanced down at her hands and I made a face at my aunts over her bowed head.

'Well, I wore white the second time I was wed,' declared Isabelle.

'Lucy must have it however she prefers it,' Mama granted. 'I understand it's too soon after . . . after the tragedy for us to invite comment with anything lavish.'

'So we will have a quiet little country ceremony as befits a by-blow of our ancient and honourable family,' I said cruelly.

It silenced both my mothers – Isabelle, whose concealed

12

bastard I was, and Mama, who had had me foisted on her to save the family's black sheep.

'I am truly sorry,' I said instantly after. 'That was quite uncalled for. I am proud of my Sedgwick blood, and everlastingly grateful for how Mama and Papa fostered me. Ultimately the whole affair has had a most fortunate outcome. I've been blessed in you all.'

My older aunt Mildred had been silent, but now she rose from the window seat and came across to take me in her arms. She bent her long, amiable sheep-face over me. 'I for one am so happy that we can all share in you, Lucy. You've been a joy to us, and all we wish now is for your continued well-being. I pray that one day you will lose all the hidden anger in you.'

As ever, she had given me something to think about.

'Listen,' I said impulsively, 'since we are almost on the subject of little Eugenie's origins, I should tell you that I intend her to be given an extra name at her christening: one for everyday use. It is Petra, and I'm sure you will all guess why.'

'For Peter,' Mama said in a low voice, 'as a special memorial. It would have made him very proud, Lucy.'

I had dreaded explaining all I owed to my dead lover, but my decision was accepted without a murmur. I could safely leave it to her to break it to Papa.

Two

E dwin's continued absence was the first mishap of the day, but only a lesser one until Mama took me aside to explain the probable reason for it. There had been a telegram from Ireland intended for me, but as the sender had economised on the wording, it was addressed simply to Sedgwick, Stakerleys, Buckinghamshire, England; and Papa, as head of the family, had opened it.

It appeared that my father – that is to say, my real father – had suffered a seizure and was unlikely to recover. Mama had telephoned Edwin at the London house, asking him to break the news to me gently. She guessed now that he had decided to take action on his own. He, knowing the other was deliberately omitted from the wedding-guest list and how matters stood between the two of us, had apparently taken pity on the old actor and felt that he should not be abandoned in his final days.

Clive had been the only one he confided his intention to when he travelled north to take ship for Ireland. It seemed that a number of those closest to me had been making decisions behind my back. It angered me briefly until I realised how unready I was to face making any move of my own.

On the single occasion when I had met my natural father, seeking him out after a lifetime of never knowing so much as his name, we silently acknowledged that if we were strangers it was only by non-association. What was so manifestly clear was that we were of the same stuff, the same impulsive temperament and passionate love of independence. It was uncanny how we both communicated this and were able to take an ironic leave of each other, a hail-and-farewell all in one. As he had abandoned Isabelle all those years before, I had abandoned him, and we were agreed on that, the unknown

14

father and the unclaimed daughter. I had walked away from his wretched cabin of a house without a backward glance, but with respect for his proud withdrawal from earlier fame – and with something more, unrecognised until now: a fierce kind of love.

It seemed an age since Mama had spoken. 'Who sent that telegram?' I demanded.

'A doctor from Londonderry who had charge of his case.'

Not the woman from his cottage then. No, I wouldn't have expected it of her. She had taken against me, probably scornful of the wealthy background which supposedly would not acknowledge her lover. It was unlikely she could even write, let alone knew about telegrams. When he had roared as Lear or agonised as Macduff over his murdered children, she would have put it down to the drink and added her own maudlin voice to his. There was no way he would ever have explained to her how two decades before he had turned his back on silly, infatuated Lady Isabelle, aware of his child that she carried.

'It was kind of Edwin to make the journey,' I said, 'but quite unnecessary.'

'He must have been afraid you would rush off to Ireland yourself.'

'Mama, I'm not as sweet-natured as my brother. Too selfish, I'm afraid.'

'Lucy, you owe that man nothing.'

'Only life itself.' My voice broke despite my brusque manner and I had to turn away to hide my brimming eyes. I don't weep easily and that always in private. Anger comes more readily. 'Oh why,' I shouted, beating on my thighs with my fists, 'must everybody get so mixed up and suffer so?'

There was a burning in my chest. I remembered what my governess had once warned me: 'Always take care what wishes you make, because they may come about.' I had wanted all my past wiped out. I wanted it dead and forgotten. Now the man who had given me that life was dying. Why hadn't I realised that the past belonged to others besides me? I had no right to wish it away for them.

From then on nothing went noticeably wrong. At least for that day. Bishop Malcolm arrived at a little before four o'clock,

15

and after he had rested in his room I went up there to ask him about the christening. He was delighted to perform it.

We walked across after dinner on a golden September evening, my baby in my arms. Mama had arranged everything. Outdoors I caught the scent of dusty grass and warm black-berries in hedgerows, but the chapel was fragrant with lilies and freesias for my wedding, with loops of white satin ribbons from column to column linking little nosegays. By the font the herbs' green aroma overcame the flowers' sweetness.

Charlotte and her father were waiting there, the widowed clergyman quite touched by the honour to his daughter. She, sensible girl, was calm and quite owlishly earnest behind her horn-rimmed spectacles. Papa was to stand in as proxy for Edwin. Telegrams had been exchanged between them earlier in the day to ensure agreement.

Eugenie Petra behaved perfectly, replete and snug in her lacy shawl, gurgling at the dribbling of water on her forehead. If she felt herself cheated of full bathtime ritual, she made no protest, and we all returned across the park with Charlotte nursing her as the very precious, fragile thing that she is.

So we drank her health in champagne, waved off the Reverend Constantine Ransom and his daughter until next day, and all retired early to bed.

My wedding day dawned in a misty drizzle, the rain hardly seeming to fall but to be held suspended in a blue mist under the distant trees. Before I was due to dress for the ceremony a message came to attend the bishop in his suite. He presented me with a flat jewel-case containing a pendant on a fine gold chain. Three amethysts were set in an intricate arabesque.

'You will certainly have other jewellery of much greater value, my dear, but this is special because it was my wife's, and my wedding gift to her. As you know, we were never blessed with children of our own. Because of my fondness for you, Lucy, and the fact that from today you will be bearing my name, I should like it to be yours. Will you accept it with my blessing?'

It touched me, and startled me too, because it hadn't struck me how, in marrying his adopted son, I should become a Malcolm too. My godfather would then be closer family, at the moment when I seemed about to lose my natural father.

'I wish you great joy,' he said.

'I should thank you for dear Clive, for your care all those years in making him what he is. I feel so completely safe with him, as if for the first time in my life.'

He regarded me solemnly. 'Safe? But marriage is more than a haven, Lucy. It is a great adventure, a risk not to be run lightly. I would rather you found it exciting.'

On leaving the bishop I returned to my room to find myself briefly alone with Isabelle. Not by accident. There was a familiar tautness in the way she moved, touching small objects, removing and replacing them slightly off-site.

'You will be all right,' she said, her voice alluringly soft; but I saw the twisted corner of her pretty mouth, belying the thistledown hair, the childlike wide eyes.

'You are a survivor. You take after your father in that. You will use this man' – she meant Clive – 'to survive on.'

I stared back, hearing clearly what she left unsaid: *See how fragile I am, how* used*! You abandon me.*

I went on looking at her, a lot left unsaid in my reply too. I was her daughter, after all, and had inherited the art; but, dear God, not the malice. Not that, ever.

'Try counting your blessings, Isabelle,' I said eventually, and – although I meant it – because it was so trite it came out sardonic. Then I shrugged and turned away, opening the door for her, leaving her worse hurt. But I wanted no part in the interminable conflict she'd first waged against Eugenie and carried now into her relations with anyone who came close.

It was a strange pre-wedding parting. Hardly a mother's blessing, and it stirred reverberations of the bishop's caution. Was I marrying Clive to use him? Surely only as much as he needed to use me. Love offered a refuge, but we'd not be blind to its challenge. Cleaving to another human creature must always bring risks.

'Goodbye,' I told Isabelle. 'Mabel will help me dress.'

These conversations were to echo like a theme more appositely than I imagined; and the first dramatic challenge came so soon after the ceremony, as we all sat over the wedding breakfast, even before the speeches and toasts.

Old Hadrill bore the wretched telegram in on a salver and stood with it behind Clive's chair. We assumed it would join others for Jeremy to read out later, but instead my new husband opened it and the colour left his face. With the barest of apologies he begged leave to withdraw, taking me with him.

Then, in the hall, while Papa hovered and his valet was despatched to collect Clive's luggage, my husband took rapid leave of me, advised by his partner at the clinic, Dr Stanley Atkinson, of a most serious setback to a patient.

The rest of the celebration was a bitter travesty and my own departure subdued. I was to follow on to London later, in the bridal car, under escort of his best man. It was unspeakably cruel and, as we travelled, I was viciously aware of the little man darting me uncertain glances from the corner of his eyes. I scorned his pity and I feared his derision, which was probably unfair. Since we spoke little on the journey I had no idea what was in his head then. The car was a French limousine hired from a firm in London. Had it been Forbes driving, I would have joined him in the front. It was distasteful having Jeremy sitting by me in my husband's place.

As soon as we neared London I told him, 'Let me know where I can drop you, Dr Owen. We will go there first.'

He tried to override it, but I wasn't standing any further interference. When he protested that he would see me safely into my new home, I frostily pointed out how unsuitable it would be. 'I suppose you would expect to carry me over the threshold too?'

After that what could he say? The driver made a detour across the Thames to Battersea, where Jeremy was decanted outside a shabby terrace house. I let him thank me for my company. It was uncouth not to make some similar remark in return, but I had to make someone suffer for my spleen. I nodded coolly, leaving him baffled and smouldering on the pavement.

When the motor arrived at my future home, I sat there for a moment petrified. It was alien. What had I rushed into? Why, for a second time, had I gone through that Christian ceremony already proved hollow? If my path and Clive's had not crossed again I could have gone on happily enough, living out my life at Stakerleys among the familiar and the trusted. Couldn't I?

I had told the bishop I felt safe now. With Clive himself, perhaps. But here, away from family and friends, alone? I felt deserted, filled with dread, and there came to me then something more than doubt, more of a premonition: that I would find terror, even danger here. I – reputed to be rash and headstrong – sat and shuddered for my very life.

It took courage to make the first move, alight and go to knock at the door I had no key for. I steeled myself to appear nonchalant.

Even indoors I wasn't free to release the impacted emotions that filled me. Our new housekeeper-cook opened the door to me and took my luggage from the driver. She had discretion enough not to remark on the fact that I was alone.

'Your husband has telephoned twice, madam,' she said, my wrap over her arm. 'He will do so again as near on the hour as possible.'

'Thank you, Mrs Bowyer. I'm afraid a doctor hasn't total control over his own life.' She smiled and went to prepare a tray of tea things.

Clive's excuse, when he did ring, was that the emergency continued. An outpatient had attempted to harm himself and his life still hung in the balance. It was essential that he should find Clive at his bedside when he came round.

The rest of his message was love-talk meant to win me over, but although I couldn't dispute the priority of his medical duty, I was still put out. 'Come and tell me in person,' I told him. 'I think I shall turn in now for an early night. Don't trouble to ring again.'

So that was my wedding night. I asked myself what Freud would have made of it.

Three

I thought I must be dreaming when I was wakened at eight next morning by my baby crying, but Mabel was standing there in the doorway with Petra in her arms.

'Madam, your husband telephoned your mama from the hospital last night to explain that you were alone, so she insisted we should set out at first light,' Mabel explained. Petra was red-faced with protest. Her little fists pumped at the air as she roared.

'She was an angel on the journey, slept all the way,' Mabel said proudly. 'I must give her a bottle, but I don't like to ask the lady in the kitchen.'

I reached out my arms. 'She's probably soaking. Let me change her.' I undid the bundle that was my squalling daughter, wiped her clean and dressed her afresh with one of the towelling squares produced from Mabel's capacious carpet-bag. Lying on the bed beside me Petra stared up solemnly, then a smile broke out and she waved one arm like a wild cancan dancer. Her rosy face dimpled.

'Let's go down,' I said, 'and I'll introduce you both properly to Mrs Bowyer.'

I left them all together while I bathed and dressed. Dear Mabel, she was trying so hard to do the right thing and live up to Sedgwick standards. She had come a long way to improve herself since she had stumbled on me in Covent Garden when we were both at our lowest ebb, she freshly widowed, homeless, and seeking employment in alien London, I in flight from the police and an accusation of murder.* Only a few months back, but already it seemed an age ago, because so much had happened in between.

* *The Colour of Blood*

20

Clive arrived home exhausted at a little before ten that morning, having spent all night watching over his patient. As morning broke Patrick Garston had blearily regained consciousness, so Clive had stayed with him a while until a natural sleep overtook him.

There could be no doubt that the man had attempted to kill himself, using a rope with a running noose attached to the upper banisters at his home. When he had jumped, the fall had failed to break any bones in his neck, so when his wife returned unexpectedly, poor woman, she had found him still hideously kicking as he slowly choked to death. She had run to call a man digging up drains in the road outside, and he had cut the rope through with a kitchen knife.

Clive told me apologetically as though it were his fault.

'You feel responsible,' I said.

'He was my outpatient. I was treating his neurosis and believed it was safe to leave him for a while. To be honest, I never thought he would act like this, even when almost senseless with drink. Unfortunately, for that reason, he is quite unable to remember what happened.'

'But you can still cure him? Clive, I'm not at all sure what a neurosis is. It sounds like something physical, to do with the central nervous system.'

'In psychology nowadays it can mean almost whatever you wish it to. When I use the term, it's usually to indicate mental instability arising from a conflict caused by trauma or suppressed guilt.'

'Perhaps because he's ashamed of being a drunk.'

'But he's never been an alcoholic. His behaviour on that day was atypical. His employers and neighbours speak highly of him. He appears to have been a hard worker with little interest outside his home life until this recent breakdown.'

'So now that he has committed a criminal offence by attempting suicide he will have increased the guilt and so compounded the conflict in his mind?'

'He certainly hasn't made his life any easier. I shall have to work with him to bring out whatever lies under the surface. And now the attempt itself is something further he has expunged from his mind. I'm sorry, my darling, but this has become a serious case and does demand my absence from you when we had most cause to be together. This is hardly the honeymoon I planned.'

I slid into his arms and hugged him. 'The Alps have stood there quite a time. They can wait a little longer for our visit. For a while I too can be patient. I'll find things to distract me. But get some rest now. I shall take Petra with us when I show Mabel round the neighbourhood, so there'll be no disturbance for you.'

'Petra's here with us?' His delight warmed me. I explained how Mama had sent the two of them on, knowing I was alone. Then there was no sending him to bed before he had dandled my baby in his lap and joined in her chortling laughter.

He slept soundly until four, took a light meal and was away again by six.

I spent a while in my studio rooms after that, Mabel helping me drag chests and easels about to where I should be using them for the best natural light. Then I set about planning the next day Cliveless.

'Mabel,' I asked, 'how would you like to spend a day in the country? It was Hampshire, I think, that you came from. I thought to hire a motor tomorrow to take you back to see your childhood friends and the farmer's wife who was kind when you had to give up the tied cottage.'

She almost wept with pleasure. So I arranged for the same driver who had brought me up from Stakerleys, quite proud of myself that I'd found a way of being absent while the main part of our furniture was being delivered from a store in Tottenham Court Road. We had managed so far with a bare minimum taken from Clive's earlier lodgings in Putney. Chilvers had offered us a footman from the house at Eaton Place just for the day, to lend authority and save Mrs Bowyer any anxiety during the delivery.

Clive returned at a quarter to midnight and reported that his patient still had no recollection of the suicide attempt. Patrick Garston was incredulous when told how he had been found, but had to accept the evidence of his injured neck and general weakness.

'Parker-Ellington's registrar from UCH is treating him for the physical injuries,' Clive said, 'and my nursing staff are strictly instructed to keep the police from distressing the poor man further. All the same, I need to be instantly available in case of some new crisis. Between sessions with him I am hoping to fit in some of my regular patients there, so I intend returning to my usual clinical hours of duty, if that is acceptable to you.'

'Acceptable, but unwelcome,' I admitted. 'I hadn't thought you would be so involved in your cases. It makes me feel I should contribute somehow. Could I be of any comfort to the poor man's wife? Visit her, perhaps?'

He smiled, coming across to sit on the arm of my chair and ruffle my red curls. 'I'm afraid you speak different languages, Lucy. You inhabit different worlds. It could put more strain on her. Already she's under great pressure, with no wages coming in and three young children to care for, one of them sickly.'

'So this Mr Garston is one of your charity cases? I understand. So may I send her a hamper?'

'No. That could hurt their pride. Fortunately, they've regularly paid money into the Foresters' Friendly Society, so some benefit will be available as their right. It goes nowhere near covering the real costs of hospital treatment, but they are comfortable with that arrangement, although goodness knows what the family will live on if there's no pay over a long period. They're the sort of people who, however needy, would find "charity" insulting. Their whole lives are based on worthy effort.'

'Yet this Patrick Garston has a mental breakdown like a rich man!'

The words seemed to echo in the shocked silence that followed them. Clive rose and shook his head. 'When it comes to suffering, we're all the same under the skin. You think you have a wide acquaintance, Lucy, because of those straitened years in Fulham, but you never really entered the lives of those you lived among there, people hedged about with the demands of respectability and determined to disguise from outsiders the unpleasantnesses they endure. They prefer to show only the surface of their lives. Underneath there can be horrors enough. Believe me, the rich have no monopoly of psychiatric illnesses. They are merely better able to pay for diagnosis, so we more readily hear about it.'

He leaned over and nuzzled my hair. 'But it's late, love, and we both have plans for the morning. Let's get to bed.'

I was ashamed then, remembering his shellshock cases, officers and their men alike; but his invitation was clear enough, his eyes tender as he held out his hand for mine. I went more than willingly.

Next morning our hired car arrived half an hour after Clive had left and we headed south, with Mabel sitting up front with the driver and Petra's basket crib on the seat beside me. Soon after crossing the Thames we were bowling along through open country. The background smell of sooty chimneys was replaced by the autumn scents of cut hay, honeysuckle in the hedges, and wood smoke from bonfires where the trees were being thinned. There was no sign of impending rain and the occasional clouds were little rounded shapes like grazing sheep.

At Thorndike Farm an ample woman, with her sleeves rolled up to the elbow and flour spilt over her checked apron, came out to meet us. Her amazement at seeing Mabel step down from the motor amused me, but she was genuinely happy to see her again and to coo over her little charge. She pressed us all to come in and share their midday meal, but I wouldn't intrude on the reunion. Leaving Petra to be further petted, I had myself driven to the nearby King's Head, where I was served a tasty, if rather heavy, beef shank pie followed by ripe greengages and clotted cream.

When we returned some two hours later, I found Mabel pink-cheeked and excited in a circle of local women. Not all, perhaps, were real friends. I thought I detected one or two sidelong glances of envy that she had fallen so surely on her feet. It was almost as though some thought that because she had left there nearly destitute, her reversal of fortune was slightly improper.

'Oh madam,' she said, turning in her seat as we got under way towards home, 'sech a wunnerful day – best ever, so it was. I'll never forget it, never!'

It made me smile, because in just that short time she had

24

returned to her country accent and forgotten the way of speaking she'd tried to pick up from the Sedgwick servants.

Back in Chelsea all was in place. Mrs Bowyer announced that Clive had sent a note from the clinic saying he would be bringing back a guest for supper. As a result she had taken it upon herself to slip out, leaving the young footman in charge of the removal men, to order a saddle of mutton for the meal, with suitable accompaniments. She had made a duck terrine to begin with and poached some pears in wine and almonds for afterwards. She hoped she had done right.

It was after I'd told her she was a treasure that she confessed that, quite unasked, Mr Chilvers had sent us a tweeny, Jessie, from the Eaton Place house to help out with our first dinner party. The footman had apparently mentioned it to him when reporting back after the furniture delivery. I saw I should have to put restraints on the over-helpfulness of Mama's London household.

I peeped into the kitchen, sniffed the wonderful smells and saw a young girl I didn't recognise dressed as a parlourmaid. She did know me, however, blushed, bobbed and waited for instructions. I had been going to tell her she would hardly be needed, since Clive's note mentioned only one guest and referred to the meal as supper: surely an informal affair among friends. But since she appeared so earnest I hadn't the heart, just smiled and asked how she had managed to arrange the table for three. She had done well, balancing the settings with a low bowl of roses where the fourth place should have been. In the cloth's centre was a silver swan (which I recognised from its being cleaned in Chilvers' pantry but which had never, to my knowledge, been used by the family). The hollow between its half-opened wings was filled with a choice of fresh *petits pains*.

I wished Clive had given his guest's name. Last night, after speaking of his patient, he had mentioned Sir Digby Parker-Ellington. I hoped fervently we weren't to entertain him. I should have trouble being polite if he repeated his attack on Clive's researches. But it would have been no less than a five-course dinner in full fig required for that great man. So was I to entertain another, less distinguished, colleague? Surely not a patient?

The more serious omission from Clive's note was the hour at which to expect them. Time went by and the mutton was removed from the oven, the vegetables delayed. At a quarter to ten, when we had almost given up hope and I was getting anxious for my husband, a cab outside disgorged an enormously fat man followed by Clive. I met them in the hall.

'Darling, this is Dr Ignatius Barrow. Iggy, my wife Lucy.'

The newcomer nodded at me over his shoulder and continued with some high-pitched argument they'd been engaged in on their way. He broke off to hand me his overcoat, which he had sloughed off with some difficulty and much flailing of short arms. 'Take care of it,' he instructed me. 'Lost my best one somewhere last week.'

I passed it to Jessie and waved the gentlemen through to the drawing-room, where drinks were ready to be served. Clive looked at the clock and pulled a wry face at me. 'If the meal's ready, maybe we'd better start.'

I forbore to mention how over-ready it had been for some hour and a quarter. Perhaps medical men had their own hours for eating. It was part of the new world I should need to learn about.

Dr Barrow was a rapid eater, his words often volubly spluttered out while he munched, but his wine glass required to be filled even faster. At one juncture during the main course, in waving to illustrate his point, he knocked the full glass over and claret spread over the napiery. He gazed at it in misery and instantly his argument dried up.

Clive stood, went round the table and casually deposited his screwed-up napkin over the offending stain, then nodded to Jessie to bring him a replacement. Manly, it might have been, but I seethed at the unmannerliness of it all.

Worse was in store when finally the cheeseboard was brought in. As Jessie leaned over to place it between the two gentlemen, I saw our guest's hand move upwards from his lap and heard a startled gasp as the girl straightened. Her face flooded with colour.

'That will be all, thank you, Jessie,' I said. Ignatius Barrow's eyes followed her out, puckered behind their thick-lensed spectacles. I was relieved when the arrival of the port and cigars allowed me to withdraw.

Jessie brought coffee to the drawing-room, but the gentlemen never came through. When I had drunk mine, I visited the kitchen. 'Madam . . .' Mrs Bowyer started up in protest.

I held up a finger for restraint and followed Jessie into the scullery, where she was dealing with the used silver and crockery. 'You've done very well,' I told her. 'I shall recommend you to Mr Chilvers as a parlourmaid.' Then I folded her fingers over a gold sovereign, for a keepsake or to exchange for current coins, and gave her a meaningful frown. So she knew she was to say nothing, just as I'd said nothing, about my unpalatable guest's appalling behaviour.

In the dining-room the gentlemen continued their discussion into the early hours while I nodded over a book alone by my fire, trying not to visualise how under the napkin the claret stain was drying in permanently. Eventually I heard Clive phoning from the hall and some ten minutes later a cab's motor throbbing outside the open window. No goodbye: our guest departed as though I didn't exist, as indeed had been the case throughout his visit.

Clive came in with his waistcoat unbuttoned and his hair tousled. When he kneeled beside my chair, put his arms round me and leaned his head against mine, I could smell the stale wine on his breath. For a terrible moment I had a sense of history repeating itself. I thought I could hear again Julian's drunken voice, after his cronies had left, demanding more money for his debts at cards.

Clive shifted his head, gently nibbled my ear. 'You are a jewel,' he said steadily. 'Thank you so much for not making poor Iggy feel awful.'

'But he *was* awful.'

'Darling, he's a confirmed bachelor and painfully shy. Women terrify him, so he pretends they're not there. When he gets used to you, he'll forget you're female and accept you as a part of me.'

'A pity, because I quite like to be noticed as a female. But not uncouthly. And he is *your* friend,' I said, reflecting that he wasn't the only one of Clive's intimates I found bizarre.

'A good friend. When you get to know him well, you'll become fond of him, as I am. I admire and respect him for what he does.'

27

'Which is . . . ?'

'At present he's working as a prison doctor while he researches the psychological problems of our criminals and social outcasts. This is just a fresh exploration of human behaviour to complement his studies of inmates in mental hospitals.'

Whose company presumably he felt more at home with. It explained a lot. 'I just wish I'd known that before. And why are you so interested in prisoners?' I asked. But then I knew. Of course: Patrick Garston. He would be considered a criminal after they had had him up in court. He would probably be sentenced to jail without an option, because he'd have no earnings from which to pay a fine.

Clive confirmed my fear. By now we had reached the seclusion of our bedroom and I turned for him to undo the long row of little buttons at the back of my dress. 'But surely,' I said, trying to ignore the way his fingers were straying, 'if a suicide may be dismissed as having the balance of his mind temporarily disturbed, purely to permit him a grave within hallowed ground, then one who survives the attempt might use the same excuse to be kept free of a criminal sentence?'

His smile was a little sour. 'The law doesn't work like that. In the latter case you have a survivor to heap blame on. It's not a case of a Christian graveyard and heavenly forgiveness at the last. And if some enlightened judge did take mental balance into consideration, he could come down on the side of having the wretched man shut away in an asylum for God knows how long. Perhaps for life, if no doctor there was alert enough to revise his assessment.'

He broke off, his fingers gently pulling at my tangled red curls. 'Lucy, how on earth will you manage without a personal maid?'

'Adequately,' I said. 'I've become accustomed to some independence since you knew me as a little girl.'

He transferred his attention to where I had slid the frock off my shoulders. 'I hadn't realised ladies' clothes were still so restrictive. Is this some kind of corset we have here?' His hands were into my bodice now.

I explained how modern calf-length dresses demanded a

flat bosom. This camisole structure was merely dressmakers' engineering to ensure that. 'And as for a lady's maid, it seems I've acquired a rather superior model.'

He had buried his face in my shoulders and was systematically kissing his way round me. It was time to forget Patrick Garston's woes and the problem of redesigning society to accommodate him.

Next morning Mrs Bowyer introduced our new cleaner and set her to polishing all of yesterday's acquisitions. Meanwhile I was exploring the garden, to which a pretty little verandah led with cast-iron steps down to lawn, flower beds and hidden bays behind a shrubbery. It was all on a doll's-house scale after grandfather's grandiose schemes at Stakerleys, but had once been pretty, if now badly overgrown. In any case, it was a great improvement on the walled concrete yard and straggling bushes of Fulham. I should be happy planning something new here.

A glass door at the house's rear gave a direct view through the central hall, and while I sat on the verandah that afternoon, I could make out our housekeeper opening the front door from time to time as several ladies left their cards in a reassuringly conventional manner. I had heard stories about Chelsea and the wild modern ways of certain eccentrics who lived there. Apparently they were exaggerated.

When I looked the cards through after tea I was gratified to find one from the gallery where I had been exhibiting some two years back. I hadn't notified it of the move, so presumably someone there who kept abreast of the social news had requested our address from the clinic or the university. I was slightly surprised that it should have been released so freely, and mentioned this to Clive on his return, at a reasonable hour for once.

He brought with him quite a large package wrapped in brown paper with a label printed with the name of a pharmaceutical firm, but I noticed that it was re-used and the package unsealed. He made no mention of it until much later, when we sat out on the verandah with our coffee after dinner. His face was sombre as he started to tell me of his efforts with Patrick Garston and the lack of progress. 'I had really hoped to shock him into return of his memory,' he said regretfully.

Clive had taken his patient straight from his hospital bed, by cab, to the house in Bermondsey where the attempt had been made. His wife had refused to stay there and had taken the three children to lodge with a sister nearby, so they had had the place to themselves. Garston had shown some distress, but not the cataclysmic reaction hoped for. He had appeared more confused than shaken at the sight of the length of rope still attached to the upper banister rail. He had gone to sit on the stairs with his head in his hands while Clive examined the severed end and looked about for the noose itself.

It was not lying where it had been taken from his neck, nor had it been left in the kitchen. Clive had gone through to the tiny, square backyard. I could smell it myself as my husband described the odour of green mould off sunless brick walls like a premonition of prison. The meagre space there was dominated by an iron mangle with worn and saturated wooden rollers. Behind it a large zinc bath hung from a nail driven into the crumbling brickwork.

He had searched every inch there and found nothing. Nor had the noose been thrown away in the dustbin, which stood raised on three bricks to allow the passage of air underneath. He had concluded that some overzealous policeman must have removed the rope to produce in court and add horror to the grisly story.

For all its poverty the house wasn't squalid. He could see how the couple had repaired and repainted areas of rotten wood and crumbling plaster. The contents were tidily arranged. Despite the smoky air of the district the curtains were freshly clean and smelled of green soap.

He had gone back to collect Patrick Garston from where he sat hunched, to return him to the clinic. Passing back through the kitchen passage, he had noticed that the door of a cupboard under the stairs had been left unlatched and nudged it shut with one foot. Then he had reconsidered and opened it. In the dark he had just been able to make out the noose lying across an upturned household bucket. He had taken it out to the waiting cab. Back at the clinic he had wrapped it to bring home.

'Goodness knows why,' he added at the end of the story. 'It's a gruesome exhibit. Perhaps in some dim way I thought it might inspire me, and yet it's a symbol of my failure, because its effect on the poor man was negative. He was shocked all right, repulsed at the sight of the thing, but he swore he had never seen it before in his life.

'I believed him,' Clive admitted, turning to me, almost incredulous at his own gullibility. 'I'd counted on shock at its sudden reappearance to bring him out of the hysterical reaction which blocked out the hideous act itself. I pressed him gently to tell me what he remembered of its purchase. Had this rope been about the house for some period, or bought for a specific purpose? He was nonplussed. He could tell me nothing.'

'Will this save him in court?' I asked. 'Could it be supposed that the poor man is *non compos mentis*?'

'So that they have him locked away for life in an asylum? That would be no solution at all. The man is as sane as you or I – just sick. I certainly hope to assure him a better future than the madhouse.'

Despite the calm, rose-scented evening there on the verandah, I was chilled inside, remembering too much. I had never actually reached court on the charge of murder, but this was only because the police had not amassed sufficient evidence against me when the case had exploded and I had almost become a victim myself. But I had known all the fear, suffered the humiliation of being locked away behind the clanging iron door of a police cell, denied access to my family, and without real knowledge of the evidence they were to mount against me. Now it overwhelmed me anew and I began to shake.

Startled, Clive swore suddenly, realising what had brought this on. He picked me up and held me fiercely close. 'Dear God, what have I done? I should have my tongue cut out. Dearest Lucy, it's all over and done with. You're safe now. I should never have brought my problems home and shared them with you like this.'

'Why not?' I demanded, suddenly calm because I saw the way ahead. It was like an electric switch lighting a room. 'Who better should you bring this to than to me? I have been this way before. It's in my own experience. Put me down, love, and let's consider this sensibly.'

He did so, and looked at me with wonder. I examined the noose, holding it in my hands to show him how I had control over my fear of hanging. 'It's just a length of strong rope which has been wound around several times and secured to itself. Can one buy it like this? Surely that's unlikely; so did he sit down and carefully construct it? It's not an amateur-looking effort. Wouldn't you expect him to have some memory of making a thing like that? Show me how it's done.'

'This may be needed for evidence,' he warned. 'I'll see if we have another piece in the house, left over from the unpacking. That's if you really insist on pursuing this grisly business.'

Mrs Bowyer had tidily folded all wrapping paper and conserved the string that came with it. She found us a length of heavy twine that was at least half the thickness of the noose, and Clive settled to copy the construction. He had almost finished when he stopped. 'No, I've gone wrong somewhere.'

'Let me,' I offered. 'I used to be quite good at knots when I was crewing for Papa on sailing holidays.' So I tried my hand with another length and it ended up the same way. By then Clive had undone his own effort and risen to his feet. He left the room and came back with Mabel, to whom he set the same task. Her effort and mine were identical.

'It's not so simple,' I said. 'Where did we all go wrong?'

'It's in the initial direction,' Clive said, examining the real noose again.

'And we're all right-handed,' I reminded him. 'So Patrick Garston must be left-handed. That would explain it.'

'But he isn't. I was watching when he signed the permit for me to run some experiments. I would have noticed because I am interested in left-handedness as a mental phenomenon.'

I shook my head. 'Our generation weren't allowed to write with the wrong hand, so he'd certainly be the same. It could be suppressed but come out when he tackled practical tasks.'

'That's possible, I suppose. I could find out by experiment.'

'Certainly you should,' I said heatedly, 'because if Garston isn't left-handed, somebody else is. I hardly think he would ask a friend to make a noose for him to kill himself. And that could mean,' I went on triumphantly, 'that he didn't attempt suicide at all. Someone set out to murder him.'

Four

C live was slow to accept my theory, but he couldn't deny the logic of it. It left him considering its relevance to his own intuitive feeling that Patrick Garston spoke the truth.

Because of his lingering doubts and his anxiety for me, I thought that he would close the subject down and forbid me to meddle in it any more; but fortunately, since I still occasionally suffered nightmares over the attempt on my own life, he saw it as therapeutic – which it was – and as I spread my suspicions about where the guilt might lie in Garston's hanging, he began to appreciate that I might be right.

Under pressure he even gave permission for me to enter the holy precinct of the clinic to observe his methods at first hand. I was to keep strictly to student rules and stay silent, at all times in the background. On those conditions, and with some trepidation, I infiltrated his workplace three days after first hearing of Patrick Garston.

While Clive checked on a patient in the small women's ward, Dr Atkinson escorted me to the door of the men's. Two of its four occupants were sitting out, being offered tea. We paused by the first bed where a man lay with closed eyes. The name above the headboard was 'Garston, Patrick'. Dr Atkinson explained that the man's memory was impaired.

That was something I knew the enormity of. Not so many months ago I had awoken to knowing nothing: total void. Clive had called it amnesia, the name giving it the authority of a positive state, which it wasn't. Memory is almost all one is. Remove it and one no longer exists. This man had lost a vital part of himself.

This was the patient who so concerned Clive that he had abandoned our wedding guests. There looked to be nothing urgent about him as he lay withdrawn, ashen-faced, mute.

Dr Atkinson was called away, so I left the ward, found an empty room and put on the white cooking overall I had borrowed from Mrs Bowyer, but the man's drained face remained in my mind.

Why need to die when you don't exist? I had been desperate to survive. In his present state there should be no danger of Garston's repeating the attempt, if suicide had been his original intention.

I heard voices approaching, waited for them to pass and then, covered by the white coat, was able to attach myself to a small group of students who followed Clive around. There were only two wards of four beds at the clinic, one for male patients and the other for female, besides two single rooms reserved for emergencies. I caught up with the teaching group at the far end of the men's ward. As we stood round the last patient's bed, the cubicle curtains were drawn to ensure privacy. Without noticing an extra attachment behind his back Clive began a résumé of the man's symptoms and his findings on them.

I stared at the recumbent form. This man lay on his back, his mouth slightly open and emitting unmistakable snores. Clive made no move to wake him. I had missed the introductory sentences but I picked up on the phrase 'continuous narcosis'. I had flirted with enough classical Greek to know that Clive referred to the man's sleeping state. So was his malaise an inability to wake up?

We stood around while my husband took a chair by the man's head, reached out and pricked the back of the patient's left hand several times with a pin. The gentle snores continued unchanged.

So was Clive's little party piece to prove that the sleep was impenetrable? Apparently so, but the trick wasn't over. 'Dennis, can you hear me?' he asked in a quiet monotone.

There was no answer, but there seemed to be a momentary pause in the steady breathing. 'We are going back a long, long way,' Clive droned. 'You are coming into the clinic for the first time. You do not like the smell of carbolic. The nurses wear starched uniforms. It is like the field hospital where you were taken four years ago – after you escaped from the Germans. You want to escape from here too, but you've promised to let us help you. Nancy wants you to co-operate, and soon you will feel well. No more headaches, no nightmares, no fits of anger, no black tunnels.'

Clive shifted slightly in his chair and took the man's hand in his own. 'So we are walking together, you and I, and we are going back in time, out of the clinic, through the traffic, down to the coast, back across the stormy Channel to France. You have felt sick on the boat, but not now. We are going farther back. It is July and you can feel the sun on your face. You have already been eleven months in France. You are longing to return to Blighty, and to something else. Is it seeing Nancy again? Yes, because you have been away too long. But we are back in that time of being a soldier.

'It doesn't feel right, because you are really a London omnibus driver, but you want to serve your country and your king.'

'King,' murmured the sleeping man.

'You don't want to kill anyone. You don't want to be killed yourself, but perhaps you can drive a lorry, a tank. There must be some way to be of service, and you have come here willingly, a volunteer. But terrible things are happening all around. The guns are getting louder. Your lorry has broken down. You have had to abandon the convoy and take to the fields on foot.'

A spasm ran through the man's body. Convulsions, I thought: that's what he suffers from, then, and Clive is keeping him in a drugged sleep to prevent him harming himself. But why disturb him so with these reminders of a terrifying time he would rather forget? Surely that's cruel?

There was no second spasm, but the man's face was working, becoming livid. He panted as though he had run and run until he could barely draw breath. I heard a murmur go round the students as they pressed forward, watching – a sort of gasp, as though this was something they'd waited for but scarcely believed they'd ever see.

So I strained to look too, and it was incredible. As we watched, the man's body underwent a change, seemed to swell, becoming more substantial.

'They are waiting in the wood,' Clive breathed. 'In hiding. A German scouting party, cut off from the rest. And you are alone. They have found you. There is something they want to know. Desperately. You have to tell them. Name, rank, number.'

The man writhed horribly. Sweat was rolling off his face. '*Fowler, Dennis, Private, 7298,*' he shouted over and over.

Then the shouts became screams of pain, and on the man's chest appeared scarlet weals, criss-crossed, as if invisible attackers beat him with rifle butts. His back arched. His arms, pinioned against his sides, showed deep, livid grooves where ropes had tightly bound him and his tortured flesh bulged over.

Clive waved dismissively and the students dispersed behind the curtains, drawing me with them. We stood silent outside and heard Clive guide the man back.

'Dennis, it's over. You're safe now. We've rescued you. Go to sleep. When you wake up in two hours' time, you will remember everything and not be afraid any more. You have overcome. You will feel refreshed, at peace, with your vigour renewed.'

There were no other sounds now except steady breathing. 'What happened?' I begged of the student next to me. He smiled. 'Fowler's brought the repressed incident up from his subconscious. He'll be able to deal with it now. Is this your first time here?'

That was when I began to see what an extraordinary man my husband was, and why he believed so intensely in what he was doing. But not so extraordinary that on pulling back the curtain he wasn't shocked to find me facing him. 'Lucy,' he said, his face like thunder, 'what in heaven's name are you doing here?'

'You said I might come and see your work.'

'As a visitor, by my specific invitation.'

So I had violated some professional ethic in donning a white coat and passing myself off as a student. 'You will kindly wait for me in my office,' he said coldly, and waved his little flock on to the women's ward.

I walked back towards the door I had come in by, past the three other beds, all of which had long windows between and faced a grey, distempered wall. It struck me how much more agreeable their recovery would be if the patients had something more cheerful to gaze at. I would raise it with Clive when he had done with reprimanding me.

Meanwhile, I smiled at the patients as I passed, glanced at the name-boards above their beds and halted at the last. Patrick Garston was awake, a fine-featured man, but now hollow-eyed, sunken-cheeked and appearing bloodless. I saw then the terrible purple bruising at the neck. One thin hand lay on the green coverlet as though reaching half-heartedly towards the woman who now sat tensed in the chair at his bedside. They weren't talking, but she seemed to devour him with her eyes.

'Mrs Garston,' I heard myself saying, 'how do you find your husband today?'

She started to rise but I waved her back.

'Much the same, Doctor, thank you. P'raps a li'el tired after 'is – 'is visit yesterdye.'

'To the house? Yes, it must have been an unnerving experience for him.' I should have pointed out the natural mistake that my white overall had caused, but it suited me not to then. 'How are the children?' I asked, mother to mother.

Her once pretty face broke into a smile. 'Nicely, thank yer, ma'am. I mean doctor. Except the littlest. She's awful asthmatic.'

'That can be wearing for you as well. I had a little brother who was a terrible wheezer. But fortunately he grew out of it.' (Only to die of pneumonia, away at school, but I wouldn't be telling the poor woman that.)

''Appen li'el Sophie'll get better, then. I 'ope to Gawd she do.'

'I hope so too.' I put out my hand for hers. 'Goodbye, Mrs Garston. It was nice meeting you. And I'm not actually a doctor, just Dr Malcolm's wife, visiting.'

Reaching the door I saw Matron at the corridor's end, blocking the way for two constables. As ever, I experienced an icy surge go through me. Even now that I am proved innocent, and since the Hastings police helped when I was rescued from the sea, it was still fear that their uniforms evoked; and now on behalf of Patrick Garston too, because surely they had come for him. Too soon for his recovery.

I darted back to the ward and snatched the name-board from its hook over his bed. I took Mrs Garston by the arm

38

and hustled her to where the farthest man lay safely asleep for the prescribed two hours. Seating the bewildered woman on his visitor's chair, I said, 'Hold his hand. If the police ask questions, just say who you are and then weep. You must pretend this is your husband.'

Then I helped myself to Dennis Fowler's name-board and hung up the other. I almost ran back to the door. Too late, a sternly starched Matron and the two policemen faced me. I concealed the board behind my back, presumed on my white coat and said, 'Matron, a word with you, please.'

She looked uncertain. 'Doctor?'

I spoke across her. 'If you are looking for Mrs Garston,' I told the older of the two policemen, 'she is at the far end. As for her husband, I'm afraid he's unconscious again.'

As they went past, I drew Matron aside. 'Have those two been here before?'

Her gaze now was full of suspicion. 'No, it was a different constable brought him in.'

'Good; they won't notice the difference then.'

She stared hard at me. 'Dr Malcolm didn't mention any lady doctor attending today.'

'That's because I'm not – a lady doctor, I mean. I'm *Mrs* Malcolm. And I shall get into really hot water over this when my husband finds out. But please, will you button Mr Garston's pyjama jacket right up to his chin, just in case those policemen come back and notice the bruising.'

She didn't hesitate, but hurried to do as I asked. At the far end of the ward I heard a man's deep voice followed by a woman's faltering reply, and I silently prayed that she had been quick-witted enough to grasp what she must do. Another rumble of male voices and then the visitors were returning. Matron and I put ourselves into consultation stance, she nodding wisely over some utter gibberish that I was pouring forth until they reached us. 'Good day, constables,' I said dismissively. They left, looking slightly baffled.

Matron drew a deep breath. 'Oh, well done, Mrs Malcolm! That saw them off properly.'

Feeling somewhat ashamed, however, I handed her back the concealed name-board. Then I went to sit like a disgraced schoolchild in my husband's office. He kept me waiting twenty minutes before he saw fit to come and explain the enormity of my earlier crime.

I could appreciate that by wearing the white coat and joining the students I had been guilty of impersonation; also that for such an intrusion to be ignored could be dangerous. Who knew what unsuitable people might attempt to infiltrate a psychiatric unit, perhaps intending to harm one of the patients?

I imagined he was ignorant of my more daring coup, but when he had checked his watch for the time, he said, 'I think we might go home now. I've completed my rounds and had a further word with Mrs Garston who, incidentally, is full of admiration for your enterprising tactics.'

I felt myself blush, knowing I should have made a full confession to him. However, the corners of his lips were doing what I could only describe as squirming; and then he broke into a broad grin, his eyes half-closed in laughter. So I contented myself with complaining, 'You said we lived in different worlds and spoke two different languages. Well, we don't. Mrs Garston and I had no difficulty at all in understanding one another.'

After that, since Clive said nothing further, I was determined to find out a little more about the Garston family, but discreetly; and next morning, as soon as he was out of the house and safely en route for work, I telephoned the clinic and asked to speak to Matron. She recognised my voice at once and hers warmed in tone, but just the same she was reluctant to give me the address I was after.

'I had hoped,' I said, 'to do something to help the family, but it seems I can't, in that case.'

'Which does seem a pity,' she admitted. And then she proved that she could be as devious as I. 'Perhaps if I were to be going over my notes near the telephone and muttering to myself, you might happen to pick up something inadvertently, so to speak.'

'So to speak indeed,' I said with enthusiasm. Which is how we managed it, and at half past ten that morning, which was a Saturday, I walked up to Sloane Street and caught a cab out to Bermondsey.

The Garstons' house was narrow-fronted and two-storeyed, part of a grim and smoky Victorian terrace, with a front door that opened on to the pavement. Nobody came when I knocked repeatedly. Eventually the sash was raised at an upstairs window of the next-door house and a woman leaned out, her hoarse voice almost lost against the squalling of an infant. 'They gorn a-wye. Din't yer know? Acaws of 'im stringing 'issell up.'

'Yes, I did know, but Mrs Garston forgot to leave me her new address.' Then, as the woman eyed me with suspicion: 'I'm from the clinic. Where Patrick is.'

'She's stying at 'er sister's. I s'pose yer don't know where that is neither?'

'You're right about that.'

She pulled a face of disgust. 'Orright, I'll come down then.'

While I waited, I searched my handbag for a piece of paper, tore a cheque out, folded it with the blank side outermost. ''Ere, come in,' the woman said gruffly and I followed her into a narrow hall where torn wallpaper hung from one stained corner in a great tongue-shaped flap. There was a powerful smell made up of mould, sweat, urine, overboiled cabbage and old rubber boots.

'You won't want that,' she said, scornfully eyeing the paper and pencil. 'It's jes' round the corner. Well, two streets orf.' She waved her arm to direct me, sniffed derisively and said, 'Nummer forty-one. It's got a green front door.'

I had better luck at Coronation Row. A flushed and perspiring woman opened the door and stared at me when I asked for her sister. The likeness was marked, this one weighing considerably more, with her cheeks pleasantly plumped out and the buttons straining on her purple blouse. 'Ethel,' she called over her shoulder, 'there's a lyedy 'ere askin' for yer.'

I didn't think I'd get much out of Mrs Garston under this woman's roof, so when she anxiously appeared I said, 'Hello, it's me again. Can you spare me a few minutes? I've got a cab waiting. We could take the children for a run in the park.'

She looked at me as if I were mad. 'What park?' And of course I didn't know. This side of London could have been Africa or Japan.

'The cabbie will find somewhere,' I said to reassure her.

It took a while to sort them out, and then what round-eyed

wonder as they swarmed into the cab's rear. The driver was a family man and wonderfully patient as the two older ones whooped and slithered on the seats. He drove us right out to Greenwich, where I recognised the Royal Observatory on its hill, and the children spilled out to roll on the grass and shriek with laughter.

I told the man to come back in an hour, but he said he'd take his time off then and maybe find a whelk stall – which he didn't, but gave up and started to play with the children, showing them how to make daisy chains and grass pop-guns. Meanwhile Mrs Garston and I spread ourselves over the lawn, rested on our elbows and settled to talk.

I had asked Clive the previous night whether he intended to mention my murder theory to his patient, but he impressed on me how necessary it was to stay silent on any defence the man might want to use later in court. Then it would have surprise value and could help to get him released, provided the police hadn't much forewarning to challenge the evidence.

So I assumed I must be as discreet with the wife. I did, however, hint that her Patrick had been led astray, and that we should try to find out whose company he had been in immediately before the attempt. 'Where would he have been drinking?' I asked her. 'Would it be at your local public house?'

''E'd never go there,' she asserted stoutly. 'That Billy Barton is a dreadful blasphemer. My Patrick wouldn't never 'ave put up with that. No, it stumps me where 'e'd 'ave got 'old of that much drink. 'E's such a sober man. Only ever 'as a little tiddly with me and Maisie at Chrismuss, s'posing we can afford a bo'el o' port.'

Which wasn't much help. 'If we could find out who he was with,' I pressed her, 'that might halve the blame levelled against him in court. Couldn't you ask around among neighbours and see if anyone noticed him in the street with a companion?'

'If you fink it could 'elp.'

'I know it could. And aren't you curious anyway?' I watched her closely and saw a change in her eyes. They came more alive. She lifted her chin. 'You mean I could do somefink what might 'elp get 'im orf?'

'The two of us together,' I said. 'If you sniff out who it was, I might be in a position to find out something more about him.'

Now she really lit up. 'Cor,' she exclaimed, 'you ain't arfa one, you are! I tole Maisie what you done at the clinic and she laughed fit to bust.'

I could imagine it, the buttons flying off in all directions as she heaved and wheezed.

'I'm glad you've got her to be with just now,' I said. 'She seems a nice, comfortable woman.'

'Oh, she is. We always bin close, me and Maisie, specially since the war. 'Er Bert died, gassed by them awful Germans at Ypres. Dirty old war, that was. Didn't do poor Patrick no good neither.'

So we got round to his military service with the Yeomanry and his job back home, which was as a junior clerk with a local soap factory. By now the cabbie was getting restless, so we picked ourselves up and brushed loose grass off our skirts.

'How'll I let yer know if I finds out what yer wants?' she asked; so I told her to cross the Thames by the Tower Bridge where she could easily pick up a cab to my address, which I wrote down for her. Then I, or someone at the house, would pay for the journey when she arrived and see that she got safely home again.

'I 'ope,' Mrs Garston said, as she was dropped off with her little brood at Maisie's door, 'as yer didn't get a wiggin' from yer 'usband over what yer done for Patrick with them perlice.'

'Not a very serious one,' I assured her. 'He may be impressive, but he's very kind at heart.'

'Yor a lucky lyedy,' she said, her head tilted, and smiling. It made her look quite pretty.

Lucky, yes. And indeed I know it, I kept telling myself on my way home in the cab; *but how am I to break it to Clive, all I've been up to today?*

Five

Next morning I awoke to find the bed empty beside me and cool to the touch. Considering Clive's admirable athleticism during the night hours, I had thought he might benefit from lying in late for once. With my bathrobe round me I went downstairs to find him sitting on the verandah steps with a neat line of footwear beside him and a velvet buffer-pad in one hand, with which he was raising a bright polish on my indoor shoes.

'Surely, Clive,' I said, 'there's no call for you to take on a boot-boy's job. Can't we get a lad in to do that? Or what's wrong with Mrs Bowyer? She's very competent and willing.'

'Nothing's wrong with her, but she never had this imposed on her in the bishop's employment, and I'd rather she didn't handle the poisonous stuff. It takes a deal of soaping to remove it.'

The word 'soap' made a little buzz in my mind. 'Did you know that Patrick Garston works at a soap factory?' I asked my husband.

He stopped polishing and stared at his hands. 'I believe he did, but I'm afraid they'll not be holding his position open. They can't afford to be short-handed while he's away, and there are plenty of ex-soldiers still on the streets who'd be glad of a working wage. But how did you find out so much about him?'

'I think his wife mentioned it,' I said casually. 'But about the shoes: I don't think you should have to clean them.'

'We haven't the staff of a Stakerleys,' he said humorously. No; nor had he a batman like Julian's right-hand man. That was something to feel relieved about.

'Actually,' Clive said, substituting one of his own brown

44

Oxfords for my black pump and selecting a hard brush, 'it gives me time to think before I'm swallowed up by the hurly-burly of the day. And do you know what I've been thinking? That I have treated you abominably in haring back here to throw myself into my work. I'm quite ashamed. We should be honeymooning together and spending every hour God sends to get to know each other more intimately.'

I squatted beside him. 'Just how much more intimate could we possibly get?' I asked seductively. 'And as for honeymoons, and gently introducing me into the wifely state, I think I have already qualified on that score, wouldn't you say?'

Pretending exasperation, he waved a shoe at me in one hand and the tin of black stain in the other. 'What a time to ask! Just wait until I'm clean of this stuff and I will check on that thoroughly.'

I hugged him and danced off, to take a tour of the little garden, crunching on windfalls under the medlar and soaking my slippers in the dewy grass. Already it was early autumn and the late roses looked softly crumpled like damp tissue paper. Back at Stakerleys it would soon be bonfire time. If I attempted it here I should probably have my near neighbours complaining of the smoke ruining their precious curtains.

Oh dear; those neighbours! I'd done nothing about returning their calls. I supposed I must act on that today, when I'd rather be talking to folk in Patrick Garston's street, seeking anyone who'd seen him brought back drunk to his house on the day he'd ended hanging from the banisters. Or had almost ended.

Clive moved aside as I climbed the steps to the house. He had completed his self-imposed duty and lined up seven pairs of shoes ready for disposal by Mrs Bowyer. No less than four of them were mine, and I recognised one of them as hers. I must, it seemed, come off my high horse and start living in a way more suited to my husband's egalitarian ideas.

We breakfasted together, I in my négligée, at least until he carried me back to our bed and kissed me goodbye for the day. Kissed me all over, and rolled me naked in the eiderdown. Then he left, for more serious matters.

For myself there was the frivolous business of making

myself presentable for the ladies of the neighbourhood. An advantage of Sedgwick life at Stakerleys had been that one made the rules and everyone automatically accepted them. At shabby Fulham we had ignored our neighbours, keeping a decent privacy about our affairs for fear of tittle-tattle; and God knew, there was scandal enough in our household, finally blazoned abroad by the newspapers.

Here in Chelsea I expected a different social stratum, a mixture of middle-class snobs and consciously classless professionals of the arty variety. So what on earth rules would apply?

I would try my own mix, employing the little case of die-stamped cards printed in my married name, which Mama had supplied me with; but first I must go and buy a fantastically modern hat. That should keep tongues wagging and hopefully encourage the overlooking of other aspects, on which I still felt vulnerable.

So had I begun to mind public opinion? The thought startled me. Wasn't I safe enough now, sheltered by a new name and Clive's presence? What had happened to the daredevil girl of yesteryear? Was she transformed into a mouse, after one impulsive act too many? The trouble was that I couldn't foresee what they would see me as, these new people I now lived among. We all slide willingly enough into roles which others suggest for us, and act them out as a sort of armour against their coming too close. I supposed now I must feel my way, listen and learn, holding my counsel until I'd sniffed out the atmosphere. Meanwhile I would go shopping for the hat and cram my unruly red curls into some semblance of order.

I was in Knightsbridge, with my purchase in an elegant box hanging by its cord from one finger, when I recognised a small figure striding along the opposite pavement. Immediately I knew I must make amends and darted through the traffic to confront him.

'Mrs Malcolm,' he said, quite taken aback.

'Jeremy. But I'm Lucy to you, surely? I am so very glad to see you. Will you spare a few moments of your time for me to apologise for the disgruntled way I accepted your help on my wedding day?'

The monkey-face screwed wryly. 'It was unlikely you'd welcome a substitute to drive away with. I understood completely.'

'But forgive? That too? I truly am sorry.'

We spent more moments arguing over whether I was culpable or not, then: 'Well, prove it, please, by letting me take you out to lunch.' I put on my most beseeching look, which he accepted with a sardonic smile; but he accepted the invitation too, to my amazement, and promptly waved for a taxi, into which I slipped, hatbox and all, while he spoke to the cabbie.

'Where shall I tell him to take us?'

'Oh, Gianni's, I think.' They knew me there and would always free a discreet table.

Gianni himself came forward to greet us. 'Miss Sedgwick,' he breathed as if this was the most exquisite moment, 'it has been too long since you visited us.'

How diplomatic: he couldn't have missed the sensational reason for my absence, even if he wasn't aware of my recent name-change. News of the very private wedding hadn't yet reached society magazines. He found us a secluded table and I slid into place with my back to the mirrored wall. Jeremy stood there awkwardly while the elderly Italian waved waiters forward and performed balletic flourishes denoting undying admiration.

Poor Jeremy, he felt totally out of place there. I should have considered him before picking on this fashionable venue. I was to find it brought out the socialist rebel in him and did nothing to earn me his respect. When we chatted, his conversation was full of the dreadful conditions of his charity patients in this uncaring city, and the callousness of the wealthy, so different from the warm and close brotherhood of the mining valleys he'd come from.

'So how did it happen that you made the change?' I asked, frankly curious.

'I let myself be flattered into it,' he admitted, scowling. 'By my schoolteachers, and the local minister. Then, when I won a scholarship to Oxford, my father, a coal-miner, was quite overwhelmed. I couldn't have refused it then. For him it was a passport to Eden, where I'd not die in middle age of consumption or a blood disease, but forever breathe good, clean air and live upright in the daylight. And besides, it would be something for him to talk about in the long winter evenings after being scrubbed up in front of the kitchen fire.'

He had set out to be deliberately provocative. 'And for you,' I pursued, 'where did you think it would lead? To a chance to benefit mankind?'

He took it for sarcasm and almost threw down his napkin in disgust. It was then that I was knocked hopelessly off course because, through the fronds of a brass-potted palm to my left, I recognised a woman across the restaurant floor. It was the unspeakable Selina Holland-Douglas.

We had met as small children, she a quiet, skinny, dark-haired little thing who wouldn't say boo to a goose; I the redhead madcap ever upsetting the formalities under which our nannies made us mix, while they exchanged adult secrets still within scolding range. At the close of these enforced engagements Selina would emerge cool, unruffled, immaculate, with not a seam twisted or a gaiter snagged. I was the one who grazed her knees, tore her dress, ranted and was taken home in muddy disgrace.

Fortunately Mama was quick to spot that we were natural antagonists and, probably more to protect our little guest than to please me, she put an end to the visits. Like me, Selina was fourteen when the Great War began, and for the duration was despatched with her mama to the United States, from where she emerged for New Year 1919 as a gorgeous butterfly to dazzle London society.

One saw her photographs in all the glossy periodicals (at the very time when my portraits and tortured abstracts were gaining notice). More recently there had been a request to paint a likeness of the new Selina for her father, a minister in the Colonial Office. Had I accepted the commission, it could have resulted in a cruel caricature of a tasselled and beaded flapper displaying her slender thighs in a frisky two-step while she tapped ash from a long cigarette holder over her fawning partner. Actually I did commit a sketch to paper, but later destroyed it in a rare rush of charity.

There must have been a great store of suppressed vitality in the uncommunicative child, which, with maturity, had burst out. She was totally modern, the post-war socialite, daring, outrageous, drawlingly contemptuous of convention. There had been one or two minor scandals from which she was always extricated at the eleventh hour to survive almost unblemished. Mostly they involved men not quite out of the top drawer, whose heads had been turned by a taste of military life and the uncertainty of survival (a situation familiar to me). There was also the legal contretemps with a perfume company which she claimed had published 'unauthorised' photographs of her in their advertising. Their use had eventually been suppressed after an agreed withdrawal of the charges, and of counter-charges against her for libel of the company's good name. It was understood to have cost her father a considerable sum to settle. What Selina had done with the quite enticing fee she had already received for the posed shots remained a secret.

Doubtless to the family's relief she had made a successful marriage, or at any rate one that enriched her materially. Her husband was a good fifteen years her senior, a newly created baron with a wartime fortune made in the steel industry. For a while, during my Fulham years, she had disappeared to his estate in Northumberland and produced an heir, but now it seemed she was back on the London scene, unaccompanied and doubtless again taking a certain level of society by storm.

What I should not have expected of her was that she would be lunching *à deux* with my husband at Gianni's that very day.

With his back to their table across the room, Jeremy had not noticed them. I tried to arrange myself as amply as possible across the mirror behind me to ensure he caught no glimpse of their reflection; and I waited with some curiosity for them to recognise me in their turn.

It seemed their conversation was so absorbing that nothing and no one around them existed. Clive's head was inclined towards her as she spoke at length, his curly brown hair only a brushstroke away from the single osprey feather in her silk turban. She seemed dressed more for evening than midday. I saw the diamonds on her too-fine fingers sparkle as she gestured with her wine glass. Her face was alabaster white, her bosom fashionably flat under several long strings of beads. The smooth, black hair, once long and obscuring her narrow face, had been bobbed and the tips flicked roguishly forward over the high cheekbones. It left her ears naked, and the rubies suspended from them picked up the colour of her painted mouth.

She ceased speaking and leaned back, eyes hooded, unnaturally still but for the swing of one sandalled foot. Its floating motion held me quite mesmerised. My gaze was persistently drawn to the creamy shoe, up the fine leg to the slender, crossed knees just free of the tablecloth's draping. That toe kept up its mesmeric sway under her companion's eyes.

As Clive began to reply, she turned away her head, drained her wine and raised the empty glass towards some waiter across the room. Clive put out a finger on her wrist and she slammed the glass down. Her hand flew up to fumble among the necklaces, twisting them between frenzied fingers. She appeared to be under some consuming emotion, or even quite drunk. It amazed me that Clive should care to be seen in a public place with a woman in that condition. It could scarcely do much for his professional reputation.

But what locked chillingly about my heart was the intimacy of that single movement of his finger on her wrist. He must have known her very well to take such a liberty.

I sensed rather than heard Jeremy's impatient question to me. 'I'm sorry,' I said. 'I was momentarily distracted.' I stared in the opposite direction for fear he might turn in his seat and look where the couple were. No, not a couple. Surely not that. But Jeremy didn't move.

'It must be that I'm boring you,' he said coldly.

'Jeremy,' I plunged in, 'I have a problem I wish to consult you on. It's so much on my mind at present that I fear it makes me appear quite rude.'

He looked cautious. 'I can't imagine what I might be in a position to help you with.'

'But you are. Better than anyone' – which, I suddenly knew, was quite true. Who else whom I knew concerned himself so much with the misfortunes of the poor and wretched? I was certain his motives sprang from basic caring quite as much as from political balderdash.

50

'It concerns one of Clive's patients I've got to know a little. While he's under treatment at the clinic, he's likely to lose his job, not that it's a very grand one. They live in Bermondsey and his wife is barely managing with their threee young children.'

'You wish me to find him employment?' Rightly he sounded incredulous.

'That isn't the immediate worry. It's something far worse, to my mind. You see, the police are about to charge him with attempted suicide, but in reality it seems that someone had meant to murder him.'

His frown was almost intimidating. ' "In reality"? Or "it seems"? Which do you mean?'

That is the trouble with intelligent people. They tend to split hairs. 'Judge for yourself,' I said impatiently, and poured out the whole story, including my visit to Ethel Garston, which I had managed to keep from Clive.

Jeremy listened intently, almost forgetting to eat until he became aware of the waiter hovering for our plates. Then he cleared his own briskly as if that were the next item on an agenda to be tackled without delay.

When he spoke again he sounded sombre. 'I've been out of touch with Clive since the wedding, to tell the truth. Otherwise I'm sure he would have mentioned this. Garston was the patient who had him rushing back to London and leaving you to follow on later,' he admitted. 'So I know he takes this case most seriously.'

'Perhaps it was indiscreet of me to disclose so much,' I confessed. 'I've yet to discover what is, and what isn't, proper for a doctor's wife to involve herself in. But I would value your opinion on what I may do for the poor man' – which led me on to confess how I'd deceived the police when they visited the clinic to take poor Garston away.

His face screwed into a mass of wrinkles and he almost howled with laughter. 'But you took a risk there,' he cautioned.

'It's what I do,' I admitted. 'Rather often. But there are things a woman can't manage on her own, and obviously I don't want to drag Clive into my underhand dealings. You see, I've set my heart on finding out who was last with Patrick Garston before he was found hanging.'

Jeremy said he would have to think about it, but I could see he was intrigued by the mystery, even while not completely believing my theory was correct. 'You might, by burrowing, find out something not to the man's advantage,' he warned me. 'Then if it was revealed, he'd be in a worse plight. You must consider this: if someone had reason to kill him, it could be on account of something evil he had done. If we exposed this, where would his dependent family be?'

'I knew I was right to approach you,' I told him. 'You've got just the right sort of mind to sift the thing out.'

He sat back and managed to look a foot taller. Then I knew I had him baited. 'Please come to dinner with us one evening soon, and Clive can give you all the medical details you will need. It's time anyway you saw him settled into the married state.'

His wrinkles stretched into a smile then. 'I could drop into the clinic tomorrow. Then perhaps the subject will come up of itself,' he granted. Which is how we left it, and enjoyed the rest of our meal in companionable silence. Next time I looked across the restaurant to Clive's table, it was vacated.

When I strolled in the garden with him that evening, I mentioned how I'd run into Jeremy by chance and we'd had a meal out together. It seemed quite to please him; but he said nothing about himself having gone to Gianni's – or that he had entertained a lady friend to lunch there.

Until then I hadn't discovered in him that male prerogative of an undisclosed private life. Although resentful, I had to admit that I'd met infinitely worse traits in a husband than secretiveness. So I pretended to myself that I didn't mind, and went on to describe how well I'd fared later that afternoon with the ladies of our neighbourhood.

'I even discovered how their lines of battle lay,' I said, 'because the snobs made a fuss of me as a Sedgwick, and the arty ones accepted me as an equal toiler. Anyway, I've performed my social duty by them, so now I can simply get on with my own life.'

'If they'll allow it,' he said with a vague smile; but I

could see his mind was elsewhere. His day had started with shoes. I wondered now if he was still as mesmerised as I by the insistent flirting of Selina's elegant toe-cap.

Six

Jeremy was as good as his word. He dropped by the clinic next morning and, after a brief discussion with Clive, visited Garston's bedside and was introduced as a colleague of my husband's. He got little or nothing from the man, but just as he was on the point of leaving, Mrs Garston arrived, dragging the toddler by the hand. Then, apparently, he contrived to kill two birds with a single stone, by leading her aside for questioning.

She was slightly tearful and in a state to unburden herself, so not only did she again pour out the full story of discovering her husband hanging from the banisters, but she also bemoaned her sister's refusal that day to look after the little one, who was too young to attend Sunday school.

'It's acaws of 'er cough, y'see,' she explained. 'I'm used enough to it meself, but Maisie never 'aving 'ad kiddies of 'er own, it gets 'er down like.'

As it might well do, Jeremy decided, because he didn't need more than a minute with Sophie to suspect that the poor little mite displayed early signs of consumption. Tuberculosis was a disease he still met too often in his work in London's East End.

Children, healthy or not, weren't allowed in the wards, and a nurse was ordered to take her away, which was the signal for an even more pathetic fit of coughing on the child's part and distress on the mother's. No persuasion from me could ever have such an effect as that scene in convincing Jeremy he should renew an interest in the Garston family. He consulted with Clive, who agreed that Mrs Garston should be advised about X-ray photography for the child's chest, with a view to special treatment under a charity scheme recently set up for just such needs. If possible, Sophie should be sent away from the city to breathe cleaner country air, but at present it seemed unlikely she could be separated from her mother.

'I never meant to stir up such a hornets' nest,' I told Clive when he reported to me that evening. He had invited Jeremy back for a meal but he had declined, being obliged to catch up on work he had neglected in visiting the clinic.

'It's essential to catch the disease at an early stage,' Clive said. 'If Mrs Garston hadn't brought the child with her and Jeremy hadn't happened along, the child's suspected condition might not have come to light for some time. You did well to get him interested. With so much anxiety over the father, not to mention the extra expense, it's unlikely the mother would have much time to worry over a persistent cough.'

'Poor Mrs Garston. Yet another burden on her shoulders.'

'Which is why we must do all we can for her Patrick. Which reminds me: Jeremy had an afterthought on the point of leaving and scribbled a note for you. I have it in one of my pockets.' He patted his jacket and produced a folded scrap of paper.

'Don't overlook the road-worker,' I read off it. 'Perhaps Mrs Garston would know who he is.'

For a second or so it made no sense; then I remembered Clive's description of how Garston had been cut down. His wife had run out into the street and called in a council workman renewing drains in the road; but that was over a week back now, and when I visited her house there was no hole to be seen outside. The work was completed, the men gone.

Yet that was a point to start from. The road-digger could well have been a witness to Garston's drunken return to the house with a companion. I resolved to chase after that myself next day. Meanwhile I questioned Clive on his patient's condition, secretly hoping that it might permit him to be moved. If so, there was no reason why the whole family shouldn't be put up in a vacant cottage on the Stakerleys estate and Patrick attend the cottage hospital as an outpatient. Then little Sophie's consumption could be tackled in a more healthy setting.

Clive wasn't optimistic. He had barely begun to scratch the surface of Garston's problem.

'Why can't you deal with him like you did with that other patient, Dennis Fowler?' I demanded, eager for the man's mind to be cleared of damaging memories in the same way. Apparently, though, it wasn't that simple.

'Because I don't know enough about him yet. Psychoanalysis – the talking cure, as they call it – is a dangerous practice because of the power of suggestion. I may lead him only so far, but for the sake of truth mustn't influence any experience he recalls. Interference could lead him on to a wrong track and risk misinterpreting his neurosis. This could cause real damage to the man. There's already evidence of this happening with practitioners in too much of a hurry, who intrude their own ideas into over-receptive patients. Enough horror can come from suppressed bad memories, without suffering false ones as well.

'With Fowler I had researched his army career with the War Office and with others serving in the ranks with him. In that way I believed I had identified the incident that was the basis of his disorder.

'Patrick Garston is a quite different case, with less known of his past. All I've discovered so far is his present employment and a clean record of wartime service with the Yeomanry. For over two years, until he was invalided home with a badly crushed leg, he saw active service outside Europe, was promoted from trooper to corporal, was never captured, never charged under King's Regulations with any misdemeanour. I haven't managed to speak with any of his officers or comrades in the field, owing to the heavy losses incurred. It could even be that the source of his trauma was not a wartime incident, so I may need to delve farther back, into his childhood.'

Certainly that didn't promise any instant cure. Meanwhile, his family stood in need of assistance, and whatever danger threatened – whether an obsessive wish to end his own life or another's intention to murder him – the man must still be present.

Without any of Clive's medical knowledge, I'd nevertheless enough of my own harsh experience to convince me that the second alternative was no wild fantasy. Hadn't I barely survived an equally horrific fate? Didn't I even now, daily, dread the coming summons to stand to witness in a murder trial? Soon Julian, my supposed first husband, would be tried for his attempt on my life and the killing of my lover.

It was an inescapable reality. Clive's protective arms and a change of name couldn't save me from reliving that horror; but with my own past unalterable, there might still be a chance to save this unfortunate family. Tomorrow I would tackle Mrs Garston again at the clinic, because now I had an official reason to be haunting the place: Clive had approved my offer to paint a mural on the blank wall facing the row of four beds in the men's ward. He believed that watching the artwork progress might be therapeutic. It seemed I was to perform like a theatre-queue busker, but without finally passing round the hat. The only proviso was that I should not employ strong-smelling materials that might cause the patients difficulty with their breathing.

Accordingly, on Monday I collected tools for the initial measurings and plaster treatment, then telephoned a decorator who had helped me with a similar project at Stakerleys a few years back. He promised to send along a workman with the necessary planks and trestles for my scaffolding.

Clive set no rules for the painting's subject matter, happy for me to consult with the patients on this. We ended with an eclectic demand for a country scene with mountains; a kitchen interior; and – from Dennis Fowler, then packing for home and to return only as an outpatient – a man fishing. Garston made no request, turning his head away when I suggested he choose in his turn. His shoulders and right arm were juddering badly while his mouth gobbled soundlessly like an idiot's. Matron quietly confided that he had woken in a tortured sweat and shouting no less than three times during the night. I wished he had at least given me some idea of what he'd prefer *not* to see in my mural.

I thought at first that Mrs Garston had decided against visiting that day, but at a little before noon she appeared alone, having left Sophie with an elderly neighbour. She wasn't happy about that, but would have felt worse not checking on her Patrick's progress – which was negative, as ever.

At the time I was overseeing the wall's cleaning. Its surface showed a few hairline cracks which required filling here and there. When it was done and half dry, I got the decorator to seal it with a pleasant sap-green as a background to work on. Then I took my sketchboard over to where Mrs Garston sat, hunched and passive. I let her watch me block in a frame in scale with the wall, and while I tried out an idea, I questioned her in a casual-seeming way about the road-worker.

'Oh, the navvy,' she said. 'Yes, Alan Durrant 'e's called. I dread to think what would've 'appened without 'im being there.'

'So you know him? Is he a neighbour of yours then?'

'Was once, as a kiddy. The fam'ly moved over the river to Wapping 'bout seven years back. 'E told me 'is dad was killed on the Somme and 'is old mum never pulled round from that Spanish flu the winter of the armistice. So there's only 'im now. Never a very friendly sort of boy, but 'e did all 'e could that day and I'm grateful.'

I admitted I didn't know Wapping and asked if it was nice there. So Mrs Garston described the waterside and even the road where the Durrant family had moved to. It sounded grim, but I thought what she gave me should suffice to track the man down.

I packed up my things, promising to be back next morning when the wall's surface had dried out thoroughly. To my relief, none of the patients or staff seemed upset by the smell of paint undercoat or new plaster.

Back home I roughed out several ideas in charcoal for a composite picture showing a laid table and the corner of a kitchen range. To one side a door stood open on to a river bank with willows and a man sitting under a fishing umbrella with a rod in his hands, reeling in a fish.

It was useless, mundane – a poor composition. The door took up too much height and constricted the outdoor scene. I decided to scrap it and devote the afternoon to researching *l'affaire Garston.*

Taxicabs were as rare as zebras in the straitened area the Durrants had moved to. It caused us to be something of a curiosity as the cabbie inched us past a row of low-fronted houses with the soot and grime of centuries ingrained in their scarred brickwork. There was a stench off the Thames at low tide redolent of long-rotted vegetation and ordure. Even Bermondsey had had a kind of shabby dignity in comparison. I kept the cab waiting while I knocked at doors to ask for Alan Durrant and was met overall with refusal and surly suspicion.

I tried to imitate the way Ethel Garston spoke; but for that, I believed I'd have got open insult, because it was clear that hereabouts they didn't care for the likes of me to come poking into their business.

''Ere,' the cabbie offered eventually, tiring of my failure to get any help. 'Best let me drop in the local and ask for the man in there. Wotcha say then?'

I could have argued that, since the war, women had proved they could venture wherever their menfolk went, but I wasn't convinced that Wapping had quite caught up with the West End on that. Certainly the louche public house that he pulled up by didn't promise an elegant welcome.

With the cab window open I sat back in the shadows, hearing the rumble of throaty voices coming from inside and aware that here the mingled smell of ale, tobacco smoke and oak casks, which I normally found companionable, was stale and nauseous. When my cabbie reappeared to say that he had the basement number I needed, but that Durrant wouldn't likely be back until sometime after midnight, I was forced to admit defeat. Never in a month of Sundays could I hope to slip away from Clive's bed to make an early-hours call on the elusive road-worker.

All the way back to Chelsea I sat and fumed at the impotence of being female. Choices that a man never needed a second thought to take on could be quite out of the question for us women. And why? Because some men were crude brutes and might force themselves on a lone, unknown female. Any visit here after dark would be folly, exposing me to obvious risk. How long would it take before the message of equality reached these poorer streets, where a woman was too often seen as no more than a punchbag, a whore and someone to scrub the floors clean?

It was unfair, of course, to condemn so widely, but it struck me then that the social revolution the Reds went on about could be better directed towards the male proletariat than to lopping heads off the effete and despised aristos; but then that showed my prejudice, didn't it? Admittedly – but at least it could make a valid point against little Jeremy with his Welsh left-wing views.

Dear God, what must he have made of Stakerleys? Hadn't

Clive ever considered that? – that once introduced into the enemy camp he might set about blowing it up, if only verbally? Lenin was a little man too, and look how far the Bolsheviks had gone with his oratory.

Catching myself concerned with such world-size themes, I instantly saw the comedy of it, so I was in a better mood on arriving home to observe that another cab was already drawn up outside. I had an unexpected visitor.

As the gentleman inside bowed his lanky form out on to the pavement, I recognised my half-brother. 'Edwin!' And then instantly I knew: my father was dead. Edwin had come to break the news to me.

His face crinkled in a wide smile, but he looked pale. He insisted on paying off both cabs before he had more to say than my name. Then we went indoors, where Mrs Bowyer was waiting to take his hat and gloves. His only luggage was the single bag Chilvers had mentioned him packing. That seemed an age ago, when he'd run out on my wedding. I would have teased him about that but I saw he wasn't in the mood for it, or for any light talk for that matter.

I ordered tea and we sat, our chairs close, in the salon overlooking the garden. He took my hands in his own, which, like the rest of him, were noticeably thinner. 'Lucy dear,' he said. 'I stayed until the end, and then there were matters to see to.'

'His woman,' I said, nodding. 'Had he made proper provision for her?'

'As far as he could. He didn't leave much.'

I knew what that implied: she would become another Stakerleys' pensioner. 'And so he's died, my father.'

'It wasn't easy for him. He fought like a giant – but with the strength of a pixie.'

That last phrase sounded like a quotation, but I didn't recognise it. Edwin smiled. 'That is what *she* said – Finvola. She was a natural poet.'

I remembered her bony, hard-done-by face and the black looks she'd given me. 'I never knew,' I admitted. I had taken her for an unschooled peasant; but then she might have been that and a 'natural poet' too.

Would she have given the old actor precious lines to

declaim? Suddenly I couldn't hold back my tears at recall of him standing there like Lear, the wind tugging at his grizzled red beard; all the irony in him, as we proudly turned our backs on each other. The man who, ages before, had seduced the young, widowed Isabelle and abandoned me, their baby, to the winds of fate. There was I being poetical now. It was the contagion of the Irish. Edwin had brought it back with him.

'He was a wonderful man,' my half-brother said. 'Through meeting him I understand you now so much better than I did.' Then I was silently weeping in his arms and the tea going cold all the while.

'I loved him, fiercely,' I said, 'just from that single meeting. But I could never have gone back.'

'He wouldn't have allowed it. With me it didn't matter. He employed all his ironic humour on the situation, mocked me in pseudo-Shakespearean verse. I played the page and the Fool for him, and the prince in rags. He seemed to come a little more alive for a while, and then suddenly one day all the energy was used up. We held his hands, Finvola and I, while he went across. All he whispered was, 'Final curtain.'

I moaned in my brother's arms and he stroked my hair, the unruly red curls I'd inherited from an Irish mummer, until we were both over the open grief. Then I collected myself and made the right social remarks, showed off my new home, and displayed myself, at last, as a legitimately married woman. Then I brought Petra down from the nursery and reintroduced her by the new name. So, until Clive came home, we spent the brief hours in a Sedgwick huddle. The world of Wapping and Bermondsey slipped from my mind.

When the two men met, there was a deal of boisterous grasping of each other's shoulders and mock pugilistics. I hadn't imagined grown men went on like that. While they caught up with each other's news I interrupted to beg Jeremy's telephone number from Clive, with the excuse that I must ring to thank him for last night's note.

He hadn't reached home and I began leaving a message with a frosty-voiced female when he took over at the other end of the line. He listened, grunting, while I ran through my inability to reach the man Durrant. 'It was a good idea following him up,' I said. 'I did all I could, but I had to give up there.'

'Perhaps one of Mrs Garston's neighbours will remember noticing something,' he said. 'We must hope for that.' And he ended by curtly wishing me goodnight. He sounded impatient with my spinelessness and I felt a fresh surge of resentment against him.

Edwin left at a little after eleven, refusing the offer of our guest room because he had already notified Chilvers that he would stay at the family's Eaton Place house. 'Did you know Isabelle was in residence at present, while Geoffrey's abroad?' he asked as he took his leave. 'I'm sure you'll be hearing from her shortly.'

Isabelle let loose in London was not good news. Even less her likely intention to get in touch with me here. Then I pulled myself up. It was enough to have turned my back on one of my natural parents. I supposed that I should really make an effort with the other.

At some moment in the night the aftershock struck and I awoke choking with emotion. Whatever dream I'd been involved in left me unsure of everything, especially myself. I seemed to be just some version of the person I might have been but had somewhere missed out on becoming; yet a detached part of that ghost-shadow knew all my failings, my petty concerns, and seemed to be watching steely-eyed while I floundered, miserably unable to articulate what was wrong.

Clive stirred alongside and I felt instant anger that he hadn't wakened with me. This must have communicated itself through the sheets, for his arms came round me and I felt his heart leap to the speed of my own. 'Lucy, dearest girl.'

I didn't have to find the words. He knew grief. It was the awful black finality, because now it was too late to do things differently. 'I never told him,' I managed to get out.

'I'm sure he knew. There was no need to tell him. You went looking for him and that said enough.'

'I left it to Edwin. Why is it so hard to say "I love you", when I meant it so unbearably much?'

He said nothing then, simply held me. 'Clive,' I said timidly a little while later. 'All the times you've told me how much you love me, I've stayed silent, haven't I? I've let you say that and said nothing in return, as if it's just my right to be loved. I want you to know . . . I think I was afraid. Now I can't bear it to be too late again. Do you understand?'

'So tell me.'

'I love you, Clive – so much that it hurts.'

He rocked me slowly in his arms. 'That's wonderful, but you mustn't be hurt. I don't want that. Be happy, as I am. I think that just now I have everything I want in the world.'

We stayed that way, locked together until later he said, over my head, 'You are wrong to remember your father guying Lear. He wasn't mocking you. The tragedy of Lear and Cordelia was one of love without understanding. Your father and you were wiser to the world. Each saw the other clearly, and the love was self-evident in that. He wouldn't have had you any other way.'

I supposed Clive was right, as so often. Robert Grainger had been a proud man. He had abandoned me before my birth; I had turned my back on him as a dying man. He would have seen it as just. We wanted no Victorian melodrama.

Then I had to smile. 'I can imagine his roar if I'd sent him funeral lilies!'

Clive didn't laugh. 'Remembering our own failings towards the dead is a needed part of mourning,' he said sombrely. 'I still feel the same about my own father. It is something we have to live with, and survive.'

Seven

The grief remained with me next morning, but dulled. Despite it I awoke feeling challenged, resolving to sort out my priorities and plan how best to divide the day between my home, my husband and baby, the projected mural and concern for the Garston family. The programme seemed simple and satisfying enough, but could more than fill the available hours.

In my notebook I rapidly sketched a new plan for the mural. It was a reversal of the old, with a calm country scene foremost, having the exterior of a white cottage slightly to right of centre in mid-ground. An open door threw golden light over the threshold, picking out a corner of a laid table with a checked cloth. Framed in the lattice window was the darker outline of a woman. Since this was for a men's ward, they could conclude she was suitably busy at the kitchen sink. A black Labrador was sprawled, sunning itself, outside, and I completed the composition with grouped trees, a hint of water, the fisherman, a distant view of low mountains and various other artistic clichés. It wasn't something I'd care to put my name to, but should serve the anodyne purpose.

Soon after ten, having accompanied Mabel on a riverside stroll with the baby's pram and a lively Petra propped up inside to observe the outer world, I set off by cab with all my painting paraphernalia, and a thermos of coffee to induce a talkative mood in Mrs Garston.

As the outline of my picture progressed, she began to relax, joining the three men seated as audience just out of my hearing as I teetered on the makeshift scaffolding. The fourth, farthest bed was now occupied by a newcomer, who was semi-comatose.

A little before noon Dr Atkinson came in with a lecturer

64

in psychology from University College and three students to observe whatever therapeutic effect the new interest might be having. I had an opportunity to study my husband's partner while his attention was off me: a tall, wispy man with thin, greying, sandy hair; large-nosed; his mouth invisible under a tea-stained, whitish moustache and trimmed beard. He seemed to lack confidence and if I'd had to choose which of the two should treat me for some mental trouble, I'd never have hesitated a second. It struck me that he might have resented his younger colleague's popularity, but he was invariably courteous, and in his own quiet way almost distinguished.

The students chatted with the patients and left favourably impressed by the experiment. At that I declared work over for the day and invited Mrs Garston to join me for coffee outside in the little garden shaded by a giant plane tree. My request to see any of her husband's wartime correspondence that she still held was naturally an embarrassment because of the very personal contents.

'I kept all 'is letters, every one,' she said. 'Even them cards that don't say nothink but just fill in the blanks. Only 'e's me 'usband, see, and some of the things what 'e said were . . . you know.'

I assured her that I did know, being very newly married myself, but that she could cover over the private bits if only she'd let me see anything regarding his war experiences with the Yeomanry's Hussars.

'Only they wasn't all 'ussars by then,' she said. 'Acaws of so many 'orses dying or getting sick on the boat going over. Near broke 'is 'eart, it did. Must've been seventy at least including 'is Cherry. Ship pneumonia they called it. First thing off the boat at Alexandria 'e was on fatigues 'elping get rid of the last lot. 'Orrible job, but 'e done what 'e 'ad to. Got commended by the vet officer, Captain Williams.'

I knew what it was to lose a much-loved horse. When I was sixteen, my dear Carob had had to be shot after breaking both forelegs under me in taking a fence badly; but such a loss wouldn't have been enough to land Garston in the state he was in now. 'So did he get another mount?' I asked.

He hadn't done. His war, from then on, had been fought

as an infantryman, first at Gallipoli, advancing on foot under gruelling Turkish shellfire at Suvla Bay.

I returned with Ethel Garston to her abandoned home so that she could show me the letters. They were in several bundles tied with white tape, one lot from Hounslow Heath, where he had first been in training with his mare Cherry; a second bunch from Egypt, full of complaints about flies, raiding Bedouins and wells run dry that kept fatigue pickets working all day on futile pumping. The third and fourth were from active service in Gallipoli and the last set from Salonika where he had been wounded with shrapnel in the right leg and finally transported home in 1917, by then promoted to corporal.

As I read the Gallipoli letters, I felt sick to my soul. It amazed me how much had been allowed to come through, as though even the censors had been so stressed that they hadn't cared to function any more. Or else the ships that carried the mail back to Egypt had fled the hellhole in a hasty turn-around and the men's letters were thrown in unchecked.

Garston had not shied away from sharing details of danger or horror with Ethel, but wrote directly as if still shaken by what he had just been through. I hadn't forgotten letters of the same kind shown me by other distraught women during the war, and no longer found it shameful that men passed on their agonies to those they regarded as weaker than themselves. I could see now it was a necessary release of emotion, as though they held out their arms for comfort and wept openly on their women's shoulders.

Between themselves, under constant stress, they must have imposed a stricter self-discipline, monastic and brusque, not daring to lower their own defences or endanger their comrades' endurance. Instead, they would have sworn and cursed the enemy, the NCOs, their officers, the flies, the mud, the shellfire, the empty water bottle, then crawled hopelessly on to the next entrenchment, laden with their shovels and two sandbags, their mess kit, their Lee-Enfield and 200 rounds, their wretched little crate of carrier pigeons. I could smell their sweat and feel it on my body. In my turn I cursed along with them.

I read with horror of the futile sorties, yard by yard on

their bellies over open plain with sparse, dry scrub; crawling over boulders and the rotted bodies unclaimed from earlier aborted attacks, while Turkish artillery pounded the area with long-distance shellfire; the petty advances and enforced withdrawals; the sacrifice of hundreds, thousands of British, Australian and New Zealand men for the sake of taking a bare hillside, lost again in a matter of days. In the rains the men had trench foot from prolonged crouching in waterlogged bolt-holes. By mid-August the tinder-dry scrub was continually torched by the heavy Turkish shellfire as they advanced to 'Chocolate Hill' or the desolate 'Hill W'. The encroaching flames consumed the wounded where they lay beyond all hope of rescue, and still the pathetic sorties must go on.

'I think us few lasted through that day,' Garston had written in one letter, 'because as we advanced towards their guns the sun was so bright behind us.' It recalled Peter describing the advantage of surprise as he'd flown out of the sun's glare to score on a Zeppelin over the Thames. My dear Peter, who had survived the war crippled, only to be brutally murdered in the peace. It was bitter, remembering.

Then, abruptly, it occurred to me that for Patrick Garston perhaps death had threatened him just days ago in much the same way. It could be that this late 'shell-shock' had its origin in something outside the war zone; some quite recent gruelling experience that had earned him an enemy back home. Hadn't Clive, in his recent lecture, said that any individual could be devastated by less earth-shaking events *in everyday life, at work, or even within the apparent security of the close family*?

It seemed less likely, considering the greater wartime hardships of Patrick Garston, yet the idea persisted. Clive had also hinted that he might now look for some alternative trauma but – true to the Freudian system – from farther back, perhaps in Garston's childhood. While he covered that angle I could perhaps pursue more recent problems as the source of the man's neurosis.

I stayed in Bermondsey until almost seven, making notes which might be of use to Clive if he needed to take Garston's mind back to those war experiences. I also smuggled out a photograph of a younger, happier Patrick Garston in uniform and mounted on a solid little chestnut mare.

By then Ethel had long given up and gone back to collect her children and cook a meal for them at sister Maisie's. It hadn't taken her any time to realise where my true interests lay and that the private pages of her correspondence were safe from my prying.

Ethel had left me to lock up, which I did, taking one last look at the sinister cut rope still trailing from the banister rail, before closing the front door on the silent house. I had asked whether her husband ever tackled any practical tasks left-handed and she had told me no; also that Clive had already questioned her on that. It seemed to puzzle her, but I didn't explain.

By the time I had walked round to Maisie's to return the key, and then continued on foot across the river to catch a cab, it was quite dark and possibly Clive would be impatient for my return home. However, when I arrived – still in the breeches I'd worn to keep myself decent on the scaffolding that morning, and ravenously hungry – I found only Mrs Bowyer downstairs. Mabel was bathing Petra in the nursery, ready for her final bottle and bed.

'Madam,' Mrs Bowyer said in an ominously firm voice, 'Lady Isabelle Penrhydd called in your absence. She declined to leave a note but impressed upon me that you should join her in dining at the Cavendish with her party at eight o'clock.'

Nicely put. Isabelle had clearly been throwing her weight about and probably not disguising her scorn at the modesty of my present establishment. 'I'm afraid she does tend to patronise terribly,' I said comfortingly. 'We usually take little notice of it, Mrs Bowyer. I'm sorry if she was a nuisance.'

Tired as I was I should have ignored the message entirely except that I still felt guilty over neglect of my father – my late father. So I telephoned the hotel and conveyed my regrets through their maître d'. He offered to bring Isabelle to the phone, but I wouldn't let him disturb her party.

Intending to soak long in the bath, I expected Clive would be home by the time I came downstairs, but Mrs Bowyer told me he had telephoned regarding yet another emergency on hand and would not be back at all that night. It really was too bad. His wretched patients would wear him out at this rate. Perhaps I had begun my marriage quite wrongly and should have refused to let him postpone the honeymoon, starting as I hoped things would go on. Now he would think he could fob me off at any time with excuses – and how could I be sure he was actually with a patient, since he allowed himself the prerogative of taking meals in fashionable restaurants with fascinating women, and never a word of it to me? There was so much about this man I had married that was still unknown to me. I had taken him so readily on Edwin's recommendation. Was this to be a case of marrying in haste and . . . ?

While a part of my mind travelled these caustic routes I wasn't really convinced. I was just gorging myself on resentment as though it was a box of chocolates I craved.

Perhaps I was mentally more tired than I knew, but the warm, scented water had revived me enough so that, once I'd wrapped myself in a soft towel, the fancy came to dress myself again. Since my husband wasn't present to entertain me I decided that others should. I had the excuse to present myself at the Cavendish. If Isabelle's little party had already moved on elsewhere, I might still be welcomed by other acquaintances dining there after a theatre.

On a whim, but also because I still had little else in the way of up-to-date formal clothes, I took out the dress I'd been married in, added a sequinned and feathered headband and my ermine cape.

As my cab drew up at the hotel's doorway it was noisily hailed by a little knot of revellers just leaving. Then, 'Darling! *Mi carissima Lucia!*' Isabelle was crying extravagantly from among them.

She was only expansive-drunk, but I knew the phases that must surely follow. Her companions, milling anonymously under the dim street lighting, scarcely impressed me as responsible.

I let her crowd us all into the taxi, six or seven despite the cabbie's protests, and we were decanted after only a few minutes at a nightclub in Frith Street, Soho, which one of them – a young man with sleeked-back black hair and an effeminate, made-up face – swore was sheer wizardry. Besides this person there were two giggly young women, one in powder blue, the other lilac; a puffy-faced, middle-aged man whom I wrongly took to be Isabelle's escort, and a gaunt woman in wispy black chiffon who looked vaguely familiar. As we sorted ourselves on the pavement I recognised her as 'Poppy' Oppenheimer – daughter of a circuit judge and married to a law lord.

In the world of jurisprudence it seems they like to preserve the legal genes exclusively. Someday our new eugenists may condemn that as unhealthy inbreeding.

When we were debutantes, Poppy had despised me for not being a true Sedgwick (accepting that Mama had produced me in an earlier, middle-class marriage). Now I couldn't claim the Sedgwick bloodline without branding myself a bastard. In this modern age, I wondered, which would she consider the greater solecism? And would she then find it necessary to patronise Isabelle as a fallen woman?

Not that I would ever enlighten her on the subject. Her opinion was of no importance. Nevertheless, if Isabelle continued fawning on me and reached the sentimental stage, she might well drop her guard and admit to more than she would care to have made public. It seemed that, having once joined the group, I must keep my wits about me and a restraining hand on Isabelle.

The nightclub was quite awful, in a cramped and tobacco-smoky basement, with sinister, subdued lighting, the members and their guests a bizarre mixture of the world-weary and the desperately exhibitionist. Isabelle was dancing with her young man, with wild swooping back to our table for champagne between circlings of the floor.

I sat, rejoicing that my painting had left me little time for socialising with my peers, and reminded myself that alcohol on an empty stomach could have a disastrous effect. Since the others had already dined, I did not care to order a meal.

The middle-aged man sat to my left and the two flappers beyond him, which left an empty chair to either side of Poppy, who was smoking one of those cigarillos Isabelle always carried with her. 'For God's sake, George,' she sniped, grinding it out in an ashtray, 'show some life and take one of the bunnies out on the floor.'

'I'll do better. Take 'em both' – which he did, the three of them rotating with their arms about each other's shoulders like home-going drunks. Poppy regarded their antics ironically before turning her attention to me, shouting to be heard above the wailing band. 'I hear you're married again. This time to a doctor.'

There seemed no point in saying that gossip had it right. I waited for some adverse comment, but all she said was, 'Lucky you, then.'

'Correct again,' I granted.

She gave a twisted little smile. She had a black, beaded purse on a silver chain, and now she fumbled inside it for a small pillbox, shook out a trail of white powder on to the side of her left hand, tickled it with a fine glass tube and lifted it towards her face. I looked away as she sniffed. I could not believe that she would dare in such a public place.

It was just then that their tango brought Isabelle and her partner so close that in bending extravagantly back, her loose, blonde hair brushed the table. I looked up at the mask-like face of the man curved over her and had my second shock in as many seconds.

So close, I couldn't be mistaken. The figure in immaculate white tie and tails was a woman. And not just any woman, but Selina Holland-Douglas.

Fortunately the dance had come to an end and a crescendo on the drums announced the start of the cabaret. The lights dimmed even further and I was able to hide my consternation. At least, I consoled myself in the dark, if Selina was here with me she wasn't elsewhere with my husband.

So is that what I'd actually suspected? Perhaps momentarily, in that subconscious mind which the psychologists consider so important. There would be time enough later to consider the implications of that. My present practical concern was to get Isabelle safely back to Eaton Place before she made a total fool of herself.

It meant sitting through a spectacular show of fan-dancing and sword-swallowing with a background tableau of decorative nymphs who appeared in the semi-dark to be totally naked. There followed an erotic *pas de deux* during which I found Isabelle had moved next to me and was squeezing my hand between her own two. Understanding that she'd reached the maudlin stage and I would quickly need to spirit her away, I slid a supportive arm round her and that is how we were exposed when the lights went up again.

I had not suspected the effect this would have on Selina. She bent over my chair and hissed something I couldn't catch. I stood up, my arm still supporting Isabelle. 'I'm taking her home now,' I said; and that was when the virago slapped my face.

It was the signal for some at neighbouring tables to raise a ragged sort of cheer and rumbles of embarrassed laughter. Our two flappers were ecstatic at the prospect of an open fight between jealous lesbians.

'You will excuse us: my *aunt* is tired,' I said distinctly. 'It has been a long day for her and she has not been in the best of health.'

Two waiters were hovering anxiously, fearful of a female free-for-all with damage to property, but Selina had drawn back and was staring at me with strangely concentrated pupils. 'Goody Two-Shoes,' she whispered. 'Bloody – Goody – Two-Shoes. For Godsake, it's Lucy Sedgwick!'

The doorman fetched our cloaks and from nowhere a taxi appeared as Isabelle and I shivered on the kerb. My slapped cheek was flaming in the chill night air, oozing a little blood where Selina's ring had cut me, but I encountered no resistance from Isabelle. In the cab she curled up on the rear seat like the dormouse in *Alice.* By the time we reached Eaton Place she was fast asleep. While I warned the cabbie to wait, a footman came down the house steps and helped to lift her out. 'I shan't come in,' I told him, 'but be sure I shall call here tomorrow. See that someone helps her to bed.'

'Estelle is waiting up, madam,' he assured me. He sounded distant, as though he imagined I was responsible for her state. Well, let him think that. Not, as Isabelle herself would say, that he was paid to think anything at all.

I gave the cabbie directions back to the Chelsea house, furious with Isabelle for the wild company she kept and even more furious with myself for having joined her party. I had intended making such good use of my day and just look how it had ended. As Mabel, in her dressing gown, let me in, the ormolu clock in the drawing-room chimed three clear strokes. I slunk off to bed as if I were a child in disgrace.

Sleeping heavily through the rest of the night, I awoke to a sense of frustration, missing out on seeing my baby before Mabel took her off in the pram, and leaving later than I'd wished for work at the clinic. All the time that I laid on glazes of paint my mind was full of the previous night and Isabelle's stupid situation. Her friends were worthless. Not one of them had had any concern for her, but only looked for easy entertainment. I wondered how far she had picked up their casual habits: whether she too carried cocaine in her evening purse. And what was her relationship with the androgynous Selina, a female for my husband, but what exactly for her? Had my natural mother taken a young lesbian lover? Could that be the result of husband Geoffrey's absence abroad; or even the reason for it?

I was out of my depth there, an unwordly prig, as Selina had accused me of being. It required the experience of someone like Clive to assess the whole situation. Where would he stand in relation to its pivotal point, the woman he had secretly had lunch with?

When he came in for his ward round I watched him covertly; the serious, listening face, the referrals back to his students, the quiet authority with his patients. Viewed from an objective angle he was impressive. Had I seen him then for the first time he would have won my complete confidence; but I remembered this was only his professional face. Under the mask he was no more than a man, like any other, as indeed Julian had been. Must I accept being deceived again, this time by someone I believed I had truly loved? Still did love, perhaps.

Impatient at this self-taunting, I reminded myself of the doctor in him, the psychologist I would need to consult over this latest family problem. I had information on Garston's past for him too. I stood by in my stained painter's smock until he was done and then followed him out to where he spoke with Sister. On seeing that I waited, she broke off, wished me good morning and went briskly back to her office.

'Darling girl,' Clive said, holding me close and kissing the top of my head. 'I am so sorry about last night. Did you miss me? It was unavoidable: a serious case of dementia quite improperly committed to a police cell. I was required to sedate the man and then wrangle to convince the authorities that he belonged elsewhere. It was the devil's own job to get him admitted to any institution at that time of night. Why does everyone seem to switch off their common sense at eight p.m.?'

'They do,' I agreed vehemently. 'That's what I badly need to talk to you about. I've been having adventures myself.'

He drew away and stared at me. I had never seen his face look so tired and my heart went out to him – all the more because of his instant concern at what I had said. His eyes lingered on the patch of colour on my cheek where inadequately I had tried to cover the scratch with face powder, but he made no comment.

'Book me in as one of your outpatients,' I demanded, 'if that's the only way I can get half an hour of your attention.'

'Angel,' he spluttered as I produced a demonic scowl. 'I've been seriously remiss. I'll make myself available this very minute. Everything else can wait.'

So I was taken into his consulting room, with the blinds drawn; but instead of the couch I sat on his knees, held close, and poured out what had happened last night, by which time we had moved to the inadequate couch and thence frenziedly to the floor.

As the final bonbon to the banquet, while I rearranged my dress, I told him about Patrick Garston's letters from the Middle Eastern front.

'You have been busy,' he said drolly. 'I'll need to work overnight to catch up with your level of good works. But seriously, I think you may run risks in becoming so involved in the Garston case. I'd like you to leave it now to the police, or to Jeremy, who is showing an uncommon interest in the man.'

Then, promptly on cue, there was a discreet tapping at the door and, when we had sorted ourselves, Clive opened it to Jeremy himself.

'Speak of angels,' my husband quoted.

Or the devil, I thought, for no apparent reason then.

He appeared discomfited to see me there. It could have been because he wished to discuss confidential medical matters with Clive, but it made me curious.

Whatever the reason for his unscheduled visit, he was reluctant to broach it in front of me, so I plunged in with interests of my own. 'Did you follow up what I told you about the road-worker at Wapping?' I demanded.

Normally quick-witted, he was left open-mouthed a moment. 'He . . . I spoke with him last night, at his home. He was unable to tell me anything of any use, I'm afraid.'

Because his face flushed as he answered, I refused to leave it there, certain that if it wasn't a lie at least it was a blood relation to one. 'Do you mean that he hadn't observed anyone going home with Patrick Garston that day, or that he wouldn't discuss it with you?'

Jeremy hesitated, darted a glance at Clive and gave the minutest shrug. It angered me that he obviously considered it unsuitable for me to continue any interest in the man.

'Jeremy?' Clive prompted.

'I . . . I had the impression that he was unwilling to answer any questions. Which isn't surprising. There are a lot of villains in that part of the world. It's possible he had something discreditable to cover up.' Now that he deigned to speak, it all came out helter-skelter.

Not that it made good sense. 'Up to some mischief while laying drains in the road?' I demanded sarcastically. 'Where would the crime be in that?'

Jeremy scowled. '"The wicked flee when no man pursueth,"' he quoted from scripture. Born and raised in the Welsh valleys, he would have been well-grounded in his Bible. Although it wasn't entirely apposite, I yielded on that, far from satisfied but refusing to let him goad me into an exchange of proverbs.

Whatever the man had or hadn't told him, it struck me that Jeremy himself was the one who appeared to be fleeing.

Clive looked from one of us to the other and settled for peacemaking. 'Maybe he thought the information was worth trading? Do you think he might open up if he was offered a few shillings?'

'Possibly,' Jeremy said tightly. 'He struck me as the sort who would swear to anything if you paid him enough. Do you think I should go back and bribe him?'

In Latin there are questions so formed as to expect the

answer 'no'. They would have been delivered in just that tone of voice.

He was clearly not intending to speak frankly in my presence. 'I'll leave you to your professional discussions,' I said abruptly, turned on my heel and left them together.

Eight

I hurried home, changed into decent female garb and set out on foot for Eaton Place. I found Isabelle still floating around in her négligée with the back of one wrist to her forehead to indicate frailty and that I should treat her gently. I dived cruelly in.

'Just what were you up to last night with those dreadful young people?'

'*George* isn't young. He's quite old actually.'

'And of the others two were mere babes; and two grew up with me.'

'Where else can I find lively company when my own daughter chooses to turn her back on me?'

I forbore to remind her that she was the first to opt for abandonment. 'Isabelle, if you feel the time has come to advertise our relationship, by all means do so. It will make no difference to how I feel or behave. But there may well be some coolness shown towards you from those whose society you still enjoy.'

She flounced across the room, turning on me with a haughty scowl. 'Really, Lucy, to make such a fuss! Over a little outing which I thought you might find quite entertaining. Anyone would think *you* were the mother, or some paid nanny with no social sense.'

So had it been social sense for her to mix with those drifters? I was loath to protest further, understanding how Isabelle must feel herself equally aimless and isolated. While she angered me I could still feel some pity. For her safety I had to risk sounding the prig that Selina had accused me of being.

'Isabelle, under the glitter those are sad people. You don't belong with them. You have a good husband and a family that loves you.'

'You are all the family I need,' she shrieked at me. 'Who is left for me when you turn away?'

I could only leave her to answer that herself. She was the one who had given her baby up.

'Where's Geoffrey?' I asked, to divert her.

'Oh, in Provence. They've found some new weevil there with grubs that strip the vine roots.'

'You could have gone with him.'

'But Lucy, *weevils*! Do you imagine I have any interest in creatures like that? Besides, he was in such a haste to go, I couldn't have been ready in time.' She allowed her lower lip to tremble pathetically – a practice I'd been treated to before.

'So follow him there now. You know he'll be delighted to have you with him.'

'Nowadays I find it so fatiguing travelling alone. It was different,' she said pettishly, 'when I employed Eugenie as my companion. And maids are such dull company.'

'Then invite your brother and Eugenie along. You could make up a family party at the *caves*. The French make a great occasion of welcoming guests to taste their new wines.'

At last I seemed to have struck a sympathetic note. It was certain that Isabelle would overdo the sampling, but at least with her brother and sister-in-law there she would be taken good care of. She agreed to telephone Stakerleys and order Forbes to come and collect her.

She learned then that Eugenie and Laurence had left for a weekend at Polesden Lacey where the King and Queen Mary were also to be guests, and this put poor Isabelle out further, railing at the notion of 'new money' chasing the royals.

'Nonsense,' I said brusquely. 'It's good for our royal family to take an interest in people who actually do things and add to the prosperity of the country. It may be Maggie Greville's passion for porcelain and majolica that first lured Queen Mary, but there's plenty of her late father about her. It will ensure she'll also have plenty to say about industry north of the border.'

'Brewing!' Isabelle said with disgust, overlooking that but for the miserable climate it could have been wine that William McEwan had made his millions at. That, in her scale of values, would have been totally acceptable.

It appeared that Papa had elected to drive down to Surrey in the Daimler, so Forbes was still at Stakerleys and available to fetch Isabelle with another car. I made certain that he would pick her up at six o'clock that evening, then made my way home for a late luncheon. It was as well that I did so, because I found Clive already there, having taken two hours off from the clinic before returning in the afternoon.

We had the rare pleasure of lunching together, but over the meal he struck me as unusually distracted, so I asked if anything was wrong.

'Not wrong exactly,' he said. 'I'm more puzzled. It's something Jeremy told me. There's no reason why you shouldn't know: he's a really gifted physician but he's decided to give up. I've quite counted on him for a second opinion with my drugs treatments and now he'll have less time to keep abreast of new developments in pharmacology. I shall miss his help, as well as his friendship. Besides, I'm not convinced it's a wise move for him to make.'

'Why's that? What is he to do instead? Is he leaving London?'

'He's transferring to surgery. Both he and I felt some fascination for the scalpel as students. In fact, Sir Digby expected one or other of us to join his team on qualifying. Eventually I found psychiatry a greater attraction, but I think it was a clash of personalities that made it impossible for Jeremy – at least then. Now he seems to have overcome his distaste for Sir Digby.'

I recalled my first meeting with the little man and his glee in mocking 'old Park Railings' as a dinosaur of the medical profession. It was amazing that so soon after that he should be accepting a position in the professor's team. The change of direction was a total *volte face*.

'I'm sorry you'll see less of him,' I consoled my husband. 'Let's give a special farewell dinner for him, shall we? As soon as we can fix it.'

Clive seemed to hesitate a moment, then smiled. 'That's a great idea, darling. I'll find a day that will suit him and we'll discuss who else to invite.'

With that settled, Clive's spirits recovered somewhat and,

as we set out to hunt down a cab for our return to the clinic, I raised the subject of a motor of our own.

'The bishop wanted to give us one,' he admitted, 'but there are several reasons why I turned the offer down, mainly the fact that we have nowhere to keep it. But I did wonder about the alternative of a motorcycle.' This last was suggested almost shyly.

Exclusive transport for himself? I wondered. Did he already find a need to escape from me? 'I suppose I could ride postillion,' I remarked.

Clive halted in mid-stride and chuckled. 'You mean on the pillion. And no, that could be dangerous. Your papa would be horrified. And I can't imagine you cramped in a bumpy sidecar.'

'Then I'll have a motorbike of my own,' I told him. 'It can't be much different from driving a car.'

My husband looked appalled, but as a cab hove into view just then, the discussion was dropped. Only temporarily, I had decided. In this case, what was sauce for the gander should also be sauce for the goose.

We had no sooner entered the building and I had donned my smock than there was a great commotion as Ethel Garston arrived. She hadn't visited her husband that morning, but then there were days when she didn't, so I had thought nothing of it.

She was in a terrible state, her hands and bodice stained with soot and her hair hanging wispily down from under her straw hat. 'Mrs Malcolm,' she cried, 'oh truly we're real lost now. Everythink's gawn. Not a stick left to call our own. Whatever is to become of us?'

Matron forced her on to a chair and loosened her dress at the throat. 'Now take long, deep breaths,' she commanded, while a nurse ran up with a tumbler of water. After a deal of calming, and between floods of tears, the tale came out.

It had been after midnight that the fire engine's clanging had woken her. A stench of burning was in the air. From Maisie's front windows they had seen the black smoke only streets away, and suddenly with a great explosion it had become a wall of flames rising over the houses in between.

She had known then, instinctively. It was her own home.

This was the final blow to her accursed family. She had thrown on some clothes and rushed out to see the worst. Nothing could be done, nothing. The fire had taken hold so long before. Jets of water from the hoses simply dropped into the inferno and were swallowed up. The firemen worked their souls out but it did no good at all. In the end they were satisfied with trying to damp down the neighbouring houses so that they shouldn't catch in their turn. It was still smoking and steaming even now, a pile of stinking, blackened timber and broken slates.

By now Clive was with us and took over, guiding the hysterical woman out of the hearing of his patients. I caught a glimpse of Garston, sitting out in a chair. His face seemed frozen in a ghastly grin, his eyes wild.

I had been in that house only a few hours before it had occurred, and she'd said that at midnight the fire had long taken hold. Everything had been all right when I had left. I had never lit the gas, had made no tea – nothing. I'd needed the electric light in only one room, where I was reading the letters. I had switched it off as I left. Surely I had? Yes – because at the outer door I'd turned back for that last look at the grisly severed end of rope. It had been barely visible in the gloom of the passage; and the door of the room I'd been in stood open.

So if I hadn't been responsible, who, or what, had?

Not that it mattered just then. There was tragedy enough for the poor, distracted woman. All our present efforts must be directed to keeping her sane.

And Garston? If his state had been critical before, what of it now? Any progress he'd made would surely be reversed. If he hadn't felt suicidal already, he might well do after this latest blow. We should never have let his wife into the ward with such horrific news.

At least she and the children had been safe at her sister's. They would have taken some of their clothes and toys there with them too. From my memory of the house there had been little of any real value among the Garstons' possessions. Ethel had cherished those wartime letters from her husband and they were irreplaceable, but at least I'd taken notes of their contents, and secreted that single photograph of Patrick with his horse.

How could it have happened? Fires weren't so rare in

that neighbourhood, where paraffin heaters were pressed into service when the evenings grew chill. I remembered seeing one in the room where I had been working; but it had been unlit. Could Ethel have gone back there after I had left, felt the house damp and set a match to the wick? Then, forgetting it, could she have left it burning? Even then it would have required some extraneous circumstance to cause it to tip over and set light to the sparse furnishing and carpets.

Even now, I supposed, the fire chief would be examining the house to search out the origin and cause of the fire. If accident was ruled out, would he be able to tell for certain that someone had been responsible? It beggared belief that anyone would deliberately set out to destroy a modest family home. Yet hadn't something even worse been intended when Patrick Garston had been strung up to the banisters and left to choke to death?

Could this have been a second attempt? If so, it would mean that the would-be killer didn't know that Patrick was at the clinic; but this time the intention might have been to destroy his whole family. Anyone passing by that evening when I had had the light on would have assumed that they were at home. Then, coming back later, with the house in darkness, they'd believe the mother and children were in bed asleep, and therefore defenceless. It became vital that they should immediately be spirited away from Bermondsey, preferably to the country, until the matter was quite cleared up – if ever it could be.

Clive had given Ethel Garston a sedative draught and she seemed quieter when I peeped into Sister's office; but on seeing me she started up again. 'Oh ma'am, whatever'll we do?'

'It's a terrible shock for you,' I granted, 'but thank God nobody was hurt. They are only *things* that are lost, and we will see they are all replaced. Was the house your own or rented?'

She stared at me as if I came from another planet. When she found words she said in a wondering voice, 'Rented, but it's *our 'ome*, see.'

I did see. I saw too how little I'd understood the ways of town-dwelling tenants. It wasn't like the Stakerleys estate, where our villagers earned ownership through generations of serving the family. The Garstons saw that wretched house as their own because they had never known, or hoped for, anything other than a letting from an impersonal landlord.

'I'm taking you back to Maisie's now,' I told her. 'Patrick is sedated, asleep. You will need to pick up the older children from school, and they mustn't see you still upset. I'll show you where you can make yourself tidy. Then I'll get us a cab.'

On our way she seemed subdued enough for me to venture asking, 'How would you feel about moving for a while to the country? I could find you a comfortable cottage and it would do the children good to be out of London's smoke for the winter.'

'We couldn't afford it, missus. Besides, there's Patrick. I gotta keep seeing 'im, keeping 'is spirits up, like.'

Like she had done today, bursting in with this further episode in their saga of miseries? 'I think we could safely leave his daily treatment to the clinic, don't you? And once the children have settled into the village school, you could be brought up to see him, say a couple of times each week. It would be a safe roof over your heads, and somewhere for Patrick to come to when he's convalescing. Your sister must be finding it quite difficult, having you all with her for so long.'

That last was what really hit the mark. I had suspected that Maisie's good nature was wearing thin, for several years now a childless widow and accustomed to suiting her own convenience.

'Patrick come from the country,' Ethel said wistfully. ''Is dad worked in a butcher's in 'arefield. That's where 'e grew up and learned to ride 'orses, so's 'e could join up in the Yeomanry at Uxbridge.'

'A real countryman at heart. Maybe Patrick would pick up work there and it would be better for you all in the long term.'

I knew there was a long way yet to go to persuade her, but the idea was in her mind now. Perhaps it could be left to ferment. Yet she must choose soon. I doubted it was safe for any of them to remain in an area where so much had gone tragically wrong.

As soon as we had the two older children back at Maisie's and little Sophie due to be delivered back by a neighbour, I boarded the waiting cab again and returned to the clinic, eager to get Clive's approval of my plans. Again I found him in discussion with Jeremy, who turned away with unconcealed impatience as I broke in on them.

However, I stood my ground. Friends they might be, but I considered a wife's right to her husband's attention more imperative than his. Putting on a social face, I asked if he had found a suitable date to dine with us. He made excuses. Now was not an easy time: he had decisions to make and was about to move into fresh lodgings. He barely attempted to hide the fact he found my presence disagreeable.

Just then Clive was called to an hysteric in the women's ward and the two of us were left together, Jeremy clearly not having completed his discussion with my husband.

'I hear you're changing direction in medicine,' I said as the door closed on Clive. 'Espousing surgery.'

'Indeed.' He pulled his monkey grimace and put on a show of sour humour, declaiming,

> *I'm sick of gruel and the dietetics,*
> *I'm sick of pills and sick of emetics,*
> *I'm sick of pulses, their tardiness or quickness,*
> *I'm sick of blood, its thinness or thickness –*
> *In short, in a word, I'm sick of sickness.*

He had surprised me. 'Really? Is that original?'

'Thomas Hood's verse. Mine merely the sentiment.'

'I remember my governess making me learn Hood's "Song of the Shirt". I thought even then that he was a miserable sort of person. But you aren't – not normally.'

'Perhaps I have cause to be at present.' He treated me to a stare of ferocious intensity that made me wonder how I had offended him. He stalked towards the door then turned, as though starting on a different tack. 'You've heard of the Garstons' latest disaster?'

'Yes. It's terrible. Ethel took such a pride in their home. I've just come from there. It's a blackened ruin. Perhaps there's a chance now they'll seriously consider moving to the country. I've been trying to persuade Ethel how the children would benefit from the purer air.'

His mouth tightened. 'It must be their decision. We have no

right to force our opinions on them. You seem to have become unusually involved in their affairs.'

It quite took my breath away. Next we should have him accusing me of arson to gain my point! I was so taken aback that for a moment I almost missed what he said next.

Confused, I tried to catch up. 'What witness? The road-digger, Durrant? *Dead*, you say?'

'That is what I came to tell Clive – only to learn then about the house being burned down. It is unimaginable what misfortunes can bedevil a family in a matter of days.'

'But how, *dead*?' I insisted. 'I understood you were to speak to him again, with an offer of money to refresh his memory. He was our only hope of finding out who was with Garston just before he . . .'

'. . . hanged himself,' he said callously.

'No! Before someone tried to kill him!'

Jeremy moved from the door as Clive came back into the room in time to overhear me. I was aware of my flushed face and the way he glanced between the two of us.

Still outraged, I swung on him. 'Your friend here thinks I'm manipulative. And I'm sure he thinks me responsible for the fire, because I was there just before.'

'You were at their house last night? I had no idea,' Jeremy muttered.

'I was working there on Patrick Garston's letters, which he wrote home from the war front. Ethel had left me to lock up after she returned to her sister's. Do you think I haven't questioned every move I made that could have led to the fire? I know the house was safe when I left.'

Clive came close and put a hand on my arm. 'Nobody thinks you did anything amiss. We just thank God the family were all away when it happened. And that you left when you did.

'I have spoken by telephone with the fire chief. There are further searches to be made, but he confirmed that the fire started in the hallway directly behind the front door. And there was an unmistakeable smell which he recognised at once. He implied that paraffin was poured through the letter box and then something like a burning rag dropped in on top.'

'A deliberate attempt then. Do you suppose that whoever did it thought the house was occupied? Ethel and those three little girls asleep and likely to be burned to death? Then Durrant,' I persisted, 'how did he suddenly come to die, and when?'

'He was beaten about the head with some kind of club,' Jeremy said, 'on his way home from some illicit drinking-hole, then left in the gutter by his door. He stank to high heaven of gin, so he was probably incapable of fending off any attacker.'

'Drunk,' I said, 'like Patrick Garston was before the attack on him. This is too much of a coincidence. And when did this happen?'

'A little before one in the morning.'

I thought he looked shifty, avoiding my eye. 'How did you learn all this?' I demanded. 'That he stank of drink, for example.'

He hesitated, darted a glance of complicity at Clive, shrugged and then admitted, 'He was to have met me at his lodgings at midnight but never turned up. The house was in darkness, so I went away. Then I had second thoughts and decided that, dragged from his bed, he'd be more easy to deal with. So I went back, determined to have satisfaction. I was the one who found him dead in the street, and still warm to the touch. I spent the rest of the night with the police, explaining away the blood on my cuffs. Naturally, as a doctor, I had tried to resuscitate him.'

And had little sleep at all at that rate. Small wonder that he sounded on edge. I could almost feel sorry for him.

'Fortunately – for me, at least – this sort of incident isn't so uncommon in Wapping of a night. Some rogues think little of knocking another out for whatever little is in his pockets. I managed in the end to convince the local sergeant that I was more used to mending pates than breaking them.'

'I'm sorry, Jeremy; but there goes our only chance of preventing Garston being charged with attempted suicide.'

'Exactly. And you may set your mind at rest that you have done everything possible to help the man. Now it remains with your husband alone to explore his mind and, if he is able, to save him from dementia.'

Now he was patronising me! The little woman had meddled in her feeble way with men's work and found the task too great for her limited, amateur ability.

'No,' I said defiantly. 'My mind is not at rest, nor ever will be while I can still go on looking for the truth. Garston never meant to take his own life. 'Somewhere, undetected, there is a man out there intent on murder. Although he failed with his first victim, this time he may have succeeded with Alan Durrant.'

Nine

There were things I should have done already; people I should have seen and questioned. At 4.30 p.m. there was time enough to catch one of them before the soap factory closed. The minister at the Garstons' Baptist chapel could be left until later, when I'd more likely find him at home.

It meant rushing back to change into formal clothing. I'd scarcely expect to have much authority with a factory manager if I stormed in like a wild-haired bohemian splashed with paint; but I wondered why I'd troubled as the stomach-turning fatty smells reached out to me when I located the place just a few minutes before the six o'clock hooter went.

Just inside the main gates was a sort of guardroom presided over by an elderly man with a walrus moustache. He gawped at my visiting card as if it were written in Chinese, so I simply brushed past to cross the yard, following an arrow that indicated *Manager's Office*. A lad of fifteen or so was pumping up a bicycle tyre by the office doorway and nodded me up a flight of stairs. Finding myself alone in a room with two desks and typewriters, I stood watching from the window while a flood of men in working overalls gushed from an unseen doorway below.

A harassed-looking woman appeared from the inner sanctum, asked what brought me there and muttered that the manager had a pressing appointment elsewhere, so was unable to see me. Nevertheless she retreated with the card that I handed to her. I stood my ground until the door opened again to emit a small, wiry man, fleshless as a jockey, who attempted to rush blindly by.

'I need only one moment of your busy life,' I said firmly, 'and then you'll be rid of me for all time. If you refuse, then I swear I'll haunt your doorstep, both here and at your home.'

Whether it was my words or my tone that shocked him, I couldn't tell, but he halted in full flight, blinked and peered at me myopically. 'Er, Mrs Malcom? I believe my secretary mentioned you made some enquiry about one of my staff.'

'Patrick Garston, an office clerk.'

'I'm afraid he's no longer with us. His post has been filled.'

'An ex-serviceman who fought bravely at Gallipoli and Salonika. A patriot, Mr Miles. You surely can't throw him out on the street for a temporary breakdown in health.'

The manager shrugged over the documents tucked under one arm and turned away tight-lipped. 'It is admirable to do good works where that is needed, madam. But there is a certain danger in the processes we use, and it would be folly to risk employing a man whose sanity is in doubt. Besides, if you knew the case better, you would know that he is to be the subject of a police prosecution.'

'I know the case intimately, Mr Miles, and have personally spoken to the police, who appear satisfied to leave him uncharged.' This was an imaginative reconstruction of my few words to the two constables at the door of the ward a few days back, and I kept two fingers crossed behind my back as I uttered it. 'What is more, I am working at the clinic which is treating Mr Garston at present. The opinion of the consultant dealing with his case is that he is simply suffering the aftermath of severe shock. It is my duty to investigate all circumstances leading up to this; which is why I require your co-operation. I should like to know the details of his employment with you, who his main associates were here, and how he behaved in the last week or two at work.'

He reminded me of the White Rabbit in *Alice*, the way he consulted his pocket watch and made fussy movements towards some distant bolt-hole; but I was there, between him and the door. 'It shouldn't take more than a moment or two,' I insisted.

'Madam, I really don't recall the man; he was with us so short a time. Miss Harman is in charge of all office staff. I can only pass your request to her. But I must remind you that the hooter has blown and I cannot pay her overtime on account of a non-business matter.'

I caught a flicker in the eyes of the woman standing ready to leave, gloves on and handbag suspended over one arm. I stood aside then for Mr Miles to make his escape.

'Miss Harman,' I said in honeyed tones, 'I have a cab waiting outside and should be happy to give you a lift home, if you would spare me a moment first.'

The offer was unexpected enough to make her pause, and I swept in. 'That is so very kind of you. Mr Miles mentioned that Garston hadn't been long with you. How long, precisely?'

'Not more than three months. He came to us from Hardwick and Meadows the accountants, and was extremely well qualified for the level of job we were needing to fill. He'd been with them since he was eighteen, with a break of some three years for the war.' She seemed relaxed, even motherly, now that her employer had removed himself.

'It sounds as though you knew him quite well.'

'Our duties overlapped to some extent. He was a reliable worker, kept himself to himself and no nonsense.' She sighed. 'It isn't always easy being in charge of men. They tend to test me out so, you know. We've normally had only women in the office since the war, but Mr Garston was an exception. I'm sorry to lose him. The new clerk isn't a patch on him with figures.'

'Do you remember the last day he was here?'

'It was a Friday,' she said, frowning, 'and we were late with the men's wages because of a hold-up at the bank.'

That sounded alarming. 'Do you mean a robbery?'

She clucked. 'Oh no, nothing like that. A clerical blunder over the cash remittance. By mistake we were given the money bags for the dog-biscuit factory. They were both labelled Tooley Street and the wrong one was handed over. The messenger never noticed and we only discovered it when the biscuit people rang through. A bank clerk had to be sent to make the exchange. So in the end we never started making up the envelopes until well after four o'clock. Patrick was good, dropping his own work to help out. You could rely on him like that. I couldn't believe it when they said he tried to take his own life next morning.' She looked distressed. 'I mean, he was a religious man. He would have thought it a terrible sin.'

'Had he seemed depressed – anxious?'

'I asked myself that, of course, afterwards. He hadn't struck me that way. Just the same as usual; a bit quieter perhaps, but polite and helpful.'

'Did he ever talk about outside interests? His family and so on?'

'He mentioned his wife and the kiddies; three little girls they were. Once he showed me a photograph of them taken at the seaside last Easter. Margate, I think it was.'

'So that would have been the holiday weekend when he was still with Hardwick and Meadows?'

'It must've been.'

'Did he have any special friends here? Men he might have walked home with after he knocked off of an evening?'

She thought a moment. 'Not that I ever noticed. He'd stay on a bit later than most in the office, you see. And the workers had all gone by then. Usually just me and Mr Miles left, like today.' She blushed and looked down. 'He did walk me to the bus stop once, when I had a heavy typewriter to take to be mended. Insisted on carrying it for me. That's what sort he was, poor man.'

With that I had to be content, picking up the cab again that had waited outside the factory gates, and dropping her off, with effusive thanks, at the Elephant and Castle. It seemed I'd drawn a blank there. I'd hoped that Miss Harman would have picked up any great distress in someone she worked alongside.

It left me nowhere. Perhaps, after tackling the Reverend Ieuan Roberts, I should make a few enquiries at Hardwick and Meadows. It was curious that suddenly, after long service there, Garston had changed to employment for which Miss Harman implied he was overqualified. That was twice today I'd been told of a man making career changes which seemed illogical.

Then an almost empty purse made me change my immediate intentions. It meant rushing home for more money, or I couldn't pay the cabbie; so I ordered him back to Chelsea, where I left him at the door while I ran in for change.

Unexpectedly Clive came out of the sitting-room to meet me. 'Darling,' I said, 'thank heaven you're here. I was afraid I'd need to borrow off Mrs Bowyer. There's a cab outside unpaid and I still require it for my next trip.'

My husband gave me a quizzical look. 'Good evening,' he

greeted me with exaggerated formality. 'When you ran so precipitately from the clinic, I feared it was to take to your bed, but it seems not. Instead, upstairs I found evidence of some rapid doffing and donning. It struck me I've more of a shuttlecock than a wife these days.'

Of course: in my hasty departure I'd left discarded garments scattered over the bedroom floor. It seemed an apology was required, little though it caught me in the mood for one; and clearly, for the present, I must curb my eagerness to follow where the trail was leading. It was vexing, but inevitable unless I was to put myself further in the wrong with Clive.

'Perhaps you will allow me to pay your cabbie off?' he enquired. His exquisite politeness, intended to highlight my own lack of consideration, was hardly endearing. Now I must be extra charming to win him round. What a tiresome thing marriage can be when you have other things to consider of more pressing importance!

While he was occupied with the cabbie Mrs Bowyer asked if it was convenient to serve dinner.

'I'm sorry,' I told her. 'I really hadn't taken account of the time. Please serve now if everything's ready.' Poor woman, coping single-handed, and I had been feeling aggrieved because she hadn't found time to tidy my mess in the bedroom. Even if I didn't reform for Clive's sake, I really owed it to her. One thing Mama had always insisted on was courtesy to the servants, because they couldn't answer back.

We had our meal in comparative silence. When eventually Clive slid his used napkin back into its ring with unnecessarily surgical precision, he remarked, 'You appear to have made a considerable journey this afternoon.'

Ah, the cab fare. Yes, it must have mounted up. 'I went to Bermondsey,' I admitted. 'And because I could never hope to pick a cab up there to get back, I kept the man waiting.'

'Very wise,' he nodded; 'it's not the most salubrious quarter for social visiting.'

He hadn't smiled, but at last I had the suspicion that he was laughing at me. 'Sleuthing, I presume. And what did you find out?' he enquired.

Now he was serious again, so I told him about Mr Miles and Miss Harman, and how Garston had left a superior post with an accountancy firm only three months or so back. 'Which could mean he had some specific reason for wanting to work at the factory. So I intend to have a word with the minister at his chapel, who might be in his confidence about that.'

'Or even know why Patrick Garston chose to leave the first post – or was summarily dismissed.'

I stared at him, startled at the implication. He shrugged, smiling. 'Elementary, my dear Watson. A man's choice of action can depend as much on the past as on his hopes of the future. Wouldn't you agree?'

That was logical, of course, but then wasn't he suggesting some misconduct behind Garston's leaving the accountancy firm? Either on his part or another's? In which case I should have to tread warily and not go blundering blindly in on Messrs Hardwick and Meadows. It would require some thought overnight to plan how I should tackle them. Meanwhile a change of subject was overdue.

'How did you find Jeremy this afternoon?' I asked. 'He struck me as somewhat abrasive.'

'He has a lot on his mind at present.'

'Which is no excuse for rudeness.'

Clive smiled, lifting back my chair so that I could rise. Then he guided me by the elbow towards the fireplace, where Mrs Bowyer had set the coffee things on a low table. 'Where Jeremy comes from they call a spade a spade, not soil-transference equipment. And he didn't actually employ the term "manipulative", as I understand.' So Clive had taken note of my complaint against his friend.

'But what right has he to question my interest in one of your patients? Whatever his exact words, I found him uncouth. He didn't always strike me that way. In fact, at first, he seemed eager to leave a good impression.'

I was conscious of my husband watching me with those bright, brown eyes that missed nothing. He let the silence build, and I knew him well enough by now to know that he waited for me to rush in and fill it. So I held my tongue. At least for a few minutes, while I poured coffee and offered the cream.

'Perhaps,' I said then, 'we should find some suitable young woman to bring out the sunny side of him. Nobody too tall, of course. One of those little elfin things with bobbed hair and skirts almost up to their knees.'

I'd thought Clive might gulp with laughter, but he was totally grave. 'Marry him off? That's not the answer for Jeremy, I'm afraid.'

The latter part he murmured almost to himself, with real regret. It struck me as strange then, and even more so later when the words came back to me as I brushed my hair before bed. I had only frivolously meant a lady friend he might flirt with a little and escort to theatres or concerts. Clive had gone further and spoken of marriage – marriage which, apparently, was 'not the answer' for his friend.

So if not marriage, what then? Why shouldn't Jeremy enjoy what was, after all, the normal happy state most men desired? Unless . . .

It plunged me back into the problem of Isabelle and her young friends. What was happening to the world when women passed themselves off as men, and men were – what? – not fully men any more? Since the war people were so changed. Or had they always been this way and I too young and overprotected to notice?

Certainly the war had changed the way we all behaved: there was less respect shown for rank, less formality, more outspokenness and demanding of one's 'rights'. Not entirely bad, perhaps; but there was a more political slant to personal relations.

So was the war entirely to blame for this sexual ambiguity too, because, with the men away fighting, women had taken over their work? Surely it had been there all through history, with the Ancient Romans and their slave boys as the empire declined. In Egypt Hatshepsut, the female Pharaoh, had pasted on her chin the false beard of authority; and Lady Caroline Lamb had abandoned skirts to flaunt herself in trews, though very much a woman underneath. Didn't I myself occasionally use breeches for decency and convenience?

Why then had I felt certain that Selina, in her white tie and tails, went much farther, was a sexual predator, intending to involve Isabelle in actual lovemaking? Had she gone so far in self-indulgence that there was nothing normal left to try? So Selina was perhaps a lesbian; then, too, there was Poppy and her cocaine. Living for the moment's sensation: could they be happy that way? It seemed to me so sad, so wasteful, when they'd been born to great privilege.

Clive came up behind and watched me in the mirror. He put an arm around me, bending to lift my hair and kiss my neck. 'Whatever it is that disturbs you,' he murmured, 'I know a certain cure. Come to bed now.'

He was right, as ever. So I went, and was totally comforted, even inspired.

Later I was to recall something I thought little of at the time. Before we made love he sighed, kissed me gently and said, 'You were right. It's time to use the talking cure on Patrick Garston. I shall go with him into his past and look for the evil genius that's disturbing him.'

I had the weirdest dream that night. It scared me so that I came instantly awake, sweating and yet chilled through. I could remember none of its incidents, but stayed haunted by its atmosphere of unholy terror.

There lingered a sort of phantom I recognised as my husband. He was somehow transparent, as though a passing movement of the air might blow him away. The face, so drawn and weary, had a spiritual glow. He turned his eyes mutely on me as if for help, but I was paralysed.

Suddenly I knew: Clive was mortal. Someday I might lose him.

It filled me with unspeakable fear. The whole of life was distorted, obscene. I saw that without him nothing had reason; I would be utterly lost.

My instinct was to wake him, cling fast and hold his live body close against mine for reassurance. I needed to feel his heart beating into my own; but so strong was this sense of his frailty that I forced myself to hold back. In the half-light, shocked awake, my eyes devoured his material body, as I screwed every ounce of determination into willing him well. Prayed for him – *to* him, almost.

No answering strength came. It was an impotence I had never experienced before – a sort of negative, demonic possession.

A premonition?

Clive stayed asleep, picking up no intimation of my crisis. We seemed already cut apart. I touched his cheek with the tips of my fingers and he never stirred.

After long minutes of lying there, physically alongside but denied, I slipped from our bed and fled downstairs.

I might have gone for the comfort of holding my dear baby, but I almost blamed her then for being another man's and not his.

Long hours stretched ahead before the hoped-for sanity of daylight. I had to find some way of filling them. With sleep denied, I resorted to my mother's refuge, God help me, and unlocked the tantalus in our dining-room. Eventually I stole back to bed, stupefied and doubtless stinking of brandy fumes.

Clive slept on, unknowing. We are all strangers in our private minds.

Ten

A wind must have arisen in the early hours. When I reached consciousness again, the far side of the bed was empty. It was late. I found my feet, drew back the curtains from the long windows and discovered a gale whipping loose tendrils of wistaria against panes that were awash with rain.

I remembered my unaccountable panic of the night hours and was ashamed. Even before my bath I dragged the sheets and pillowcases from the bed and was standing there uncertain what should happen to them next, when Mrs Bowyer came in with an unexpected breakfast tray. I gestured at the linen bundled in my arms and she took it from me, saying, 'I'll let Mabel have them, madam.'

Why Mabel? I thought; then I remembered that she had acted as laundry maid at Thorndike Farm before we had met up. So perhaps that was how she spent her time now when little Petra was asleep. It was neglectful of me that I'd had no idea of how the two women shared household tasks between them.

'I had assumed we used a laundry service,' I said.

Mrs Bowyer smiled. 'Not for the past week, madam. Mabel has set up a special room in the attics for drying the linen off. There's a splendid wood-burning stove, and she brought her own irons, which she heats on its top.'

'And where is the washing done?'

'In a copper in the basement, madam. It seems not to have been used for some time, but she tells me it's more than adequate. I have spoken to Dr Malcolm about the added expense for fuel and soap. He's arranged for a strong lad to come in on washdays and carry the baskets of wet things upstairs.'

It made him a better housewife than I! Or at least more aware of what was going on under his nose.

I drank two cups of tea but refused the food, feeling uncertain in my stomach; and when I had dressed, I went to explore the far attics, one of which had been newly converted to a drying room with racks suspended from ceiling pulleys. The stove was one I had noticed before when we had considered taking the house. It was old but quite a handsome affair, covered in blue and white Dutch tiles. Three heavy pressing irons hung in a wire basket beside it. Under a slanting skylight stood a large, solid deal table covered in layered padding and a topsheet that reached almost to the ground. A nearby cupboard held supplies of yellow soap, packets of starch and blue dollies with various-sized bowls for soaking out stains.

It struck me that Mabel took great pride in her skills and had set up a little kingdom of her own here. I should need to check with Clive that her wages had been raised accordingly; but no – he'd certainly have thought of that.

The wind continued to buffet the house, but the rain had lessened enough for me to consider walking a while by the river. I wrapped up warmly and went out, burrowing into the wind. The Thames was swollen and heaving like coastal waters, though without breaking waves. Barges ploughed through the water with dirty grey-green moustaches at their bows, and the helmsmen were muffled, hunched in their wheelhouses. Whistler's sombre tones were scumbled on the misty air.

In the streets of Chelsea too autumn was evident, with leaves tossed on the wind and broken branches littering the paths and gutters. Already the trees were half-stripped and I missed the bright foliage.

Revitalised by the brisk exercise, I returned to the house and dispensed with lunch, since Clive had evidently been too busy to come home. At twenty minutes past two I covered my breeches with a greatcoat, slung my painting satchel over one shoulder and set out on foot for the clinic. If I worked solidly for three or four hours, I could probably complete the mural's outlines today.

I found Dr Atkinson busying himself between the four beds of the male ward, checking the men's condition before allowing them to sit out and watch the painting's progress. Patrick Garston appeared lethargic, perhaps drugged to control the alarming judderings I'd noticed before. I assumed his wife had visited earlier and left before my arrival, so I was able to concentrate wholly on painting.

When I took a break, having cleaned my brushes, I walked through to the women's ward to see Clive, only to find that he wasn't in the building. Matron, on being asked, admitted reluctantly that he had received an emergency call from a private patient and would probably not be back that day. Normally quite open with me, she was suddenly distant and cool. I wondered if I was somehow responsible for the change, or if Clive had instructed her not to reveal his whereabouts to me.

She had darted a glance at her notice board before answering and, when I looked later, I saw Clive's initials – CM – against a telephone number that seemed vaguely familiar. I jotted it down on a corner of my sketchpad and spent the next few minutes examining my motives for doing so. Did the cruel deceptions of my earlier marriage still affect my ability to trust him? Or was I expecting a need to get in touch with him myself? Yet again, did last night's shattering realisation of his mortality leave me fearful for his safety? Whichever it was, I found myself frankly uneasy. It must have been a call of some importance that took him away, since today he'd intended leading Patrick Garston back into the past.

I had been back at my work no more than fifteen or twenty minutes when Jeremy Owen arrived, was closeted for a while with Matron in Clive's office and then came out to talk to me. Again he appeared offhand, claiming to be unable to offer a date for dinner with us owing to pressure of work, caught as he was between both areas of career interest, completing his existing obligations while preparing for the transition to Sir Digby's surgical team. Then, as though he accepted that his refusal had been boorish, he complimented me on the almost completed mural, particularly the insertion of the mare cropping in the left foreground. I doubted he knew it was a portrait of Garston's Cherry, probably regarding it as a mark of rural whimsy on my part.

To me, completing the painting's layout was an anticlimax, since my husband wasn't there to join in the general enthusiasm. The nurses were as delighted as the men were appreciative. There remained now only a few glazes, tonal and decorative touches to add, and they could wait for tomorrow.

I didn't need thanks from the silent Garston. It was enough to see his gaze focused on the figure of the mare. He seemed slightly more awake now, calm and perhaps a little more at peace, although I thought I detected moisture brimming in his eyes. Perhaps I had managed to start him on his journey back into his wartime experiences. It was a pity Clive wasn't present to observe it.

I challenged the patients to account for the story that was pictured there, and left the other three arguing over what should be the name of the woman silhouetted in the window.

It was dark outside the clinic, the weather turned chill and misted so that the lamp standards showed only bleary globes of catarrhal yellow with little effective light thrown down. I made for the brighter streets with shops, and had difficulty in hailing a cab because already most splashed by filled with theatre-goers. Eventually I came on one of the remaining hansoms and was *ker-lip ker-lopped* home behind a thin, dispirited nag.

At home the swagged curtains weren't yet drawn, giving out a rosy glow from shaded table-lamps set about the drawing-room. Inside all was warm and brightly welcoming, Mabel and Mrs Bowyer emerging from a kitchen that gave out great gusts of savoury baking smells. I was more than ready by now to mop up all the comforts on hand, being famished, having cut out both breakfast and luncheon that day.

Clive wasn't back. Curiously he'd neglected to telephone. I tried not to show that I was put out at this. 'We'll wait half an hour while I change,' I told Mrs Bowyer; 'then perhaps you would serve dinner. By which time I expect my husband will have returned.'

In the event I dined alone, sitting over my coffee and the daily newspaper until I could barely keep my eyes open, before slinking away to bed. My painting clothes lay where I had peeled them off and, as I arranged them now on hangers, I emptied the smock's pockets. A folded page torn from my sketchpad fell to the floor. I opened it and stared again at the telephone number which Clive had left with Matron.

Although it still seemed one I had been in the habit of

ringing, the actual location escaped me. There was nothing for it but to put on my négligée, go downstairs and dial it on the study telephone.

My call was answered almost instantly. 'Claridge's Hotel,' pronounced a suave male voice. It caught me unawares and I had no idea what to say next.

'Do you require Reception or Restaurant, madam?'

'Reception, I think. That is, I wish to be connected with Dr Clive Malcolm.'

'Very good, madam. Is the gentleman a guest with us?'

'Perhaps visiting a guest?' I couldn't avoid it coming out as a question.

'And the name of the guest, madam?'

I had no idea, and plunged into explanations: that the visit was a professional one in answer to an emergency call some hours earlier.

'I am afraid, madam, I have only recently come on duty. Will you allow me to make enquiries and call you back?'

I gave him our number, but he also required my name. So, ashamed to be thought a wife checking on an errant husband's whereabouts, I gave my professional one.

'The Honourable Lucy Sedgwick,' he intoned after me, adding the title I'd never owned but was often mistakenly given. I didn't correct him. If it brought speedier service, so much the better.

It was almost twenty minutes later that the call came. 'Clive,' I blurted, 'what on earth has . . . ?'

The over-genteel cough put me right. 'I am sorry, madam. Dr Malcolm did indeed attend one of our guests earlier today, but he left the hotel some time after five p.m. Is there any way in which we may be of further service to you?'

'The name of the guest?'

There was a pause while discretion fought with the desire to oblige noblesse. 'I regret, madam, that that information is not available.'

A white-gloved slap in the face. There was nothing more to be done. I had probably already overstepped Clive's professional boundaries and this would be listed as a crime alongside my impersonation of a medical student; but perhaps if I never mentioned the gaffe to anyone, he might not get to

101

know. Could I rely on Claridge's discretion working in both directions?

I supposed that I had just missed Clive when I left the clinic, and that he would eventually have returned there to catch up on the routine work he'd been obliged to postpone. Then, unwilling to disturb our household in the early hours, he would finish his night on the little truckle bed he kept there for emergency stays. With any luck he would come home after breakfast, as once before, and spend part of the day with me.

That only partly compensated for the loss I felt and the hurtful way he had failed to keep me informed. I went dissatisfied to bed, spent half an hour tossing and turning, then let fatigue have its way, and fell heavily asleep.

My first act after breakfast next morning was to search for the telephone number of Hardwick and Meadows and, having discovered the address, which was in Catherine Street off Aldwych, I rang for an appointment under my professional name. I asked specifically for Mr Meadows, assuming him to be the junior partner and possibly less skilled in opposing this 'manipulativeness' that Jeremy had accused me of. I learned later that he was the sole remaining founder of the firm, Mr Hardwick his father-in-law having died some eight years earlier.

My appointment was for twelve noon of the same day, surely an indication that the practice was not overemployed. The office, viewed from the opposite side of the street, confirmed that impression: the quarters were cramped, and although the brass plates shone like the proverbial good deed in a naughty world, it was some considerable time since the handsomely panelled outer door had seen paintbrush or sugar soap. The interior was modest in proportions, made more cramped by the oversized, rather flashy furniture. Desk tops and chair seats were covered in a plum-coloured leather which showed paler scratches and appeared to have faded from a more blatant purple. There was London grit on the window sills, and dust furred the ornate wainscotting. At the main desk a wispy young man sat behind an immense typewriter.

'Lady Lucia,' he gushed, rising and wringing thin hands – not my own, fortunately. He appeared to have delved, however imperfectly, into *Burke's Peerage*, whose covers I recognised on the higher shelf behind him. 'Lady Lucia, Mr Meadows will be delighted to see you in just two minutes. Do please take a seat.'

He subsided again behind his machine and fixed me with a simpering smile.

'A blustery day,' he ventured.

'I suppose so. One barely notices the weather in London, walled in between all these great buildings.'

'Ah, you are from the country, milady. A more robust climate there, I imagine.'

'And you are a city man.'

It appeared to flatter him. He threw out his puny chest. 'Born and bred.'

'And have you been long with Hardwick and Meadows, Mr . . . er?'

'Peel, milady. Percival Peel. My dad was a great one for alliteration. Yes, I can boast that I am quite part of the furniture here. I came straight from school.' He giggled effeminately, hand to mouth. 'A number of years ago, of course.'

Between five and seven, I should think, if he'd left at the age of fifteen – which meant that his employment here would have overlapped with Patrick Garston's. If I had little success with the accountant himself, it might be possible to contrive an accidental encounter with this Mr Peel after work hours and to bleed him of information over a cup of tea in some neighbourhood café.

I was kept waiting the required amount of time to give the impression of an earlier consultation overlapping with my appointment, but no voices reached me from the adjoining office and there was no sound of another door closing on a departing client. Eventually a handbell sounded and the secretary looped his cheeks into an ingratiating smirk. 'Allow me to show you in.'

It was hardly necessary, since there was only one alternative door to the one I had entered by, so I walked past, turned the knob, and presented myself to the head of the firm. He had struck a substantial pose against the long window, presenting his better side, I was sure.

He reminded me instantly of the famous full-length profile

of Cardinal Wolsey. There was the same effect of corpulent, self-sufficient authority. This was equally the façade of a self-made man who had risen from modest origins. The eyes turned on me were not large but set in an impressively fleshed face. I had to warn myself that this was a modern man and not one raised to sixteenth-century values.

'How kind of you to see me at such short notice,' I told him, but loftily. He took my hand in his warm, soft one; in a mellifluous tone invited me to take a seat – would I care to join him in a glass of sweet sherry or madeira?

I accepted, needing to get a full image of the man's little idiosyncrasies. As a portraitist I thought I could read, in a few moments of relaxed conversation, much of what I looked for.

He had certainly checked on my background, addressed me correctly as *Miss* Sedgwick, then paused, an eyebrow raised. 'I take it this is a consultation regarding your *professional* finances?'

'Oh indeed, yes. My family affairs look after themselves.' I waved vaguely. 'It is less clear to me how the money accrues from my art work – and, indeed, appears to dissolve of itself. It is more than time that I found some competent person to manage matters on my behalf. I have an agent who arranges with galleries for exhibitions and so on, but in addition there are private sales which do not go through his books. I must confess I am a total noddlehead when it comes to money, and sometimes I wonder if I have actually received the full amounts we contracted for.'

He nodded pontifically. 'You refer there to commissioned portraits, do you not?'

'And occasional landscapes of country estates.'

He rubbed his pudgy little paws together, beaming on me. 'A care I should be most happy to provide, Miss Sedgwick. All that we should require is a letter in each case setting out precisely the terms of your contracted work and a proviso that all monies should be paid through the named offices of Hardwick and Meadows. I can then assure you that you will have no further cause to trouble yourself at all. I take it that a quarterly statement would be preferred?'

'If that is what you normally provide. Thank you, Mr Meadows.'

He appeared quite satisfied that I was the empty-headed little society duffer I'd suggested, so how on earth could I now introduce any query concerning an ex-employee of his living in Bermondsey? It was obviously impossible. He had given me no opening at all. I'd be leaving with nothing gained.

At the office door he bent over my hand so that I lost the impression of Wolsey in a close view of his individual features, saw black hairs in his nostrils and pendulous earlobes with a sharp crease diagonally. I knew then that I would have portrayed him in black, not a cardinal's red. Not that I would really have cared to paint him at all.

'May I enquire,' he asked, retaining my hand, 'by whose recommendation we were brought to your notice?'

I gave a little pout of exasperation. 'Now who would it have been? It was at a dinner party recently. Such a host of people I hadn't met till then. Nowadays it isn't long before the talk turns to money matters – and someone said I really should be rolling in it: what on earth did I *do* with all my earnings? Then someone else said I was a dilly not to have it properly controlled. That's when the name came up. It stuck in my mind for some reason. Hardwicke Hall, you know. And then *Meadows* sounded so charmingly countrified. Well, afterwards I got one of the servants to look for you in the telephone directory, *et nous voilà*!'

The clerk was still at his desk as I left and I waved my fingers at him, hoping he felt as hungry as he looked, but afraid he was the sort to have a cheese and pickle sandwich hidden in a drawer. However, I lurked at the street's corner and sure enough, in about twenty minutes he slid from the doorway of Hardwick and Meadows, a woollen muffler round his neck and a slouch cap pulled over his greasy locks. It wasn't difficult to let him overtake me as I watched in the shop window's reflection.

As I guessed, he wouldn't let the opportunity slip and danced round in front of me, archly preening himself. 'Lady Lucia – or do you prefer to be called Lady Margherita?'

'I'm an artist, so for most purposes Miss Sedgwick does nicely, thank you, Mr Peel. But, knowing this district, could you, I wonder, advise me where I could best get a cup of tea?'

'The Waldorf's just a few steps round the corner. I believe you'd find it quite suitable.'

So I thanked him and suggested he keep me company there, if he wasn't immediately needed back at the office. He assured me he had a whole thirty minutes at our disposal, and in fact took almost half as much again before mincing back to Catherine Street, believing he had acquired more information from me than I from him.

I slyly implied that his employer had impressed me as a promising subject for a portrait, and expressed surprise that the office had none on its walls. (What it did have – and I was annoyed that I'd not been able to take a closer look – was a number of group photographs in which Meadows had surely appeared with colleagues or fellow students. One had even looked like a formal mess group of uniformed officers.)

Peel was flattered on the firm's behalf and eager to convey my opinion to the accountant. If it resulted in a commissioned portrait, I should insist on the background being that very room, where I'd then have the opportunity to pry at leisure.

On my way home by cab I began to regret putting out that feeler. My life was complicated enough and the search for a twenty-fifth hour didn't permit my making a suspect of every distant contact poor Patrick Garston had encountered; but probably Mr Meadows wouldn't rise to my bait – or if he did, I could plead pressure of other commissions until he finally lost interest.

So exercised was I by these considerations that I barely noticed it was Mabel who let me into the house, but as I handed over my coat I could see past her into the shadowed inner hall.

Mrs Bowyer stood there in evident distress – and beside her a stout police constable.

Eleven

The policeman turned to regard me, frowning. The women appeared alarmingly solicitous. Oh God, I thought, what has Isabelle been up to now?

'She's not hurt? Dead? Not that, surely?' I burst out.

There was a shocked silence. '*She?* Who would that be then?' the constable demanded.

'My mother?' I offered, not thinking how that might further confuse matters. 'I mean Lady Isabelle Penrhydd.'

'Nobody's dead, dearie,' Mabel said impetuously, almost hugging me.

Mrs Bowyer, suddenly straight-backed again, took my arm firmly. 'Come and sit down a moment, madam. We have something to tell you.'

'For God's sake, then tell me! What's wrong?'

It seemed it was Clive. He'd gone missing – but how could you miss anyone like him? He wasn't a child to go wandering off. He knew London well, or at any rate the part he worked and lived in. He would be seeing to a patient somewhere and would have lost track of the time. What was all the fuss about? Unless . . .

'He's injured. Is that what you're trying to say? In hospital himself? I must go to him!'

'No, madam,' the constable said stolidly. 'Trouble is . . . nobody knows where he's got to, like.'

'Missing? But how long? I mean . . .' Then I recalled he hadn't been home the night before. I'd assumed he would be staying over at the clinic to make up for time lost during the previous day. *When he'd also gone absent!*

'Was there any message from him, madam?' Mrs Bowyer urged. 'Can you suggest where he might be, since Dr Atkinson and Matron are at their wits' end to account for his absence. It seems he had a full diary for today. All appointments have had to be cancelled, and no one has seen hide nor hair of him.'

Of course there had been no message. That was what piqued me, feeling he took me too easily for granted. But hadn't I been just as offhand? – unable to remember clearly when I'd last set eyes on him.

That is what the policeman asked next. My confusion was clearly increasing his suspicions of me. 'Didn't you expect your husband home last night?' he demanded.

'He's a doctor,' I said angrily. 'He has to put his professional duty first at all times. I assumed there was an emergency at the clinic.'

Then I remembered that there *had* been an emergency, one that had called him to Claridge's; but that had been yesterday afternoon, and when I'd rung I'd been assured by a receptionist there that he'd left at about 5 p.m. After that he would have gone straight back to the clinic. Stumblingly I explained all this to the three of them. 'He keeps a temporary bed there for when he needs to stay near a patient.'

'He never reached there.'

They stood around me in the drawing-room as I sat crouched as though some ravening creature gnawed at my guts, until the constable decided matters had reached a critical stage and he packed the two women off. 'Now, madam, we'll have a few simple questions and some straight answers from you, if you please.' His tone was patronising, almost threatening.

'When did you last actually see your husband?'

I had to cudgel my poor brains, so crammed with other less vital matters. 'Last night, in bed,' I said. 'No, I'm wrong. It was the night before, and he had left by the time I woke up.'

Two nights back, disturbed by the sudden revelation that Clive was mortal, I'd reached a sort of psychic crisis; been so filled with pitying love for him, but let him sleep on, peacefully unaware. Instead of roaming the house and befuddling myself with brandy I should have roused him and told him fiercely how precious I at last knew he was. That terrible fear of some day losing him – that shattering knowledge of his vulnerability – hadn't that been a presentiment of what was to happen now, so soon after? I felt a sweat break out at the thought of it.

The policeman stared at me with cold, washed-out grey eyes.

'Perhaps you are a little clearer over how long you've been married, Mrs Malcolm.'

I wasn't – not instantly able to count off the days and hours as I supposed a new bride should be. The wedding had been on a Saturday and so much had happened since then. Today was either a Thursday or a Friday. So was it three weeks I'd been married? I said as much.

'A day under a fortnight,' the man stated with an air of satisfaction, as if I'd meant to deceive him and been foiled.

Could it really be? If nothing had gone wrong on my wedding day – if the wretched Patrick Garston hadn't been found hanging from the banisters in his home – I should now have been on honeymoon with my darling man, still touring Switzerland and Austria. He would have been safe and happy enough then.

'We were obliged to cancel it – the honeymoon, I mean,' escaped me, as if it could mean anything to this stranger.

Apparently it did. He insisted on knowing why, so I explained how a patient had suddenly required my husband's personal attention. He seemed to take it that I would have resented the decision and that this would have caused a distinct cooling of ardour between the two of us, if not a definite rift.

'No,' I told him. 'I knew there must be adjustments made if I became a doctor's wife. The decision to postpone travelling was one we made together.'

'And since then? This wasn't your husband's first absence overnight.'

I supposed Mrs Bowyer would have mentioned it. Or Matron. Thought of her reminded me of the phone number pinned to her notice board. It was suddenly important.

'Yesterday he was called to a patient at Claridge's. You should follow that up, constable. When I telephoned there, the receptionist could have been mistaken in saying that my husband had left. Though it's strange if Clive warned neither the clinic nor myself that he intended staying on. Or perhaps he tried to get in touch and the hotel failed to deliver his message.'

'That possibility has been investigated. Dr Malcolm was independently witnessed leaving, as the hotel claimed.'

I met the constable's eyes then, and they held harsh accusation. 'How did you know where he had gone? Matron informed me that she was forbidden to give you the name of the hotel or the patient. And that she obeyed the instruction.'

'My husband gave that order? Specifically about me?'

'It seems he felt it necessary to keep some things secret from you, Mrs Malcolm.'

'Private, not secret,' I defended him. Or was I defending myself?

'So who *was* the patient in question?' I demanded.

The man's eyes flickered, but he said nothing. We were left staring at each other, hostile as cats with their fur on end. 'For God's sake,' I cried, 'what are you doing to find him? Shouldn't you be out there asking questions of anyone who could have seen him since?' Then, seizing on any straw to clutch at: 'Who was this witness who says he saw him leave? It could have been someone of the same build and appearance, not Clive at all.'

'He was seen by a personal friend who was passing at the time. There could have been no mistake. They actually spoke together.'

'And did Clive mention where he would be going next?'

A trifle reluctantly the policeman admitted, 'He intended returning to the clinic on foot, since there was a scarcity of cabs just then.'

'And his patient at the hotel? What of him?'

At that point the policeman stood his ground and reminded me that he was the one appointed to ask the questions, not answer them, so I must be satisfied – which I was far from being.

Next he began asking where and how I had spent the thirty-six hours since yesterday morning, and then I knew: he believed I'd been either directly or indirectly responsible for Clive's disappearance. All the horrors of my past treatment by police interrogators came rushing back to overwhelm me. I found it almost impossible to still the trembling of my hands.

I answered as fully as I could without revealing the enquiries I'd embarked on. At every point he repeated the question in a slightly altered form. I think I convinced him that I was concerned about my personal finances and so had had recourse to the firm of Hardwick and Meadows. He took a note of their address, warning me that everything I claimed could be checked.

Eventually the inquisition ceased, like a child's clockwork toy that had run down; but it was clear to me that the constable left the house with one remaining question in his mind unanswered: whether I had caused my husband some serious bodily harm or merely forced him into abandoning a thoroughly distasteful marriage.

Had I not been so anxious, it would have been humiliating. My old horror of the police, the clanging cell door and the mixed scents of disinfectant and wretched unwashed humanity returned to plague me again; but it was anger that most possessed me. This time it was not myself but Clive I must direct all my energies to saving; and his danger was undefined. There was nothing to work on – no identities given for whoever was behind his disappearance.

Who had this mysterious 'patient' been and who the 'personal friend' who'd encountered him on leaving the hotel?

Jeremy and Iggy were the two who first sprang to mind, but Clive was a popular man among his colleagues and had countless friends whom I'd not yet met. It could have been someone I had never even heard of. And not necessarily a man, since I'd already proof that he still kept up with women he had known before we married. Since he'd been so adamant that I, his wife, shouldn't be told of his whereabouts, wasn't he assuming my disapproval of where he was bound and whom he was to meet? Marrying him, I had been overconfident that I was all he desired in a woman. Now it must occur to me to wonder: had he become so proficient a lover through long practice? Could my attractive husband be an obsessive womaniser?

I tried telling myself that such suspicions were unworthy. I hung on to the memory of his gentleness, the candour of his eyes. I could almost feel the touch of his hand in mine, the little roughness of a tiny scar at the heel of the thumb, already familiar and treasured. Surely I would have known if I shared that intimacy with a rival.

Mrs Bowyer had seen the policeman out, and now she appeared with a globe of brandy, which I refused. Also the offer of food. 'Perhaps a little of your good chicken soup, but later,' I promised. 'First I have some phone calls to make.'

The number for Jeremy's lodgings was on a memo pad in the hall, but I heard the telephone continue ringing unanswered before I remembered he had spoken of moving. It seemed possible he had already left Battersea and was living elsewhere. So I rang the clinic and was answered by Dr Atkinson, who provided the new address from Clive's desk diary, but regretted that a telephone line had not yet been installed there.

'Then I must call on him in person,' I said. 'It's likely he can offer some suggestion where my husband has gone.' I rang for Mabel to run out and find me a cab, which she did while I dressed for outdoors, and within twenty minutes I found myself in Bloomsbury, quite close to the University Hospital.

The house was a stuccoed, three-storeyed Regency one, a definite improvement on the earlier lodgings. Here it seemed Jeremy had a whole floor to himself, with his name in a brass card-holder at the outer door. I pressed his bell and waited. After a few moments I heard someone descending the inner stairs and he opened the door to me.

'Lucy! Mrs Malcolm,' he exclaimed. 'What on earth has brought you here?'

'Clive's gone missing, or so it seems. I hoped you might know where he could be.'

'I've no idea. It's inexplicable, as I told the police. Let me . . .'

'They've been to see you already? What did you tell them?'

'Just that . . . Look, we can't stand here. Please come in. Is that your cab waiting? Let me pay him off and I'll get you another later.'

I allowed his masterly briskness to take me over, standing suddenly quite droopy and lifeless in the hall. 'Right at the top,' he told me tersely as he came back, and he chose to follow behind, as though he thought I might stumble and need support. On the first landing I passed a handsome mahogany door with a brass knocker fashioned like a mermaid, then continued up by a narrower staircase to where a vee of light spilled from an open doorway. It gave on to a tiny hall and beyond it a largish, square room with two long windows overlooking the street below.

He led me to a sofa upholstered in a dark kingfisher-blue silk, and even in my dazed state I observed that all the furnishings in the elegant room were matching, in figured brocade or heavy velvet, lit with little touches of lemon yellow. There was even a boudoir grand piano half-covered by an exotic fringed shawl which I took to be Indian. In his new life Jeremy appeared to have fallen securely on his feet.

He had disappeared towards what I assumed was his kitchen or dining-room, because he came back with a carafe of water and a tumbler of brandy, which he insisted I should drink barely diluted. It burned into me and I let its warmth run through, giving me the courage I needed to face him out over what secrets Clive had been withholding.

He denied knowledge of any. 'If your husband chose not to offer particular details of his work, it was purely from professional discretion and to shield you from the harsher aspects of what could seem unpalatable to a non-medical person.'

'So he would have no scruples about confiding such matters to you? In which case, did you know he was to visit Claridge's Hotel and the identity of his patient there?'

I could see he wanted to refuse me an answer, but I insisted. So, reluctantly, he admitted, 'I had no foreknowledge, but when I dropped in to see Matron she did explain why Clive was absent.'

'And although you next spoke to me, you never mentioned this.'

'I saw no reason to.'

'Because it was no business of mine? Or because, had I known, I would have . . .' I almost said 'disapproved', but warned myself off in time After all, who was I, a mere wife, to censure my husband's comings and goings? That's certainly how a confirmed bachelor would have seen it. '. . . questioned it?' I substituted.

The monkey mask was quite rigid with protocol: I was an outsider. What medical confidences Clive shared with him, or with Matron for that matter, they were clearly to go over my head.

'The police,' I reminded him. 'Didn't they demand to know? What did you tell them?'

'Simply that he intended catching up on his work at the clinic.'

I stared at him. 'So you were the "friend" he ran into as he left Claridges's?'

'I happened by just then, yes.' The admission seemed to embarrass him. Evidently he was unaware that this had been kept from me.

'He was on foot, I understand.'

'At that point, yes. He might have caught a cab later in Oxford Street or farther.'

'And that was the last you saw of him?'

He hesitated a little too long. 'You saw him again!'

'From my seat in the omnibus. I caught one in the next street and it passed him. He had gone about a hundred yards, then stopped to search through his pockets.'

'As though he'd lost something?'

'Perhaps looking for some note or prescription he'd made out.'

'Or an address or telephone number.'

'It could have been anything.'

'Yet he had stopped in his tracks – might have had second thoughts about where he would go next. Isn't that possible? It would account for his not returning to the clinic.' I was desperate for some logical explanation.

'This was over twenty-four hours ago,' he reminded me sombrely.

He was right. It did nothing to allay my anxiety. I wanted to blame him for Clive's absence.

'You hadn't offered to accompany him?'

Jeremy looked puzzled. 'There was no need. He had completed his examination of the patient at the hotel, and all was in order. I had work of my own to catch up on.'

No need? It sounded as though Jeremy had expected to be called in professionally. 'So you didn't just happen upon him, but had intended to catch him at the hotel and help him with whatever treatment was required.'

'Something like that.'

That wasn't what he had said before. I was left wondering in which of his two capacities he'd expected to help: as Clive's adviser on drugs or as a surgeon? But it seemed hardly appropriate for me to ask so much. We appeared to have arrived at some impasse. My questions had dried up and I was no further forward. I looked about me for a way to end the conversation. 'This is a beautiful room. You seem to have settled in comfortably.'

He coloured and was momentarily at a loss for words, then admitted, 'I was fortunate in having a friend who no longer required this apartment. I'm not sure that it's quite what I was looking for. I'm no Sybarite.'

Perhaps not, but persons of his kind were reputedly very artistic, so he would appreciate the elegance. Doubtless Jeremy would enjoy being moulded to his surroundings, rather than altering them to his humbler style – which reminded me of Clive's other friend, the extreme of inelegance. 'Would you happen to know how I could contact Ignatius?' I enquired.

'Iggy?' He seemed astonished that I should know of him. 'I heard that he's currently working at Pentonville prison. If you write to him there, it should reach him safely.'

I could do better than that. I would telephone or call on him in person. If Clive was in difficulties or danger no time must be lost; and Iggy struck me as someone who would spare no pains to find out what had happened.

On the way home by cab I considered Jeremy's cool attitude – or attitudes, plural, because there had been moments when my questions had caught him out in embarrassment. He was keeping something from me, and I was not entirely sure that it was out of consideration for my feelings. Even if it was, surely there was something slightly sinister in that fact? Did he, or the police, suspect that some terrible misfortune had overcome my husband? An attack by some vagrant? Or had Clive *enemies*, even, that I had never dreamed of?

115

Twelve

At home I threw my coat on a hall chair and seized the telephone, jiggled the hook frantically and asked the operator to connect me with Pentonville prison. She passed me to someone else, who took her time finding the number; but at last I was through to a male voice who told me that the Governor's office was closed until eight thirty the following morning.

'This could be a matter of life or death,' I hissed back.

A new voice took over. 'Governor James,' he said with authority. I had heard the click of a ring on metal as he was passed the telephone.

'I'm sorry to disturb you,' I said. 'This is an emergency call for Dr Ignatius . . .' Dear God, what had the man's surname been? Suddenly it sprang back into my mind, as its image trundled by, filled with unlovely garden rubbish. '. . . *Barrow*! This concerns Dr Clive Malcolm's disappearance.'

Whatever he made of my hectic message he wasted no time – obviously a man accustomed to dealing with crises. There were a few muffled words, then several clicks and another voice answered. 'Dr Barrow here. Can I help you?'

'Oh, Iggy, if only you can!' I burst out, abandoning all formality. 'It's Lucy Malcolm, Clive's wife. I'm afraid he's gone missing, since five yesterday afternoon. Would you have any idea where he might be?'

'*Disappeared*? Since *five* yesterday? No; he was here with me until almost seven, my dear. He left in some haste, fearing he'd be late for dinner with you. Do you mean that no one has seen him since? This is most disturbing. Most unlike him. He certainly intended to return home immediately. Rushed out to catch a cab. Even left his cap behind in his haste. Oh dear, oh dear! I really think you must inform the police.'

116

'They know already. I've had them here questioning me and the servants. I think someone at the clinic must have raised the alarm.'

'So they aren't aware that he was here? I must get in touch with them at once. They'll need to scour the hospitals in case there's been an accident. Leave it with me, my dear. I'll get on to that now and telephone you as soon as we have news.'

Bless the man for not beating about the bush and wasting time on sympathy. Thank God it had sprung into my mind to appeal to him. I could understand that Clive might have some professional business to seek his opinion on, but anywhere beyond King's Cross station was an unsavoury district to be walking back from at night. Some tramp might have been hanging about ready to attack and rob a stranger; and anyone well dressed hastening from the prison could seem fair game for a criminal. Clive would have been on foot until a cab appeared. Oh why hadn't he been a spendthrift like me and kept his cab waiting?

As soon as Iggy had rung off I thought of a dozen things I should have asked him, but didn't dare call him back and so delay his contact with the police. What would Clive have needed to see him about? Was it connected with the mysterious patient he had just attended at Claridge's, or some other case?

The more I considered it the more I came to believe that this must be some further research he'd required on prisoners or prison conditions, and the only person I knew of at risk of being convicted was poor Patrick Garston, unjustly accused of attempted suicide. Clive would have been as uneasy as I was about the troubles the Garstons had suffered. First there had been the man's near-death from hanging; next, the murder of the man who might have led us to the one responsible; thirdly, and on the same night, the torching of the Garstons' house. Lightning might strike twice in the same spot, but not three times in so short a period. Surely those incidents were linked. And now – possibly – a fourth: the disappearance of the one man who might have drawn the truth from poor, shattered Patrick Garston.

It smacked of desperation as though, having failed to murder Garston, someone had tried again with the house fire, only to discover that none of the family had been at home. Afterwards there would have been talk among the neighbours, and Ethel's sister, or someone else, would surely have mentioned the clinic and how my husband, a psychotherapist, was working on a cure for the man's amnesia. This would have drawn Clive into the endangered circle.

As he made his way back from the prison, Clive could have been recognised, followed and attacked in some dark alley; and if it had happened like that – not a random victim, but targeted by a man already a murderer – what hope remained that Clive had survived a day later? Dear God, the killer could have dragged his lifeless body away and disposed of him in the Thames!

I was sick with worry and maddened by inactivity. I should have been out searching the streets myself, but was forced to stay by the telephone, waiting for the promised message from Iggy. When it came, how could it be anything but bad news? Or at the very best just negative: nothing known; nobody found wandering who resembled my husband.

Was there no one else I could turn to? I had tried the only two of Clive's medical friends I had met. My adoptive father would be abroad now with Eugenie and Isabelle; Geoffrey busy in Provence with his weevil grubs; Edwin back at Eton for his important final year. Sooner or later I should have to warn the bishop that his one-time ward was missing, but he could do nothing to help. He was an old man, retired, and if not unworldly, yet out of touch with present harsh realities.

Back at Stakerleys there remained only Aunt Mildred and Dr Millson. There was a matter they could help me with, but I didn't dare clutter the wires with it while there might be news coming through on Clive's whereabouts.

It was an hour and three-quarters after I'd returned when the telephone at last rang. Even expected, it startled me and I fumbled over lifting the receiver.

'It's me,' Iggy mumbled, gauche again because he had to deal with a woman.

'Iggy,' I pleaded, 'is there news?'

'He's here, with me.'

'For God's sake, put him on. Let me hear him.'

'I can't. I mean, he's . . . Fact is, we're at Bart's, m'dear.'

So who was this Bart, that he wouldn't allow my husband to use his telephone?

'St. Bartholomew's – the hospital. I'm afraid there's been an accident.'

Only an accident? Not an attempt on his life then? Thank God for so much, but how bad was it? 'Iggy, how is he? He's going to be all right, surely?'

'He's in very good hands. Getting the best treatment the country can offer. They'll be taking him up to theatre at any moment now. Sir Digby's promised to deal with it himself.'

'Wait there, will you? I'm on my way. Where exactly is Bart's? North or south of the river?'

'Not far from St Paul's, but you needn't—'

'I'm coming. I must talk to you. Please stay on.'

'I'm not going anywhere.' He sounded offended. Well, a good friend would be.

'Just a moment, Mrs M. Something's happening.' He broke off and I heard a murmur of voices, some discussion, then Iggy more clearly saying, 'Um, right then.'

'What's going on?' I demanded.

'A change of venue. Sir Digby wants him moved to the East London Hospital instead. In Whitechapel Road. He'll get a private room there and the theatre's come free.'

'Is that as good?'

'Excellent. I'm to travel with him. Must go now.'

I snatched up my coat, shouted to Mrs Bowyer that Clive was injured, in hospital, and I would ring from there. Then I ran from the house.

By now it was raining steadily, falling straight and steely against the black sealskin of wet roads. Headlights from traffic were reflected like barley-sugar twists on puddled surfaces. All the taxis which passed had passengers aboard. I searched in vain for one that was free. It wasn't until Sloane Street that I caught a cab being paid off, and then I was quite out of breath, wheezing to get out the words, and with rain running down my face. The driver sat stolidly waiting while I held on to the door. When I did speak he grunted, 'You didden oughter get in a state like that.' Perhaps he thought I needed the hospital for myself.

Sitting alone there in the confined, smoky space, my teeth

gritted, I wished I'd asked Iggy more. I needed to be prepared. If Sir Digby had been sent for, it must be serious indeed. Or was it because Clive was a doctor? – a thank-you case, as they'd call it, with the fee waived for a colleague. Not that it mattered. I'd most willingly give every penny we possessed to get Clive safely back on his feet again. The journey was taking for ever, struggling against the evening tide of traffic returning westward. As we reached the Strand, there was a procession of brewers' drays drawn by great Suffolk punches clogging the way of the motors. I thought of the motorcycle Clive had suggested buying. It would be the only sensible way of threading through at this time of evening. But would dear Clive ever recover to ride one?

'Go round about!' I shouted through the glass partition.

The driver hunched his shoulders. 'Covent Garden'll be worse.' But he had heeded and turned down to Victoria Embankment where we made better progress for a few minutes before coming up behind Smithfield market. Even there we were halted by pedestrians, who flung themselves heedlessly into the roadway to gain the opposite pavements. I could well see why central London was famous for its many hospitals. I couldn't argue with the cabbie's modest speed when it seemed that Clive might himself have become a victim of the traffic scrum.

I was dropped off a little short of the entrance, behind other vehicles being paid off by their fares. This time there was no point in retaining the cab. I could be here overnight or longer.

Real hospitals make me uneasy, and I'm not easily intimidated. The clinic is different, more human and without that aggressively disinfected atmosphere that locates the solar plexus via the nostrils. The nurses here were so cool, so tall, immaculately starched, with their leg-of-mutton sleeves, crisp lilac stripes and stiff little hooped pillboxes on their heads. I wanted them to be goddesses. Anything, so that they performed miracles for Clive.

Iggy was seated in the reception hall, stumpy little legs planted wide and his rounded belly hanging down between, undistinguished and a little crumpled, but just then so reassuring. A younger man in a white coat, a stethoscope hanging from his neck, was in conversation with him, standing and respectful. As Iggy caught my eye and *harrumphed*, the other smiled and held out his hand. 'Thank you, sir,' he said and bowed towards me. Then he took off.

Iggy struggled to rise, but I put a hand on his shoulder and forced him back, slipping into the seat beside him. 'What of Clive?'

'Sir Digby's just arrived. He's scrubbing up.'

Never mind old Parker-Rillington. It was Clive I'd asked after. I must suppose he was sedated ready for the knife. 'What exactly happened?' I demanded. 'To my husband.'

'He was discovered unconscious in a cab,' Iggy said shortly. 'The police aren't sure how he came to be there.'

'There'd been a crash?'

'No. The vehicle wasn't damaged – just parked in a little alley off Holborn. No driver. Apparently a robbery, because all Clive's money and papers were gone. He was taken into Bart's as an unknown. The clothes he was wearing weren't what I saw him in the previous day. His jacket was missing and they were old, patched trousers, none too clean. His attacker could have exchanged with him during the time he was missing.'

'But his injuries?'

'We'll know more when Sir Digby's completed his exploration.' He was going to leave it at that, but I clamped my hand firmly on his arm and increased the pressure until it must have hurt.

'A couple of broken ribs, a blow to the occiput, and stab wounds to the thigh and abdomen.'

'Someone meant to kill him.'

'They might have succeeded if he hadn't been a doctor. The thigh wound had nicked the artery. He was left to bleed to death, but must have been conscious enough to fix a makeshift tourniquet with his torn-off sleeve. He hung on with both hands and crossed the other leg over. The weight was enough to stem the heavy flow for a while, but some circulation continued – perhaps enough to have saved the limb from certain amputation. You understand that it could have . . .'

'Mortified, yes. So Sir Digby may be able to save it?'

Iggy nodded sombrely.

'That's not all, is it?' I could tell from his dour expression. 'The other injuries? His head?'

'We don't know yet. We can only pray.'

For an instant the hall and its moving figures blurred and receded. I felt Iggy's hands on my shoulders. 'Don't faint on me,' he pleaded. It was grotesque; he the learned doctor, but still socially inept with women.

'I'm all right,' I promised; and then, bitterly: 'If all we can do is pray, I must let his guardian know. The bishop is well qualified for that. It's not a skill I've had much practice in just lately.'

There was a great deal of waiting to endure. The young doctor returned, having arranged for a tiny office to be vacated for Iggy and me to sit in. There was a telephone, and on the desk a tray with tea things and a plate of sandwiches.

'When did you last eat?' Iggy enquired sternly. 'Just get some of this down you pretty sharpish.' He seemed more his bristly self now, and I remembered Clive saying that this ungainly man would overcome his embarrassment of my being female once he accepted me as a friend.

I discovered after the first few bites that I was famished, devoured most of the sandwiches and accepted two cups of tea, Iggy playing mother. What else, when he normally had no one at home to pour for him? As the waiting dragged on, I settled my head against the side of a bookshelf and must have drifted off.

Suddenly, like a fluttering of doves, there were two nurses at the door ushering in Sir Digby in his shirtsleeves with cufflinks dangling. Even as he stood there, frowning importantly, his fingers were wrestling with pushing the little gold discs through their holes.

To see him in such undress I feared the worst, but his haste in coming was all to set our minds at rest. Or as far as he was able. It seemed that a smashed rib had been removed in order to mend a small puncture to Clive's left lung. The femoral artery had been repaired, the thigh wound stitched up and the abdominal lesion dressed but, having lost so much blood, my husband remained in a very weak state.

All this information was delivered over my head to Iggy, as

a medical man, but it seemed that my permission was required before Clive could be given a transfusion of blood.

'Of course it must be done, and at once. For heaven's sake, take some of mine,' I insisted before Iggy could put it to me.

'We have suitable sources,' the surgeon said shortly. 'It is more than likely that your blood would be inappropriate. There are certain risks attached. Your part is simply to sign the form of permission.'

Even as he spoke a nurse was setting pen, ink and paper on the desk where the tea tray had been.

'Iggy,' I pleaded, 'what must I do? If there are risks in it . . .'

'Greater risks in leaving him without,' he almost snorted.

'But why me? Can't Clive decide on this for himself?'

The two men gave each other stare for stare. 'The patient,' Sir Digby intoned as if from a great height, 'is still unconscious.'

Iggy's lips tightened. 'Under sedation?'

'Comatose,' the surgeon murmured, not for my ears.

'Sign, there's a good fellow,' Iggy urged me, his face a tragic mask. I complied, still unhappy at the fashion-swings of medicine when in one age the panacea for all ills was to leech blood, and in another to open the veins and pour someone else's in.

In an instant the room was emptied of the invasion. Iggy and I were again left together. I would have given anything for Clive to pull through and be restored to what he was before, but the risks were unknown to me. As a doctor's wife I should have been more aware of innovations in medical procedures. I was left like some primitive aborigine too ignorant to do more than fear the shaman's mystic powers.

I appealed to Clive's friend. 'Iggy, I don't understand. What will they do to him? People have died, haven't they, after receiving another person's blood?'

He looked quite fierce for a moment. 'We're learning more and more all the time,' he said, 'widening the horizons of knowledge. It's known that not all types of blood mix safely, but certain persons are born with a type of blood that can be used for anyone at all. In emergencies suitable volunteers are brought here for this very purpose, their blood having been examined microscopically and analysed. You may be certain that the blood given to Clive will do him no harm but build up his ability to withstand the existing injuries.'

So it seemed that I had done the right thing. All the same, if Clive pulled through – and he must – it would be grotesque for my husband's body to have part of an alien person in it.

Iggy was blinking at me through his thick-pebbled spectacles. He had softened, and I remembered that he worked with jailbirds and lunatics. There was a deal of sympathy in the man – almost the antithesis of the detached and arrogant Sir Digby. Doctors, I reflected, came in all shapes, sizes and personalities. This one would forgive me for my ignorance.

'I think,' he said slowly, 'you should come and watch. It will reassure you. We can observe the ward through a glass panel in the door. No one will be aware of us.'

So I went with him to an upper floor and gazed through a sort of porthole that gave on to a small, brightly lit room with two iron beds set parallel in it. Two figures lay there under sheets and attached to each other by rubber tubes interrupted by a slim glass vessel. All was orderly and quite undramatic. Simply life being poured from one body into another.

I could see little of the stranger who was doing this incredible thing for my husband – just his large, rather knobbly, stockinged feet protruding from the sheet that barely covered him. He must have been well over six feet tall. Then he raised his head from the pillow as a nurse spoke to him and I saw he had a shock of curly black hair.

'How much will he give?' I asked.

'A little less than a pint. Then another donor will take his place. And so it goes on until the recipient's blood content reaches a safe level.'

I couldn't imagine any more worthwhile sacrifice that could be made. 'When it's all over,' I whispered, 'and Clive's well again – or even if something worse happens – I want to do this. Will a woman's blood do?'

'It's every bit as good. But you'd need to be tested to make sure it is the kind the haematologists want. There are never enough volunteers. Since the war so much blood is required for repairs.'

He sighed. When he spoke again his voice held an almost

religious reverence. 'We're hoping that some day a way will be found to preserve supplies, so that each hospital can keep a stock of its own; but up until now all experiments have led to killing its essential nature. Whether heated or frozen, it dries and dies. To do any good it must be passed on fresh.'

We moved away from the doors as the donor began to sit up, his arm freed of the tubing. A nurse had started to bandage where the hollow needle had gone in. 'I want to thank him,' I whispered.

'Better not. We like to keep it anonymous.'

I stared at him. 'You do it, don't you? You give your blood.'

'Such as it is,' he admitted. 'Many doctors and students offer. Mine is only good for a small minority of patients.'

'What happens now?' I asked as we descended the staircase.

'You'll be a good chap and go home. There's no chance of Clive having visitors yet awhile. But come back at midday tomorrow, when doctors' rounds are over. I'll arrange then that you get to see your man.'

He had a cab whistled up by a porter and, surprisingly, climbed in after me. 'I shall drop you off,' he offered, almost huffily.

'Chelsea's hardly on your way to Pentonville prison. Not unless we take a circular route by way of Birmingham and Norwich.'

'Doesn't matter, woman,' he grumbled. 'It's a pleasant night for a ride.' Then he frowned. 'How is it you know where the prison is but not any of the hospitals?'

I knew because I had gone to spy out where they'd first taken Julian. I'd stood outside and tried to imagine the cell he would be in. But I'd no intention of admitting as much to this kindly man.

'I do know the Westminster Hospital,' I said. 'Mama was taken there injured by shrapnel during a Zeppelin raid. As for the prison, that's a long story. Maybe I'll tell it to you some day.'

Thirteen

I felt hustled away. They could at least have allowed me to sit at Clive's bedside for a few moments. I'd had only a glimpse of his still, bandaged head beyond the man who was giving blood to keep him alive.

A phantom haunted me – an image of Clive in that taxicab, fighting for his life while consciousness slid inexorably away. I clearly saw his face drawn with pain, the desperate efforts of his fingers to tear off his shirtsleeve and use it as a tourniquet. I swear I could smell the blood, sticky and decadently sweet. I felt myself confined in the same stale cab, but like a ghost incapable of any action.

It had already happened, was over; but the echo of it kept coming back, angering me because it was negative. I should be looking ahead, trying to plan. For what, though? There was nothing I could do physically to aid his recovery – that was the concern of doctors and nurses at the East London Hospital – but there were others who must be told: Bishop Malcolm, my family, the staff of the clinic. So the next hours must be spent at the telephone, but first I must decide how much – or how little – to confide.

I rang the bishop, retired now to Bognor. He took the news quietly but was obviously shocked. 'And you, Lucy, how are you? Have you family to stay with you?'

Mrs Bowyer and Mabel, I told him; and little Petra too. My parents being away, I'd had recourse to Clive's colleagues, who had done all that was possible. Sir Digby Parker-Ellington had operated and we must wait until daylight for news, when Clive would be fully conscious.

At that time I wasn't aware of lying, and certainly hadn't meant to deceive the dear old man, but it seemed to me then that if there was any justice under the sun Clive must come out of this well.

The bishop gave me his blessing and asked for a word with Mrs Bowyer. I left them talking together while I went to hang over my sleeping baby's cot. She looked so secure that I could barely believe it was the same night that these terrible things had happened.

When I came downstairs again, Mrs Bowyer insisted I should eat the supper she had saved, but the salmon had no more taste for me than flaked cardboard, and the hock was vinegar. Pecking at it did give me time, however, to consider what precautions should be taken. Without Clive to treat him, keeping Garston at the clinic had no point. Ethel and the children were homeless. It seemed the ideal moment to whisk them out of London altogether and set them up on the Stakerleys estate. To begin with they could be put up at Forge Cottage (where Big Dan's wife took in summer paying guests) while Grandfather's agent found the Garstons a suitable place of their own. Any general medical care Patrick needed could be arranged by Uncle Millson.

With this in mind I telephoned Aunt Mildred, not mentioning Clive's condition, but only that circumstances demanded one of his patients should be sent at once to the country together with his wife and three little daughters. No, there was no danger of infection. The man had suffered a mental breakdown, which was why Clive had been treating him. He needed peace, rest and to feel secure with his little family.

As I had been sure she would be, Mildred was happy to be of use, promising to arrange everything after breakfast. She asked after Petra and then suggested that perhaps I should be getting some rest myself since it was almost two thirty in the morning. I'd had no idea how waiting at the hospital had eaten into the time, and apologised profusely. Not knowing the circumstances, she must have thought I'd turned into a nightbird like Isabelle.

There was no alternative to her suggestion, although I was certain sleep would be impossible, but even as I stripped off, weariness overtook me and I had only to crawl between the sheets to go out like a snuffed candle.

Over a late breakfast, at which I asked Mrs Bowyer and Mabel to lay places for themselves alongside mine, I gave a fuller explanation than I'd been capable of the night before. They were already distressed that Clive was in some danger and I tried to sound hopeful. I then explained how I would send the Garstons to Stakerleys by hired car, but I needed Mabel to go with them, since I must keep vigil over Clive at the hospital. Mrs Bowyer assured me she would be delighted to take over nursemaid duties until either of us returned. When I rang the East London, it was to be told that there was no change in Clive's condition.

The car was ordered for eleven o'clock, by which time I hoped to have rounded up the Garstons and brought them back by taxi. The main obstacle, I expected, would be opposition by Matron to removing Patrick from her care, but I was relying on her seeing the advantage of one less responsibility while Clive's absence left them short-handed. So, taking the bull by the horns, I went there first and waited while Matron was filling in acceptance forms for a youngish woman who sat hunched, miserably rocking forward and backward, while she counted aloud. Every now and again, when she was asked a direct question, she would halt for a moment, appalled, shake her head, then resume the obsessive movement, starting to count again from one.

As I had expected, Matron expressed doubts over Garston's removal, but I won her round by claiming that he would be transferred to the personal care of a distinguished doctor Clive had every confidence in. Dr Atkinson anxiously took over the ordering of an ambulance so that Garston should travel in comfort, but I instructed the driver myself on where to deliver him and how to find Dan Partridge's smithy. To minimise confusion, the patient was to receive a mild injection of sedative.

I wasn't entirely truthful with Ethel Garston. By claiming that Matron had sanctioned Patrick's transfer to the country I made it sound like recuperation, and implied it had been part of Clive's plan for him. However, once she knew that the family would be together again, Ethel was most willing, swiftly collecting their few remaining possessions and tying them in a borrowed sheet. Our cab deposited us back in Chelsea before the hired car was due.

Mabel at once made friends with the children and I felt

confident that, lulled by the car's warmth and comfort, Ethel would most likely get some well-needed sleep on the two-hour journey. At ten minutes short of eleven we heard a motor's throbbing in the road outside, but when Mrs Bowyer opened to the chauffeur's knock, I heard her give a glad cry of surprise. 'Oh madam,' she called, 'it's His Grace.'

The bishop, stiffly alighting from his Daimler, was astonished by the children who had rushed out to surround him. 'Well, bless my soul,' he exclaimed. 'What have we here, eh? Where have these cherubs sprung from?'

Then there were squeals of panic as a huge, shaggy shape bounded after him on to the path, shook itself, and advanced with grinning jaws. Accustomed as I was to country dogs, even I quailed before the fearsome-looking Irish wolfhound. 'Gentle as a lamb,' the bishop assured me. 'This is Cuchulain. He's your husband's, but Clive thought better than to burden you with the hairy monster in your love nest.'

He had come to comfort me, bless him, and meant to leave the wolfhound with us as guard dog until such time as my husband was home again. Certainly, although the beast's hackles rose if the excited children approached too close, he was lamb-like in his approach to Mrs Bowyer, a friend of long standing. At her command he established himself under a console cabinet, nose on paws, to keep an eye on comings and goings.

Mabel had run upstairs to fetch little Petra, and when she came back with my baby in her arms, the wolfhound raised his head and treated the pair to a fierce stare which alarmed me afresh. However, with the hired car's arrival just then, all was bustle and excitement getting Ethel, Mabel and the children aboard. We all stood at the door to wave them off, then returned to the morning-room where Petra, wrapped in her lacy shawl, had been tucked safely against the cushions of a sofa. As I ran to pick her up, the wolfhound leapt between, snarling and slit-eyed. He was only a pace away from her and I was terrified that he might seize the little bundle and sink his fangs into her tender body.

'Leave him to me, madam,' Mrs Bowyer whispered, with a restraining hand on my elbow. 'Down, Cuchulain,' she ordered and he allowed her to sweep past, bend over the little bundle on the sofa and pick up my baby safely.

The bishop had paused in the doorway. 'He was guarding her,' he claimed; but I wasn't so sure. He moved stiffly to a chair and the dog went to him. 'You know a helpless puppy when you see one, old fellow, don't you. You must trust him, Lucy, and he'll take care of the whole household. May I suggest now that I accompany you to the hospital?'

I had only to put together a few night things for Clive: slippers, toiletries and socks. Then we settled in my god-father's capacious motor and, more rapidly than yesterday's ride, we drove east across town, I having been assured that Mrs Bowyer would not leave Petra unattended in any room with the dog.

At the East London Hospital a house surgeon described my husband's condition as 'critical but stable', which gave little encouragement, except that yesterday there had been greater cause for alarm. The infusions of blood were reinforcing his body's general resistance, but it would take time before it was known how damaging was the injury to his head. Meanwhile, he lay inert in a coma. His face was a stranger's, all animation suspended, so much blanker than when I had watched over him asleep. He could have been the carved stone effigy of a Crusader in some village church.

The bishop stayed beside me a while, then made an excuse of needing to speak with the hospital's chaplain. It left me alone, holding my husband's hand. I talked to him, told him all the things that might be poured out too late over a loved one's grave; but there was no shadow of reaction in the still face.

It was agony, being incapable of any kind of help. Since the doctors could give no assurance that he would regain consciousness soon, I decided I'd do better to try tracing his movements from when he'd left Pentonville prison two days before.

In the corridor a police sergeant stood waiting, his helmet under his arm. 'It's no use,' I said. 'He's not likely to be talking for a while.'

'Mrs Malcolm,' he said, 'could I have a word with you? Would you mind coming this way?'

He led me to the chapel, which was dimly lit by two altar candles. My godfather was there on his knees, but he rose stiffly and came across to us. It seemed he had met the sergeant already, for they nodded to each other and we sat in a pew together, I between the two men.

'My name is Bradley, ma'am,' the policeman began. 'Sergeant Bradley. I don't know if your husband ever mentioned me.'

I stared at him, uncomprehending. When had Clive had occasion to speak to him? He'd been unconscious since he was brought in.

'A few months ago,' he explained, 'when you had trouble of your own.'

'Of course. You must be the sergeant from Scotland Yard. You were so helpful to him over clearing my name.'

'I did little enough. It was Dr Malcolm's efforts that led us to the real killer. Today, when I saw the report that he'd been attacked, I thought I should look into what happened. A highly respected gentleman, your husband, ma'am. There's a chance he met up with a villain we have on our books. Could you tell me what actually happened?'

'We don't know. It could have been a random attempt to rob him, although he seldom carries much of value on him. On the other hand, there's a chance that . . .'

'A connection with something else?'

'It's a long story, but I'd so welcome your opinion on it – a sequence of vicious crimes which must surely be linked. First there was a poor man in Bermondsey who was thought to have tried to hang himself.'

'Thought to?'

'By the police there, who intend to charge him with it; but the circumstances were strange and the man has no memory at all of what happened, which is how my husband came to be treating him for severe shock.'

So while Sergeant Bradley sat patiently listening beside me, his helmet carefully placed between his boots, I outlined the Garstons' misfortunes and our suspicions about them.

At the end the bishop raised a mild protest. 'But Lucy, my dear, has all this happened to you and there was no word to me of it?'

Sergeant Bradley tutted and shook his head. 'You do take some terrible risks, ma'am. Seems you're not able to keep out of trouble. Last time it's Dr Malcolm looking out for you, and now you're both the other way about.'

'The point is, we can't wait for Clive to come round and tell us who attacked him. We must find out for ourselves, and then if the other crimes *are* linked . . .'

'We may find it's the same instigator for them all. Well, until the good doctor's able to tell us himself, I'd like a word with this Patrick Garston. Seems the story started with his hanging.'

'I don't think it did,' I contradicted. 'That wasn't the real beginning because, if someone did string him up to die, there'd surely have been a reason for it: one imperative enough to merit killing the one possible witness too. Because there's a charge outstanding, I'm afraid the very sight of a police uniform could have an adverse effect on Garston at present. I'm counting on the peace and security of the countryside to help heal him while my husband can't offer any treatment.'

We discussed what other measures the good sergeant might take, because he was determined to do what he could. Clive had certainly impressed him on the occasion when they'd met. It struck all three of us that the logical starting point of any investigation was to tackle the Pentonville end independently of the earlier incidents. Then, if it came to light that the attack on Clive had indeed been made by some local villain, it could rule out any connection with the train of events involving the Garstons.

Sergeant Bradley left us at the hospital door and we went back to my husband's bedside for a further half-hour's vigil. 'Will you stay a while with us?' I asked my godfather as we were driven back towards Chelsea, but he declined. He was expected back in Bognor that evening, where he had begun a course of confirmation classes for adults who had slipped through the parish net there. It seemed that, like artists, bishops never totally retired. Since there was nothing he could do for Clive on the spot, he might as well be concerned with the saving of souls and praying for a specific miracle.

Mrs Bowyer produced a late lunch at three o'clock, and it was already getting dark when the bishop's car drove off. The house felt empty afterwards as I waited for someone to telephone from Stakerleys that the Garstons had settled in.

It was Aunt Mildred who made the call. All had gone well. The ambulance had arrived first and Garston had already been installed in a bedroom overlooking the smithy's rear yard when the rest of his family arrived. Ethel had seemed bewildered at first, but so thankful to be again with her husband. A truckle bed had been put in his room so that she could be with him overnight. The three girls were sharing a second room. Dr Millson had visited them all and suggested that Mabel should stay over for at least two nights, at the big house, until the family felt properly at home. Tomorrow Deakin, the land steward, would drive her with Ethel to see two cottages which were vacant on the estate.

I took the opportunity to mention that Clive was spending a couple of days in hospital after an attack on the street. He was healing well, but it was nothing the Garstons needed to know about. I would get in touch later – perhaps come down myself and see how they had taken to country life.

It left me with a superstitious fear that my white lies were tempting fate, but I suppose that under it all I had a weird belief that making light of Clive's injuries might cause them to become so. Evidently Jeremy had been right about the manipulator in me. Now I was expecting not only people but events to go according to my wishes.

Jeremy – I hadn't heard from him since my visit to his new apartment in Bloomsbury. Doubtless Sir Digby was keeping him well occupied as his registrar. Iggy had telephoned twice while I was out and had left messages, but I put off returning his calls until I could be sure that Sergeant Bradley had caught up with him. Meanwhile I hunted through Clive's desk for a map of London, and marked with a pencil the alley near Holborn where Clive had been found unconscious in the cab.

It struck me then that the police must already have identified the taxi from its licence number. Its owner's name would be registered by the local authority. What had happened to the man, that he hadn't reported his vehicle missing? If Clive had disappeared for almost twenty-four hours, had the cab done the same?

Not necessarily. His injuries must have occurred only a short time before he was found, or he would have died from blood loss. So had he spent most of the missing hours elsewhere, only to be dumped unconscious in the cab as somewhere convenient to hide the body?

I pored over the map, found Caledonian Road and made another pencil mark for the prison, which was almost due north of Holborn. A considerable area lay between the two points: all the length of Gray's Inn Road, with Bloomsbury to the west of it and Clerkenwell to the east. Clive had told Iggy he was in a hurry to be home but it was a busy time of evening. He might have thought a cab easier to pick up near King's Cross station. So had he walked in that direction? Had he actually found one and been taken elsewhere? But why? In order to rob him? If so, where had he been all the time in between? Held captive? For what reason?

All I could be sure of was that Clive had never intended to stay away so long, or to end up in the way he'd done. *End up?* No, it wasn't the *end* – couldn't be. Clive was going to be all right. He had to recover.

My attempts at reasoning had led nowhere. Perhaps I should tackle it from the point where he'd been found. I held a magnifying glass over the tiny streets marked on the map and found myself staring at Aldwych. It brought to mind the office of Hardwick and Meadows, Accountants, which I'd visited so recently. Yes, there it was, in the narrow street leading off to the left, no more than four or five minutes' walk from Holborn itself; but that could be forcing the facts, to make a connection. Clive had intended coming straight home. Whatever happened to him would have happened early on his journey on foot, well to the north of Aldwych.

There were so many negatives. I must wait and contact Iggy again. Perhaps Sergeant Bradley had learnt something useful from him by now.

I telephoned the hospital a little after eleven that night and was connected with Sister Hendry in charge of Clive's case. She repeated the report I'd been given that morning: my husband's condition was 'critical but stable'. She added that no change was expected over the next twenty-four hours.

When I went up to bed I found Cuchulain spread on the landing between the closed doors of the nursery and Mrs Bowyer's bedroom. He showed the whites of his eyes, growling almost under his breath, as I slipped into my own room. I thought better of looking in on Petra, knowing he would let in only someone he was utterly sure of.

What I hadn't been prepared for was being barred from the bathroom as well. In my nightdress, having brushed my hair and reopened my bedroom window, I attempted to slide past him; but he rose to his full height, hackles raised, and displayed his yellow fangs in a menacing snarl.

I was obliged during the night to make use of a rather splendid chamber pot hand-painted in blue with Gloire de Dijon roses, one of a pair Clive and I had laughed over as curious wedding presents. Just then I was nearer to tears.

Fourteen

When Mrs Bowyer brought in my tea next morning, she listened to my complaint with a little smile on her lips. 'He's no fool, that dog, but he does make up his mind rather fast and with his own kind of logic. He knows he's here on guard duty and he has yet to discover the villains. Since little Petra is the most fragile, to his eyes she must be defended against everyone he hasn't already learned to trust.'

'He didn't take against Mabel,' I reminded her.

'But she came in carrying the baby. Perhaps he saw her as the mother.'

As many might do, I thought, *since Mabel is far more involved with my little one than I.* What a shamer for me. Even at Stakerleys, with all those nursery servants between, no one could ever have doubted who was closest to us children. Eugenie was the perfect mother I had shown no sign yet of becoming.

'So how do we put him right about me?' I asked wretchedly.

Her smile broadened. 'Well, madam, you know dogs, and what makes most sense to them.'

'Eating and following their noses. You mean I should put his food down for him and then let him sniff my hands? I hope you're right. But doesn't that mean that anyone can win him round with the same kind of bribery?'

'No, because I shall tell him when he may eat. He won't take it from a stranger unless he's given permission.'

'So we'll try that as soon as I'm dressed.'

'Very good, madam. Meanwhile I'll let him out into the garden.'

All the same that wasn't the first thing I did when I was ready. With nothing now to be a barrier, I went into the nursery

136

and took little Petra in my arms. She had been given her early bottle and was quite sleepy again, despite all those hours of uninterrupted night. I buried my face in the sweet milkiness of her, hugging her close and vowing to make amends. 'The trouble is, my darling, that so much is going wrong all around that I have been horribly neglectful of you – and of my good husband too. Have patience and I really will prove how very much I love you both.' I kissed her forehead and laid her back in her soft nest.

As I reached the kitchen, Mrs Bowyer opened the door to the garden and Cuchulain came in. He stopped just short of me and his nose went up. A little quiver went through his lanky frame and then his tail made an involuntary swish from side to side, immediately halted. His gaping mouth looked different now: more of a grin than a snarl. I had not even reached for the box of dog biscuits, yet he seemed to know I meant well. When I filled the bowl and laid it before him, he went on staring at me and the tail movement began again. His grin almost begged me to let him eat. 'He's changed towards me already,' I said. 'What did you tell him?'

'Nothing. He's worked it out for himself.'

Then I guessed. 'It's Petra,' I said. 'I've just cuddled my baby. He must smell her off me.' I took a step closer and held out my hands, which he nuzzled, then quested up towards my blouse. Even without accepting food from me he was won over. I nodded towards his bowl. 'Eat, then.'

He stared at me, swung his shaggy head towards Mrs Bowyer, who only had to nod. Then he was into the mush of meat and biscuits without another word spoken.

The day had started well. If only that should prove an augury for more critical matters. I held on to the thought as I went to ring the hospital.

'Little change,' I was told; but that was better than *no* change, surely. I wanted to break through the starchy formality and demand, 'So what improvement is there?' but at the clinic Matron had already trained me sufficiently to know that no information can be granted beyond the formula the doctors hand down.

It was too early yet to expect news of the Garstons' settling in at Stakerleys' forge. Aunt Mildred and the good doctor would take breakfast before driving down to check on them. I must wait for their call and meanwhile present some semblance of normal domestic life, helping out Mrs Bowyer with the extra tasks Mabel's absence had dropped on her.

I began straight after my own breakfast by wrapping Petra against the chill wind that had arisen and taking her along the river promenade in her perambulator, with Cuchulain on a leash alongside. I guessed that the ocasional 'accidental' encounters with female neighbours on our return route followed surreptitious peeping from behind their seemly Chelsea curtains. At least in this one of London's many overgrown villages they were much akin to our country friends. Perhaps it was a relaxation of formality due to their arty and literary backgrounds. It didn't escape me that Cuchulain's presence ensured they didn't coo too closely over my baby or prolong their conversations.

I handed over my two charges, assured Mrs Bowyer that I should lunch out and expected to return soon after dark. If any of the family were to ring, she could inform them that Clive was a little better. My first visit was to the clinic, ostensibly to enquire how Dr Atkinson was managing on his own, but really to find out if the medical network had brought him further news of Clive's progress.

I caught him sternly rebuking Jefferson for the muddied state of a trolley used to carry patients between ambulance and ward. The porter's surly face was flushed as he turned away muttering. The doctor stood stooped, frowning and nervously rubbing his thin hands together. 'One must maintain standards,' he insisted apologetically.

'Of course,' I agreed. He looked gaunt and tired, unable to control the slight trembling of his hands, but was still his usual mild and kindly self. I found that he had indeed received some technical details from Jeremy concerning the operation by Sir Digby, but appeared little reassured. He pressed me for information about Garston, which surprised me, because I had thought he was exclusively Clive's patient. I said as much to Matron later, but she explained that Dr Atkinson had heard of the case first through his charity work in the East End and had caused him to be admitted free of charge when the police wished to hold him. This caused me some regret over keeping secret the Garstons' whereabouts, but I told myself it was safer so. The poor old chap, blinking away behind his pebble lenses, was nervous and overworked enough as it was. He might prove a weak co-conspirator if the police came again demanding to know where their would-be suicide had been whisked away to. If they were referred to me, I would think up some likely story – or so I hoped.

Matron too enquired how Garston had settled into his new hospital, so I stretched the truth to assure both her and Dr Atkinson that he was under the care of a Dr Ignatius Barrow, and was relieved to see that the name provoked no reaction in either of them. Doubtless Iggy's unpublished researches among prisoners and the criminally insane were outside their experience.

All four beds in the men's ward were filled again, their occupants at various stages of being prepared for sitting out or receiving treatment. Matron and her nurses appeared to be worked off their feet, although it was Sunday and duties should have been lighter. There was no occupation for me there, now that my assistant had applied a transparent finish over the mural, so I made myself scarce.

Seated in a cab, I was half-minded to return to Chelsea and devote the day to painting, but even the knowledge that Sergeant Bradley was fully informed of my suspicions failed to overcome the urge to stick my own clumsy oar farther into the investigation. I tapped on the glass partition and ordered the cabbie to make for New Scotland Yard.

It seemed he had no weekend dispensation. The sergeant received me most civilly despite a desk covered in bulging files on existing cases. I gave him the little news I had of Clive's progress and the good man hummed with closed lips. 'I left instructions,' he told me, 'that he should be allowed no visitors except yourself, Bishop Malcolm and Dr Ignatius Barrow. We can't be too cautious, if it's at all possible these incidents are connected.'

It hadn't struck me until then that, even in hospital, a further attempt might be made on Clive's life. The prospect was horrifying. I regretted that he wasn't in a fit state to be removed, like the Garstons, to the country.

'He might be less safe there,' Bradley considered. 'To

anyone who knew the family connections, it follows that he would either be with his adoptive father in Bognor or on the Sedgwick estate at Stakerleys; and that could lay the trail to Patrick Garston himself.'

'And you think Garston is still the main intended victim?'

'Yes, until he can name the man who meant to kill him. Which is why he requires the greatest security. You will be glad to know that the police charge against him has been dropped. I have asked for the full report on the man bludgeoned to death in Wapping, and it seems there are definite links between the incidents. This Durrant was certainly the witness working outside Garston's house on the day of the hanging. Also, the man who claims to have stumbled on his body was a doctor well known to your husband. And a neighbour is quite certain she saw this very man some hours earlier, lurking outside the murdered Durrant's house.'

'Jeremy? You believe that Dr Jeremy Owen was involved in some way? But he's one of my husband's most trusted friends. It's true he was there at that time, because I had given him Durrant's address. I'd been to Wapping myself previously but couldn't find him. Jeremy decided to follow this up and save me going again. He contacted him once, but the man was unwilling to talk. So he went this second time, hoping to pay for the information we needed.'

'What you say confirms what he claims. All the same, you can't be sure what he had in mind. To pay the man to admit what he'd witnessed? Or the contrary: to bribe him to hold his tongue? We shall need to check for any previous connection between Garston and this Dr Owen.'

The suggestion almost took my breath away. 'I know his intentions from what Jeremy says. There would be no reason for him to lie. He's not that sort of person.'

Sergeant Bradley said nothing then, but went on staring at me with shadowed eyes that had seen too much and were probably accustomed to more liars than honest men. It stung me to be taken for a gullible innocent. At that moment he was more alien to my world than the rest of the Garston affair altogether. It did nothing for my confidence in his judgement. How could he succeed in finding the man behind all these crimes if he was so quick to see evil in honest efforts to get at the truth?

One mark of progress in the case was that he had particulars of the taxi in which Clive had been found. It had been stolen shortly before from a street off Covent Garden while the cabbie had a meal before the evening's theatre rush; but there was nothing to explain where Clive had spent almost a full day before being found in it, near Holborn, injured and in different clothes.

I hadn't confided to Sergeant Bradley how I'd attempted to check on Garston's wartime break in his employment with the accountants Hardwick and Meadows, and his subsequent position as a clerk at the soap factory. Since it had turned up nothing of any significance, I was sure that the sergeant, a pragmatist of the here-and-now school, would be disinclined to consider it. Yet that angle was all I had left to busy myself with, so I walked up to Trafalgar Square and ordered coffee at the Charing Cross Hotel while I thought out what next move to make.

As I sat there at one of the long windows, the Sunday pedestrians, grim-faced and miserably hunched against the east wind, passed their contagion on to me. I marvelled that I had ever returned to London after my wretched time in Fulham. The tame domesticity of our little house in Chelsea, even if my husband were restored to full health, now appeared soporific.

I had been idle too long. Painting the mural for others' therapy had satisfied a passing need, but even as I worked on it I had missed the delight of real creativity. Yet what could inspire me now, when all my anxiety and frustrated will was fixed on that silent body lying in a side ward of the East London Hospital? So much grey negativity, while my mind cried out for action and colour.

I had set up my studio on the third floor of our new home, but I'd yet even to open my tubes of oil paint there. That is what I craved now. I longed for their very smell and messiness. It seemed immaterial what I worked on, so long as I could pour my heart into it.

Meadows, I thought then. Not the lush grasslands of Stakerleys, but the man who had reminded me of Wolsey in his cardinal's robes. Since I'd tentatively mentioned it to his clerk, could I suppose he'd told his master that I'd a fancy to paint his portrait? It seemed worth my telephoning tomorrow to find out.

There remained one possible source of information on Garston that I hadn't followed up, so I decided that, after a leisurely lunch I would call on the Reverend Ieuan Roberts. By then he should have delivered his morning sermon and be relaxing at home.

The Baptist chapel, flat-fronted above five steep steps, with a gabled front in brick and flint, interrupted a long terrace of indistinguishable, soot-grimed houses. The nearest, to the chapel's left, had a varnished wooden board by the door with Roberts's name and initials under the title 'Minister'.

I rang and the door was opened by a gaunt woman wearing her thin, fair hair drawn harshly back into an unflattering bun. She greeted my request with an uncompromising stare but moved back to allow me to enter. The minister appeared just to have risen from his lunch, having pudding crumbs caught in the creases of his straining waistcoat. He was shorter than his wife and recognisably Welsh, with dark hair in tight curls and a wide, baroque mouth. Pure examples of Saxon and Celt, I thought then.

I explained that I was the wife of the doctor engaged in treating Patrick Garston. They listened to me in silence except for occasional little explosions of comprehending grunts from the man. Eventually, 'I have not been negligent,' he pointed out. 'We called twice at the house after Patrick's . . . er, tragic business, but found no one there. Then Mrs Garston was traced to her sister's house; not a member of our little community, and I regret she was most unwelcoming. So, all in all, I have met with our poor sister only the once and that under difficult circumstances. Now we learn that she has lost her home in a disastrous fire, and there is still no improvement in Patrick's condition. I greatly fear that our dear brother is lost to all reason, and we must diligently pray for Our Lord's forgiveness on him for the wickedness of his deed.'

From which I gathered that they thought the worst and hadn't considered that Patrick might have suffered at another's hands. 'So who do you imagine set fire to his house?' I demanded. 'For he certainly can't have done that himself.'

'An accident,' Mrs Roberts declared firmly.

'We had never guessed,' said the Reverend, 'that Patrick was a secret drunkard. It is my experience that so often this becomes

142

a family tragedy, as others are drawn into the demon habit. From that it is but a little step to the drunkard's nearest becoming equally lost to reason and therefore accident-prone.'

'You have no call to doubt either Patrick or his wife,' I said hotly. 'As for the fire, it was arson. I know this because I myself locked up the house after Ethel had left that night. The police have proof that the building was deliberately fired by someone who intended to destroy both it and any who might still have been indoors. I came here hoping you might be able to suggest why that unfortunate family should have any enemies, and who they might be.'

This quite shook the man, but his wife, having made up both their minds, was not to be put off course by an interfering outsider. I revised my first impression that she was colourless and he the dominant one. Now it became apparent that Ieuan Roberts was merely the plangent mouthpiece and she the *éminence grise* of the local pulpit.

There seemed little to be gained here. The Reverend could only claim that, before alcohol had disturbed the balance of Garston's mind, he had seemed in every way an exemplary member of their family in God. He now felt that they had been sorely deceived.

'I'm sorry about that,' I told them, 'because I was relying on your familiarity with Patrick to explain a few little puzzles.'

The Reverend Roberts looked embarrassed and searched in his breast pocket for his glasses. With them on, he managed a mental retreat. 'We have told you,' Mrs Roberts insisted, 'that he sadly deceived us. There is nothing we can say to explain the dreadful thing he did, except the power of the demon drink.'

'But apart from that, did he never mention why he decided to move from his post with the accountants Hardwick and Meadows to work as a less well-paid clerk at the soap factory?'

They were both struck silent; then: 'I had no idea about the difference in wages,' the Reverend admitted. 'He never asked for a reduction in his covenant with the chapel.'

'There's not much doubt,' said Mrs Roberts with some sense of satisfaction, 'that his intemperate habits had come to light and he was duly dismissed.'

Their minds were made up. Only a certain type of person was acceptable to their ministry. It was as well that they'd been unable to penetrate Maisie's stronghold with their pious comforting. It would have taken more than a Job to endure it. I thanked both coolly for their patience in listening to me and cut short the interview.

For once I'd economised on the cab by dismissing it on arrival. It took all the long trudge on foot over Tower Bridge and along Whitechapel Road to clear me of my slow-burning anger. I arrived at the East London Hospital to learn that Clive's heart rate had improved and he had received a further infusion of an unknown donor's blood. My own heart leapt at the news, but I forced myself not to hope for too much.

Dr Ignatius Barrow had visited that morning and a younger doctor had also called but been refused admission on Sergeant Bradley's instructions. There was even a constable sitting in the corridor outside Clive's private room, who required me to prove my identity before I was allowed in. So much caution reassured me in a way, but reminded me chillingly that my husband might still be in danger of attack.

From his description I guessed that the 'young doctor' denied entry was Jeremy Owen. It seemed a little hard on my husband's good friend, and I wondered that he hadn't insisted, on the strength of being a member of Sir Digby's surgical team.

I stayed by Clive's bedside, holding and stroking his hand, whispering how very much I loved him, until the evening staff came on duty. Then I was obliged to leave while they 'made him comfortable' and the lights were lowered for the night. But how can you make comfortable someone incapable of feeling anything at all?

I went back to his bedside when they had finished and while Sister was filling in the report. When I kissed him goodbye, I whispered that I should not see him next day because I had urgent business to attend to at Stakerleys. He gave no sign of having heard me, but I felt somehow that he had.

Fifteen

Next morning, before catching the train from Marylebone, I telephoned Aunt Mildred with the expected time of my arrival. She told me that her brother and sister-in-law had returned the previous day from France with Isabelle, who had been unwell over the whole period of her stay.

I wasn't particularly eager to become enmeshed in family matters while so worried about Clive, so I explained that I should be leaving Petra at home in Mrs Bowyer's charge and not staying overnight – a decision that she clearly considered odd. However, she should have the whole story once I was with her.

Next I rang the office of Hardwick and Meadows. The alliterative Mr Peel answered in his best Uriah Heep manner. He must have had some conversation with his employer about me, because this time he had my name right. He seemed to expect I would be sending on details of my finances, but I confessed they were in such a terrible muddle that it would take me some days to collect all the relevant papers. I also complained that my present sitter had suddenly gone abroad in mid-painting and thrown out my bookings – which reminded me to enquire whether he had mentioned to Mr Meadows what pleasure it would some time give me to attempt a portrait of him.

He assured me that he had done so and Mr Meadows was both flattered and delighted. At this point the conversation was taken over by the accountant himself. After a liberal airing of mutual compliments, I achieved what I was after, suggesting, as if the idea had just struck me, that although I couldn't fit in the main work for some time, yet a sitter's temporary withdrawal allowed me a half-day for exploratory sketches. If I came in, I would not upset any of his work schedules but would prefer to draw him unposed at his desk, between receiving clients, of course; the outcome of which was that we arranged an appointment for two days' time at three o'clock.

At Marylebone I had barely ten minutes to wait for my train, but during that and the half-hour journey down I again tried to fix my mind on Patrick Garston and why anyone should want to kill him. Beyond self-defence against a vicious attack, I knew there were motives the police looked for in murder: money, revenge, jealousy, frustrated sex, or fear.

Garston had no real money of his own beyond the little he earned; but could he have stood in the way of another's making a fortune? Sex seemed not to come into it. He had no reputation as a Lothario and his Ethel showed no likelihood of having taken a lover. His station in life was unlikely to provoke envy, although he had a good marriage and three children – which might be riches to someone who had none of those, but there was nothing there to account for anyone wanting to take his life. So I was forced to conclude that either he had done something callous which was worth being brutally avenged, or he knew a secret which threatened another's security.

It left the option of sifting through the whole thirty-odd years of his earlier life for a valid reason. To my mind this fell into four phases: his wartime experiences; his work with Hardwick and Meadows; later employment at the soap factory; and his personal life, which included his marriage and worship at the Baptist chapel. I had already tried dipping into each of those areas in turn but had come up with nothing of any apparent help.

The murder of Alan Durrant could have been coincidental, but I didn't believe that. Nor did Sergeant Bradley. There must be a link. If only Jeremy had got to Durrant earlier with his offer of money, we might have known by now the identity of whoever had brought Patrick home in a drunken state and left him choking on the ready-made noose.

That he had brought it with him was proof of premeditation. Had I actually encountered such a cold-blooded mentality during my enquiries into the Garstons' lives? Or a tactician, prepared to follow and attack my husband in the street to prevent his relieving a patient's dangerous blocked memory?

So could I picture the kind of killer we sought? Someone

determined, yes. One who planned in advance. And one who had contrived to make the teetotal Garston drunk, therefore persuasive and with more money in his pockets than a chance footpad would carry. He was cunning, yet not particularly effective, because Garston had been saved from death by Ethel's arrival on the scene, and Clive, God willing, would survive too, thanks to his ability to stem the worst bleeding.

A killer who twice hadn't stayed to watch his victim's end. Why was that? From squeamishness? I doubted it. Perhaps from fear of being discovered in the wrong place when he was due elsewhere? A *hurried* killer. That was a new concept. It was also the only positive element that came out of my present puzzling.

Forbes was waiting with a car for me at Great Missenden station, which was a comfort; but I wasn't prepared for the flood of emotion that swept over me at memory of so many homecomings before, when life had been less fraught. Even in the harsh days of my subjection to Julian the weights had always dropped off me as the car wound up the drive towards Stakerleys. Here, for a while, I'd known I would be safe and genuinely loved, even while I kept secret the real condition of my wretched life.

Momentarily I was quite overcome. I felt rather than saw Forbes glance swiftly at me and away as my face screwed in suppressing the tears. As ever, when I was the only passenger, I had slid in beside him, but he must have been forewarned, by my brief greeting and absence of the customary chatter, that things were badly wrong. He pressed a folded handkerchief into my hand and left me to sob freely while he drove a slow circuit until I had myself under control.

'I'm so sorry,' I said at last. 'The fact is, I'm bringing bad news. My husband's injured and in hospital. He's likely to stay unconscious for some time, or else I'd have stayed by his side.'

'Mr Clive, miss? Oh you poor lamb!' Then his goodnatured face flushed crimson and he spluttered his apologies. Even as things were, it made me laugh, and so I felt a little better prepared to have the family let loose on me.

'Let's go by way of the forge, I said. 'There are people there I need to see first.'

147

Forbes drew up before the house. He silenced the engine and I heard the clang of Dan's hammer as he worked on a horseshoe. I walked round to the smithy and there all the Garstons stood, well back from the burning coals which Dan's eldest was vigorously pumping with bellows. A Suffolk punch nearby waited stolidly to be shod.

Dan grinned across, his good-natured face shiny with sweat and crimson from the reflected fire. 'Miss Lucy, it's good to see you.'

'Don't stop, Dan,' I called. 'Strike while the iron's hot.'

It took me back over the years to when I had been as young as little Sophie and could often be found here when I'd escaped our nanny. Now Ethel Garston's three little ones were drawn in the same way to the glowing fire, the hiss of water, and the scents of leather, white-hot metal and horseflesh.

'How are you all?' I asked; and to the children: 'Isn't it a lovely din?'

They were excited and shy all at once. 'How are they finding the country?' I asked the parents. Patrick shuffled his feet and looked away, leaving it to Ethel to converse. 'Well,' she said slowly, 'there's a lot to take in. They're a mite frighted of the animals, and they're not sure they like it that milk comes out of cows.' She smiled on them fondly. 'Kate wanted to know where's the sea.'

Of course it was all new, and probably the only other place outside London they'd seen was Margate. 'I'm sorry we can't manage the sea,' I admitted, 'but we do have a lovely river. It's too late in the year for bathing, perhaps, but it's fun to go out in a boat. Maybe one day Daddy will take you. You could even try fishing.'

Then I suggested that Ethel should walk a little way with me up to the big house while the girls stayed in their father's care. Ethel seemed a little apprehensive at leaving them, but she clearly welcomed a moment to talk with me. As soon as we were out of earshot she said, 'Your Dr Millson's been that kind, and 'is lyedy too. They'd got Patrick all set up in bed by the time we was dropped 'ere. It was loverly being all together agyne. I adn't 'arf missed 'im.'

'So how do you find him?'

148

'Well, 'e don't wanta stye in bed, so I s'pose that's a good sign. Only . . .'

'Not really better yet? It's early days, Ethel.'

She stopped in her tracks while she worked out what to say. 'It's like 'e's not there most the time. Like 'is mind's gorn orff on its own.'

I explained he'd got used to the comparative quiet of ward life at the clinic. He'd need plenty of rest alone.

'Yes. I better get back. The littl'uns can be a right 'orror.'

'But first there are things I need to know, Ethel – about the day it happened. That business at the house when you found him. It was a Saturday, wasn't it?' Not that I'd any doubt of the date, since its outcome had interrupted my wedding breakfast.

'Sat'dy mid-morning, yes. I'd gorn down the market, after leaving the girls at a magic-lantern show for kiddies at the chapel. About missionaries in Africa.'

'And Patrick?'

'Went to fetch some more med'cine for Sophie's corff.'

'Where from?'

'I dunno. 'E said someone 'e knew 'ad recommended it for asthmaticky chests. We'd 'ad one bottle already, but it got knocked over and the med'cine spilt.'

'So he was going to a chemist's, or a herbalist?'

'I s'pose so. One or the other. Or the children's Sat'dy surgery, down the river.'

'Ethel, can you remember? Afterwards did you find this second bottle in the house? Because if so, he'd returned and then gone out a second time later. I need to know where, and who he would have talked to. Maybe someone walked back with him.'

'No. I didn't find no med'cine. I 'ad to give Sophie Friar's Balsam that night on a lump o' sugar. 'Er cough was that bad.'

'So perhaps he never got to where he was going, but met someone on the way.'

'And went drinking instead? Not my Patrick, 'e didn't.' Her voice was shrill with denial. Yet Patrick had been drunk when they had found him, stinking of gin, and that's why he hadn't been able to resist his attacker.

149

'There's something else I need to ask you, Ethel, but it will be painful, I'm afraid. Can you bear to describe just how he was when you entered the house and found him?'

She turned on me more angry than fearful. 'Well, *dead*, I thought. 'Is face all red and bursting, sort of. And just 'is toes touching the floor. The rope must 'ave stretched a bit, they said.'

I pictured him, suffering from compression of the jugular and windpipe; but that little bone Clive had mentioned – the hyoid, was it? – that hadn't been snapped. It seemed to imply that he hadn't suffered a sudden fall from above. More likely the noose had been fitted and then the inert body hauled up from some point on the stairs.

'You thought he was already dead? So he was totally unconscious?'

'Yes, jest the way 'e was when the perlice took 'im orff. They tried getting 'im round and said 'is 'eart was still ticking. Then yor Doctor Atkinson was called in, 'im wot does the charity cases down our way.'

That would be the point at which Clive had taken over the case and offered Patrick a free bed at the clinic. 'Thank you, Ethel,' I said. 'I believe you may only have missed the killer by a second or so. Maybe he left by the rear as you came in the front door. It's fortunate for you that there was no confrontation.'

She stared at me with huge eyes. 'But we never use the front unless there's someone special coming. I went in the back way like alwyes.'

So, possibly hearing her key in the lock, the killer could have slipped out by the front, almost opposite where Alan Durrant was working – or leaning on his spade – which made it so much more likely that he had held the clue to our killer's identity. And the police hadn't thought to check on that significant point before. There was still a vital question to ask which could unravel the whole mystery.

I took Ethel's hand in my own. 'I'm sorry to have revived all that agony for you. Look, you'd better go back now. I'll come down again before I go off tonight.'

'Yor not stying then?'

'I have to get back to my husband.'

'Remember us kindly to 'im then, ma'am. 'E's one of the best, 'e is, and you deserve each other.'

It jolted me then to recall that she didn't know what had happened: that Clive's life hung in the balance now as her own husband's had.

From a distance Forbes had kept an eye on our progress, and before I had my first glimpse of Stakerleys the car had caught me up. I sat again beside him and craned to see my dear childhood home through the trees, sunlight slanting across its honeyed stone. The great doors stood ajar, and before I could alight Mama was running down the steps towards us, with Papa just behind.

They had so much to tell me about their stay in France, and I countered with a description of Petra's progress in crawling, and how she would persist in pulling herself upright against any chair or table leg. 'I don't want her walking too soon,' I said, 'for fear she's too heavy for her soft little bones. And she chatters a lot, to anyone – friend or stranger – all in her own language. Even to the birds in our garden. And Cuchulain.'

So then I had to explain about Clive's Irish wolfhound, and how the bishop had brought him for company, since Clive wasn't at home. 'In fact,' I admitted, 'that's why I've come, to explain; that, and to check on the Garstons. You see, Clive's really quite ill in hospital after being attacked in the street.'

They were horrified, Papa exclaiming that he knew some districts were dangerous to walk in after dark, but this was an absolute outrage. Because it shouldn't happen to people like us? I wondered wryly. Certainly if there was any justice in this life, it shouldn't have happened to Clive. He was one of those who contributed so much to other people's good.

Fortunately, none of the family connected his misadventure with his work. I couldn't imagine how they would react to seeing his practice as one which could occasion risk. The attack was accepted as random without my having to trim the truth at all. I mentioned that he was found in an abandoned taxicab and everyone assumed that the driver had been guilty and would promptly be found and charged with aggravated robbery.

'So you will appreciate why I'm obliged to return to London this afternoon. I simply felt this was not something I could tell you by telephone.'

They understood I didn't wish to linger on the subject, so when the Millsons had joined us and been informed, we settled to discuss the newly arrived Garston family and how they might best be helped. A cottage had become vacant two months back, but the estate manager was ordered to delay redecoration because it was felt that, despite cramping circumstances at the smithy house, Dan and his little brood were swiftly reconciling the newcomers to country life.

I was glad of that, because if our secret enemy followed the trail here, Dan would be a formidable defence. 'I'd like Patrick to see our stables,' I said, and gave a sketchy account of his wartime service with the Yeomanry's Hussars.

'Good, splendid!' said Dr Millson. 'I've been at a loss quite how to deal with him, apart from building him up physically. His is not like any of the shellshock cases I've observed before. There's some deep and complex distress there. Not that I consider him dangerous.'

'Not even to himself?' I tempted. It was certain that Uncle Millson would have been informed of the suspected suicide attempt.

'Definitely not to himself. He is too concerned for his family. His mind is not turned inwards. That comes across clearly despite his abstraction. He finds comfort with his wife and children, and tries to provide comfort himself. It is unfortunate that he's not quite able to succeed.'

Bless him for a kind and sensitive man. I'd done well to send Patrick here to rest and find some understanding.

We talked of everything under the sun before I enquired about Isabelle. She had returned, as I'd feared, to the nursing home in London where from time to time she'd attempted a cure for her drinking. 'Was it voluntary?' I asked.

'Almost,' Papa replied grimly. As the years went by and no improvement was lasting, even he was becoming out of patience with his younger sister.

'It was I who suggested she should join Geoffrey in Provence and ask you both along,' I admitted. 'Perhaps it was a bad idea.'

'It might have worked,' Mama said, 'but in Nice she ran into some young acquaintances she'd known in Mayfair, and we scarcely saw her after that – until she was found

152

unconscious in someone's hotel bedroom. I'm afraid that this time it was more than alcohol. She seems to have acquired a more dangerous habit.'

Cocaine, I guessed. That was what the company I'd rescued her from was using. Or it was using them. This was a madness I'd never come across before the war, but it was fast increasing now among the wilder young people.

'Perhaps you might call on her, Lucy,' Mama pleaded. 'You are the one she always talks about when she's feeling low.'

Did I need to add her to my present worries? I could see my adoptive parents had been reluctant to appeal to me, but she was, by blood, nearest to me if not dearest.

'I'll visit her,' I promised, though it sounded begrudging. Clive was my real concern, not this spoilt and spineless woman. 'And what of Geoffrey?'

'He's happy enough when left to his bugs and beetles,' Papa said. 'No one can fault him in his care for her over the years. It's only fair that he should sometimes have time to himself.'

'I always thought he was the epitome of eternal, selfless love,' I said, 'but perhaps with time even that rubs thin.'

'He intended to stay with her,' Aunt Mildred granted, 'but she'd have none of it – verbally insulted him and forbade him to visit. She has always been her own worst enemy. So poor Geoffrey has gone back to Provence with his tail between his legs.'

What an epitaph for Isabelle: a drunkard and a virago – and I was her only child. Had I inherited from her? What would the fashionable geneticists make of me?

Our talking had caused lunch to be served late, to old Hadrill's obvious irritation. Mildred wheeled Grandfather in and there was a fresh fuss over me. I was allowed to sit at his side and help him eat. I saw he was using a spoon for himself. Now and again he would throw a word into the conversation and someone would respond. It was wonderful to see him recovering even so little and trying to follow the conversation.

Papa was concerned about accompanying the Prince of Wales on his imminent visit to India. It was his first important engagement abroad without his parents' support. 'I shall be thankful to get him safely home without any political gaffes having occurred,' Papa said.

I asked exactly what duties he was to perform.

'Generally smoothing things over,' he said. 'Making sure no sensibilities get irretrievably hurt.'

'Barring the stable door after the horse has bolted, more like,' Mama added under her breath.

We dawdled over coffee, then Mabel joined Mama, Mildred and me to walk back down to the forge. We spent a little time with Ethel and the children, Patrick having returned to bed exhausted. Then Forbes brought the car down to take the two of us to the station.

In the train I brought Mabel up to date with our local news, she wanting to know of every move Petra had made since she'd left Chelsea. I sat back for the last part of the journey, counting my blessings. Not everything in my life was at risk. Not everyone outside my family was capable of evil. Nevertheless, as we alighted from the cab at our door, I felt fresh anxiety for Clive press stiflingly on me.

'There is no news from the hospital,' Mrs Bowyer said quietly as she took my wrap. 'Dr Ignatius Barrow rang not more than twenty minutes ago. He said a stable condition at this point was encouraging.'

Did that mean that some crisis had been expected, even as I chose to be away? However comforting the bulletins were, I had to look for some sinister ulterior message. 'I'll visit tomorrow as early as they'll let me,' I assured her.

Silently a dark shadow appeared in the kitchen doorway. Cuchulain gave me a searching look, then his jaws gaped in what appeared to be a grin. His tail gave two solid whacks against the wooden panels.

'Hello, boy,' I said. 'We're still friends then. That's good.'

Mabel and I indulged in a little infant-worship before settling to our supper, and suddenly I felt some small return of confidence; but I wasn't fully human yet. I felt I was being driven like a motor car, and had merely been changed up into first gear from neutral.

Sixteen

I lay in bed, staring at the ceiling. Alone again, my mind, as if on a spring, leapt back to the motives I'd been considering on the train. Money, sex, revenge, fear. Surely not fear: I doubted that anyone could fear a man in Patrick Garston's position.

Although we hadn't been familiar with him before his present shocked condition, everything pointed to him being a properly modest, kindly sort of family man. So if fear was what impelled the killer, it must have been on account of some knowledge, not power, that Garston possessed.

So did this mean that the killer was someone who valued his reputation – a person of status whom scandal could destroy? If so, Garston had represented a danger to his continued well-being and had to be eliminated. A cold-blooded, intellectual choice of murder – yet one which he had not stayed to see completed.

The brutality of the two street attacks was quite unlike the premeditation over Garston. So the perpetrator might be a cerebral person whom no one would imagine behaving in such an impulsive way – which, out of my present limited list of suspects, seemed to point to Meadows the accountant or Roberts the respected Baptist minister.

There was another possibility: that the killer was a professional criminal, and what he thought Garston had access to was evidence to prove his guilt. So, which did I prefer: a man of some standing, or an established villain? From this ambivalent reasoning it appeared that I could now eliminate nobody at all.

In any case, wasn't I overstepping reason in trying to apply psychology – a science I was by no means qualified to draw upon? How badly I needed guidance now from Clive to sort out my mind and tell me if I was teetering on the verge of fantasy. Who was there I could confide my amateur ideas to? Iggy, loyal enough to Clive but with his own quirky attitudes to women that made me doubt his judgement? Elderly Dr Atkinson, already overburdened through Clive's absence from the clinic and perhaps not far from a breakdown himself? That left only Jeremy, with whom I felt I had got off on the wrong foot. I wasn't imagining the barrier between the two of us, and I felt it was my own fault. Somewhere I had done or said something that had set him against me. It was less that I failed to trust him, than that surely he wouldn't trust me.

Certainly I had refused to accept Sergeant Bradley's assumption that Jeremy Owen could have prevented Durrant disclosing who was at the house with Garston before the hanging. However mischievous, the little Welshman wasn't capable of murder. Or was he? He had hard-earned status and career to lose if his reputation were in question. No; leave him for the present. In any case, I'd not go to him for advice.

All I actually had to call upon was common sense and my own experience of evil; and the very thought of that recalled the blackest memories already reawakened when Papa had taken me aside that afternoon to announce that a date was now fixed for Julian's trial. Within a matter of weeks I should have to stand up in court and reveal all the wretchedness of my earlier life when attesting against the man I had once thought was my husband. It was insufferable, unless I knew that Clive would be well again by then and standing by my side.

Yet in this present puzzle I should be able to use my own experience in some way, having intimately known a murderer, lived in the same house with him, shared his bed, his meals, suffered financial inroads to pay for his gambling debts and unprincipled expenses. Shouldn't that have taught me enough about evil? But this was different. There must be as many kinds of murder as there were different sorts of love.

None of this reasoning was helpful in finding sleep. My mind by now was wound up tight like a clockwork spring. There was nothing for it but to get out of bed, dress and go silently downstairs, hoping not to disturb the rest of the household. Not wishing to turn on any upstairs lights, I found my way to the stairwell by moonlight, which penetrated the long window of the first-floor landing. For a few minutes I stood there, holding on to the looped velvet curtain and drinking in the silvered beauty of the little front garden. Beyond the tall brickwork of the opposite wall in Swan Walk, the Horticultural Gardens lay spread like a tidily patterned Persian carpet worked in greys and lavenders. Then some stirring of a tree's upper branches shifted the shadows under the wall and I saw a figure close against it, watching our house.

Although I couldn't make out any individual features, the hunched shoulders were a man's, as was the cap pulled low over the eyes. He moved his weight heavily from one leg to the other, then stamped as if he'd been a long while motionless and stiffness was setting in. He looked once down the Walk in the direction of the Thames, then up again at our windows. Although I knew he couldn't see me in the darkened house, I was deadly afraid of that pale, blank moon-face lifted towards me.

What was in his mind? Surely nothing good at this hour of the night. Was he waiting for something to happen, or planning some rascality against us? It might be simply some local thief intending burglary at a later date, having no connection with our present problems.

Determined to double-check that all locks were secure, I crept down to the ground floor. As I stepped off the last stair, a dark shape detached itself from the shadow of a mounted *jardinière* and came forward to nuzzle my knee: Cuchulain. I ran into the garden room to fetch his leash, clipped it on, then quietly unlocked and opened the front door.

As we suddenly appeared on the threshold it startled the man opposite. The wolfhound was growling softly in his throat, a low sort of rattle that made the hair stand up on my neck even although I knew he'd do me no harm.

The man broke cover and ran, with Cuchulain straining after him. It was all I could do to keep hold, but I didn't dare unleash him for fear he went for the throat of some possible innocent with a valid reason to be cooling his heels outside the Horticultural Gardens.

Feeling safe enough now, I put the latch up on the door and ventured out into the street. The sound of the man's running feet was dying away towards Royal Hospital Road. We turned in the same direction, following at a brisk pace, Cuchulain pulling at me until I commanded him to heel. Clive had him well trained, and I thanked heaven in my heart that Bishop Malcolm had taken thought for our safety in bringing him here.

The main road appeared empty, but then I heard a motor start up and somewhere ahead to the right – perhaps from Ormondegate – a car shot out and roared off into the night, making for Pimlico.

I guessed the man had been alone. I certainly hoped so, since I'd left the house open. We hurried back and I stood listening on the steps before entering – not that there was any need to, because the wolfhound was more than able to scent if a stranger had gone in before us.

The house was silent and still, disturbed only – or more likely calmed – by the slow-dragging tick of the hall's long-case clock. I released Cuchulain, scratched him gratefully between and behind his shaggy ears, and ordered him back to his corner. Then, trying to avoid the creaking stair, I went quietly up to check on my little one.

With daylight Mrs Bowyer appeared with my tray of early tea and I warned her that a stranger had been spying on the house overnight.

'Perhaps it was a watchman, or a beat policeman,' she suggested comfortably.

'Not the way he took to his heels when I took the dog out to check on him. And then he finally roared off in a car as though chased by the Furies.'

She looked at me sombrely. 'I wondered why Cuchulain's leash was hanging over the newel post. But that was a terrible risk you took. There might have been more than one of them out there, waiting to break in.'

She was right, of course. I'd put my household in danger, acting headstrongly again. 'Next time,' I promised, 'if there is a next time, I will rouse you or Mabel to have the door locked again after me.'

She shook her head. 'That isn't what I meant at all, madam.' She looked disturbed.

'Mrs Bowyer, I've told you: there is no need to call me that.

This is only a small establishment and I like to look on you as a friend.'

She looked down at her clasped hands a moment, then smiled. 'Thank you, but I prefer to do things properly, madam. It is a habit I became accustomed to a very long time ago.'

'Just as you wish, Mrs Bowyer, but don't let it sound like a barrier between us, please.'

'As to the watcher,' she said more briskly, 'I propose to inform the local police. It can do no harm for them to know that a stranger has been loitering around here in the night.'

Being impatient to be with Clive again, I hurried through my bath and dressing. Over a brief breakfast I took a hurried glance through the mail. There were four letters for Clive and a couple of bills. One of the two for me was from my solicitor. I was glad that Papa had forewarned me what it might contain. The trial of Julian Veal, alias Captain Julian de Verville, was set for five weeks ahead, and likely to be heard by Mr Justice Preston. Since I had not been the legal wife of my bigamous 'husband', I could be subpœnaed to attend and give my testimony. There was no mention of the woman I had glimpsed on the day he had tried to drown me in the sea at Hastings, but perhaps her trial would be held separately, after his almost certain sentencing.

Grim as this news was, five weeks seemed a lifetime away – perhaps the remainder of Clive's lifetime, I thought with a shudder of apprehension. But no, I'd woken with a sense of determination and wouldn't allow myself any negative attitudes. The most important and pressing thing was to get myself to the East London Hospital and spend the morning with him.

I was made to wait on arrival, since the surgeon was progressing on his rounds, a luxury liner with a little flotilla of lesser mortals in his wake. He gave me a grave nod as he passed me sitting in the corridor, but made no attempt to speak. So my husband's condition was unchanged. Yet as I sat at the bedside later, talking quietly to the unmoving statue, I received a shock. The hand I held between my own gave a little throb. And again there was movement, the ghost of a squeeze from his finger ends.

I called for Sister, and a houseman came with his stetho-scope, prodding all over Clive's chest. He listened fixedly and gently forced back one of Clive's eyelids. 'No,' he decided at last. 'It was probably a nervous reaction of your own hand. Take a little walk round the hospital to relax, and a nurse will bring you a cup of tea.'

I knew what had happened, though. Clive was in the silent body and he'd heard my voice. He knew I was waiting, and he was trying hard to get back.

There was a surprise visitor towards noon. Sergeant Bradley from Scotland Yard came quietly in, wearing plain clothes. I had barely time to wonder if he had been made a detective or whether he was giving up precious free time to concern himself with police matters, before he beckoned me outside. I relinquished Clive's hand to follow him.

'I understand you had some trouble at the house last night,' he began.

'I would hardly call it trouble. Not in the light of day. But I admit I was uneasy, which was how I came to go after the man.'

'It was as well you had the dog with you.' He spoke grimly and appeared to be familiar with the incident.

'How do you come to know of this?' I asked. 'It was reported only to the local police station.'

'I had put out a request to be notified of any occurrence regarding your family.'

'You are expecting further attacks, then?'

He considered his words before replying. 'Not necessarily, but it is as well to be prepared.'

'As we are, with the wolfhound. He's a splendid deterrent.'

'But not invulnerable. We know that whoever attacked your husband carries a knife. It has also been reported by the hospital – somewhat late, to my mind – that samples of urine taken from the good doctor showed that he had been injected with an anæsthetic, which was undoubtedly used to keep him docile or unconscious until the killer could dispose of his body in the taxi.'

'Can this help your investigation?'

Sergeant Bradley didn't give a direct answer but frowned warningly. 'The investigation is not mine, but the concern of the local station. My interest is a personal one because I have a great admiration for your husband. When I met him during

160

your earlier trouble, he impressed me with his integrity and determination come-what-might to counter the charges against you. To my mind he would have made an excellent policeman himself, if he hadn't chosen to take up medicine.'

It was a long speech for a man who was normally economical with words. I nodded, determined that my eyes shouldn't brim with tears. 'He is a wonderful man, sergeant. It's quite unthinkable that he should die now, again attempting to protect an innocent victim.'

'It rests with the hospital . . .' he began.

'Yes, but while they take care of him, what can *we* do? What evidence have you to follow up regarding his attack?'

'I have discussed the locality with the station involved. There must be some building the killer has access to, where your husband was kept. It would lie between the prison and the alley where he was found, and not far off the route he was walking. I suspect there may have been a car from which his attacker observed him, waiting for a convenient moment to strike.'

'Would he have glimpsed who it was? He's normally very observant. If he – *when* he – regains consciousness, he may be able to give a description.'

'His head injury indicates he was struck from behind. I doubt he suspected anything. And it is thought he was unconscious, without food, for almost a day, until he was left to bleed to death in the cab the following evening.'

'Thank God he wasn't killed instantly. But why not, if that was the final intention?'

'Possibly because it was easier to dispose of him later. There may have been pressure of time or other circumstances that required an interval. Suppose, for example, that the attacker was expected elsewhere that night and had work to do next day. He was desperately setting up a kind of alibi for himself by putting off the moment of death.'

I considered all this as I walked the corridor with the policeman. Agonising as it was, I forced myself to conjure up a picture of what had happened, like a flickering movie film: the initial attack; the bundling into a vehicle for transport elsewhere. Clive, senseless as a narcotic injection was given, lying tied up in some filthy cellar.

161

'That reminds me,' I said suddenly. 'Something I noticed. There are faint bruises on his wrists. They've only just come up today. I saw them when I held his hands. They're only dim. There's no chafing. It's as though he was bound by something soft, but tightly, so that it left an impression.'

'I should like to see that.' We checked our steps and went back to the small room Clive lay in. Sergeant Bradley took a pair of reading glasses from a pocket and examined the wrists closely. He grunted. 'Soft, as you say. Perhaps strips of cotton were used, like a torn-up shirt.'

'The clothes he was wearing weren't his. Why would anyone have stripped him and put on those dirty garments?'

'You are sure he didn't do it himself, as a disguise? No? I agree; it's too far-fetched. Dr Ignatius Barrow mentioned nothing about his changing his clothes at the prison.'

'Would the attacker have meant to sell them on, like his fob watch?'

'Possibly – or we were meant to think that. Just as whoever found him might have taken him for a tramp. Fortunately, the constable called to the scene was observant. He looked first at the hands and knew this was no vagrant. Then at Bart's the body too was found to be clean and well cared for. There was a report of a missing doctor put out by the Matron at his clinic. It all came together when Dr Barrow started telephoning the London hospitals to find his friend.'

'How lucky that the constable was alert in the first place. I must thank him.'

'Lucky indeed. As you were, madam, last night. I must insist that you take no further risks of that kind, but trust your local police to be equally alert. Now, if you will, I need to know every detail of what happened in that chase.'

I settled again in the corridor and recounted the whole story while he made notes. At the close he grunted again. 'So the watcher ran some distance, towards central London, then left the scene in a motor. And we are assuming that a vehicle of some kind was also used to transport your husband to wherever he spent the hours of his captivity.'

'The cab he was found in?' I queried.

'No. That taxi was accounted for all the previous evening and all that working day, until half an hour before it was noticed parked in the alley. There is no question of its driver being involved in the attack. We are questioning people living or working close to that spot, hoping that someone observed it being parked or a scuffle taking place inside.'

'Scuffle?' I asked sickly.

'When the stabbing took place. Dr Malcolm must have come round and struggled, fending off the knife so that it slid into the femoral artery instead of the heart, the intended coup de grâce. Supposition, of course, but it fits the facts. The stab wounds were fresh or he could not have survived.'

'Which he will do,' I said fervently. 'I'm determined that he shall.'

Seventeen

As soon as Sergeant Bradley had left, I returned to Clive's bedside, promised the inert form that I would be gone no longer than was absolutely necessary and kissed his freshly shaved cheek that smelled reassuringly of his own soap, which I had brought in that morning. Then I took my leave.

In a dim little café off Aldwych I snatched a quick coffee and a cheese omelette, then hoisted my sketching satchel on to my shoulder and made for the offices of Hardwick and Meadows.

Peel bowed me through to the presence. The accountant was much more than Wolsey this afternoon. He received me with even papal grandeur. Was I perhaps expected to kiss his ring? Before I found a chair he had seated himself at his desk, in half-profile, chin poised on one pudgy hand, the index finger aligned with his right temple, and began smiling fiercely at the opposite wall.

It wasn't unusual for my sitters to have practised in front of a mirror, but few did it with such certainty of achieving total gravitas. I had to accept that this would be a formal pose. 'Perhaps,' I suggested, 'we should place something for you to fix your gaze on,' and I snatched from its hook the group photograph that I had noticed on my earlier visit. 'Shall we get Mr Peel to move the nail?'

He was called in and performed the feat by hammering it into the grimed plaster with the heel of one badly worn-down shoe. By which time I'd discovered that the group wasn't composed of military personnel, but showed Boys' Brigade lads in uniform, some holding musical instruments, with a younger-looking Meadows seated in their midst, and the name of a Methodist church printed below.

He noticed my interest and preened himself. 'I'd taken it for an army unit,' I said offhandedly.

'No. I never had the privilege of military service, due to an infirmity of the chest, but I believe that in my own way I fulfilled some measure of duty to our fine nation.' His mouth screwed with false modesty, and as I raised my eyebrows he condescended to amplify his claim. 'By working to uphold the moral conscience of our young.'

I was disappointed, having hoped to find a wartime link with Garston; but at least his words confirmed that he set great store by being accepted as respectable – a man who might fear having any unsavoury practices exposed.

As I sketched away, the afternoon wore on without further revelations. I was thinking of putting my things together and excusing myself from more when a rumpus broke out in the outer office and a man's voice, raised in anger, came clearly through the partition wall.

'By God, it's diabolical! These wretched people – they're driven out of their minds with worry. Hanging's too good for the likes of you lot, leeching on the needy, making fortunes out of others' misery! An inch here and an inch there and suddenly they're way under, up to their necks. If there was any just—'

By then Meadows had lurched from his chair and was swiftly – considering his bulk – through the door, slamming it behind him in a single movement. The man's voice wavered. I heard Meadows' response, low and viciously intense, but I couldn't make out the words. There came a crash and then a second one even louder, as if a heavy desk had been overturned. A gasp of pain, a whimper; then scuffling followed, a cry of protest and finally the outer door slamming.

Peel and Meadows spoke together in whispers, which came through like the twittering of birds, and there was a scraping of furniture legs against the wooden floor. In a minute or so Meadows returned, still slightly out of breath and smoothing back his greased hair with one hand. I was still kneeling on the floor to pick up my scattered crayons, which he'd knocked off in rushing past.

He produced excuses, complained how very difficult it was to explain to the ignorant the follies of their ways with money. 'They are incapable, some of them, of understanding how it takes time to put right the appalling muddles they have landed themselves in. It is hard enough for financial experts' – and he

165

raised his shoulders in a beneficent shrug – 'to pull back what is lost, and yet they expect instant miracles.'

I sympathised. 'But I'm afraid you will think me every bit as silly, when you find what a muddle I've made of my affairs. Somehow expenses have a way of mounting up while one's concentrating on other matters, and then sitters can be so unreliable about paying for commissions, pretending the portrait is a gift and they have done one a favour by sitting there to be worked upon. You would be surprised at some of the noble names who have failed to honour their commissions.'

He bent over me, patting my hand. 'My dear,' he said in his fruitiest tones, 'how well I understand. It will be an honour to help settle your little difficulties. And if there is some temporary embarrassment, I am sure we can come to a helpful agreement.'

'Do you mean a loan, Mr Meadows?' I hoped I wasn't overplaying the young innocent role.

'Something of the kind, my dear, against a small security, of course – jewellery perhaps, or title deeds to property, which are quite useless mouldering away in some dusty drawer. I find often enough that my clients can be unaware of how these may be used to mend a temporary gap.'

I smiled admiringly. 'And then one can make a fresh start. That's such a relief. Of course, my family mustn't get wind of it. That would be too shaming. Such a devil of a job I had to persuade them in the first place that I should manage my own affairs.'

'Trust in me,' the old serpent said benignly, 'and you will find you surprise them how capable you have become.'

I removed my fingers from between his two plump, moist hands, made my excuses and left before his nauseating hypocrisy should make me physically sick. I returned to Chelsea, and Mrs Bowyer opened the door to me before I could pay off the cabbie. Her face betrayed that something momentous had happened.

'What is it?' I demanded.

'Dr Barrow telephoned, madam, and asked that you return to the hospital at once. But the news is good. It seems that Mr Clive is likely to regain consciousness.'

So I immediately climbed back into the taxi and set off

again for Mile End Road. As I alighted, another cab drew up behind and in it was Jeremy Owen. My earlier doubts about him resurfaced and I was instantly determined he shouldn't get to my husband's bedside before me. 'Oh there,' I exclaimed loudly, 'now I've left my purse behind! Jeremy, would you be so very kind as to pay off my cab?' and I flew ahead, to ensure his entry was barred.

Iggy was waiting there in the hall, again slouched wearily on a bench, pendulous belly hanging as ever between widespread knees. He looked up at the sound of my heels on the tiles and I saw his face was unshaven. He appeared like some exhausted old tramp but, for all that, the doctor who approached addressed him with the greatest respect.

'Clive?' I broke in. 'Has he come round?'

'Not yet. But soon, we think. Would you care to sit with him?'

'If you can ensure we're not disturbed. Jeremy Owen's outside. I don't want . . .' But by then he was upon us.

Iggy gave me a hard stare and nodded. He patted the bench beside himself. 'Dr Owen, a word, if you'd be so good' – releasing me to follow the houseman towards the stairs.

I could see little difference in my husband's condition. After a few minutes of sitting mutely, I took the damp cloth from the bowl on the nightstand, squeezed out the surplus water and dabbed it gently on his brow, then across his slightly parted lips. 'Darling Clive,' I whispered, 'I'm right beside you. Wake up, my dearest.'

A single pearl of water ran from his brow on to the bridge of his nose and down to the corner of one eye. His lid twitched, flickered. He gave a gentle sigh, seemed to murmur something unvoiced that I took for my name. I leaned across and lifted his hand, praying that again I should feel some pressure from it; but it lay flaccid in mine.

Then he smiled, just as I'd seen him do asleep at home. 'It isn't a dream,' I told him severely. 'This is real, and it's time to wake up.'

'Bully,' he said quite distinctly, and both eyelids fluttered, then opened dimly. 'Lucy?' he murmured, staring as though I were a long, long way away and he could barely make me out. 'Where are you?'

I realised then that he was blind.

A nurse appeared behind me, with the young houseman I'd met in the hall. I didn't dare voice my fears but pointed to my own eyes, then to Clive, and shook my head. The nurse put her hand on my arm, attempting to lead me off, but I resisted her.

'There are tests we must do,' she said.

'But you can wait, surely? Give us a few moments together first.'

I wasn't prepared for Clive's discovering the truth. He lifted both hands to his face, struggled to sit up, but fell back, groaning. 'Oh, dear God! No!'

His agony was too much for me. The doctor moved in between us. I let the nurse draw me away. In the corridor outside, Iggy was waiting. I buried my face in his musty-smelling old suit and howled with grief.

For me, at first, it was almost enough that Clive had survived. But not for him. He had never gone through the agony of waiting, assessing the crucial chances that hung in the balance. He simply recalled being held prisoner, blindfolded, in some unknown building, then waking to the confined space of the parked cab; finally a knife lunge in the dark, which he'd had barely the strength to ward off.

When the attacker had made off, there had been the brief illusion of safety, until the warm flooding over his thigh had made him aware of his very lifeblood running out. He had done what he could to stem the flow. Then darkness had taken over and there had been nothing until he awoke to the sound of my voice – but without sight; and that to him was the essence of living. How, blind, could he continue his work, support me and a household, be of any use to anyone any more?

I had never believed that he could be so distraught. It seemed almost as though he wished he had never returned to life at all.

Iggy moved between the pair of us, an unlikely but very real support. I longed to believe his assurances that vision was frequently impaired after injuries of the sort Clive had received. There would need to be explorations of the skull, possibly an operation to relieve pressure on the brain; but with every day, he said, we could hope to see some small improvement that would indicate a subsequent return of adequate sight.

Adequate for what? I wondered: walking again, but with a white stick and clutching someone's arm? The challenge of learning to read Braille? Accustoming himself to an existence in permanent dusk? He had been so different, so physically perfect – *whole*. I'd heard it said that doctors make the worst patients. It was more than that. Here was a psychiatrist set upon denial.

'Aye,' Iggy said in a voice of scorn, 'it's clear you've been spoilt, lad. Till now the cherries have all fallen off the tree straight into your cap. But now that the wind's blowing more chill, you'll simply have to possess your soul in patience until the leaves fall and buds shoot again. Then, if all's well, there'll be more fruit; and your good lady will make jam of 'em for yuh.'

I hadn't expected such fancy metaphors from the plain man, and certainly not mention of a soul. I might have protested at the harsh tone, but couldn't repress a wry smile at his words. Clive lay with his eyes shut and his face turned away. This was the third day after he had come round. Despite the shades that kept the daylight out of his room, I thought I caught the shine of tears on his cheek.

'So that's all I'm good for then? – to eat the jam my wife will some day make for me. I meant to be so much more for her.'

'You shall be,' I promised. 'You will fight. We shall fight this together.'

Having said his piece, Iggy had left us together. We sat for a moment in silence; then Clive struggled to sit up against his pillows.

'Do you know what I really fear?' he asked quietly. 'It's that this – *blindness* – is not of the eyes, but something else.' He touched the bandage on his head. 'The brain. That I could not bear to inflict on you. I would rather die.'

'Is that how your patients feel, do you think? Perhaps this experience will deepen your understanding of them, now that you too feel cut off, futureless. This must surely – cruel as it is – bring alive the words on the casebook pages.'

He stared back at me with empty, shadowed eyes. I felt I had said something quite unforgivable, pressed his hand, kissed his forehead and left.

Next morning there was a note delivered to me by hand. An off-duty porter had brought it from the hospital. I opened it with some apprehension, but it was short, crookedly scrawled, and said all I most wanted in the world: 'My dearest Lucy, I have been so wrong. But now with all humility I am resolved to accept each day as it comes. Please God there will be better ones which I may use well, with you beside me. There is so much left to live for.'

Two days later, bruised and still limping, he came home, with a tennis shade protecting his eyes from what sunshine the mostly overcast day provided. He could make out moving shapes, blocks of dark and light. After monochrome, I told myself, I had progressed as an artist to full colour. I was determined that, with everyone's encouragement, he should do the same.

Eighteen

At home our first visitor was Jeremy Owen, righteously simmering at having been kept at arm's length in the hospital. As Mrs Bowyer led him through to the garden room where Clive was resting on a daybed, I drew Mabel aside and gave instructions that, whatever happened, I was not to be called away until our visitor had left. Better that I should be thought oversolicitous than that I should openly reveal that I did not trust my husband's one-time friend any more.

I followed him closely in and was determined to stick like a leech, however private or professional their talk should become. Whether it was due to my presence, which clearly made him uncomfortable, or out of genuine consideration for Clive's obvious frailty, he left after only ten minutes. During that time he begged to be of service in what spare time he could wring from preparing for his new commitments. Already Sir Digby threatened to prove a most demanding chief, although Jeremy would not officially join him until the beginning of November.

'As I supposed,' he said wryly, 'my addition to his team will relieve him of most charity cases, so that he may follow up his wealthy clients. I am already inundated with lists of operations that have been cancelled for some reason or another.'

I couldn't resist saying innocently, 'How gratifying that it will allow you to exercise your preference for the poor.'

He didn't rise to the bait and Clive turned a curious, if blind, glance on me, well knowing by now when I was taunting.

'I had hoped,' the Welshman said, 'to follow up the disease of the youngest Garston girl. In fact I found a hospital bed for her, but have lost touch since the family vanished. So it has been given to another deserving case.'

'She is being treated,' I said hurriedly before Clive, who

was looking puzzled, could question how the Garstons could have disappeared. Jeremy gave me a challenging stare and I guessed he had been in touch with Dr Atkinson, who totally disapproved of my having whisked Patrick away.

'Has she seen a thoracic specialist?' Jeremy pursued.

'So I understand,' I said vaguely; then had a wild idea to divert him. 'If you wish to know more, perhaps you should ask the Reverend Ieuan Roberts, their minister.'

'What of Garston himself?' Clive demanded. 'How is Dr Atkinson dealing with his problem?'

Jeremy and I faced each other, staying equally silent. After a moment he took pity on my husband's concern. 'The case is waiting on your return,' he said noncommittally. Then he turned the conversation to other matters.

To fill an awkward gap I mentioned that Jeremy had taken an apartment in Bloomsbury, near University College Hospital; but instead of enlarging on its sophisticated allure, he dropped the subject, muttering that he found the area more convenient but expensive. 'There's a ridiculous discrepancy between prices north and south of the river,' he complained. 'The house is no better built than the one I lodged in at Battersea. It simply has snob value.'

'I thought the interior rather posh,' I said sardonically, but was not prepared for Clive's startled expression. 'You've been there? Seen it, Lucy?'

'When you went missing, I was half out of my mind,' I admitted. 'So I called on Jeremy for his help.' That had been before Sergeant Bradley's doubts had set me questioning Jeremy's version of Alan Durrant's death. By now I wasn't sure what I believed of my husband's so-called friend, except that I would never trust him alone near Clive's sickbed.

When Jeremy took his leave, Clive demanded a chair to be set by the telephone in the hall, as he had several vital calls to make. With a sinking heart I stood by, prepared to face an inquisition after he had rung the clinic to check on matters there during his absence.

I managed to overhear Matron's voice, confident and brisk, doubtless wishing him a rapid recovery and reassuring him about her duties. Then Dr Atkinson, rather halting, as presumably he rambled through a report on their shared patients. In my mind's eye I could see his bearded, lanky frame stooped over the telephone, eyes blinking nervously behind the thick lenses. It was impossible to make out the words, and Clive's reaction was one of cautious alertness. He ended by thanking the staff, and Atkinson in particular, for shouldering the added burden without assistance. Although he didn't say as much, I knew he intended to visit the clinic as his first outing from home – perhaps even next day.

When he had finished his messages, Clive sat there silently with a rug over his knees and Cuchulain's shaggy head lodged there, his tail swishing across the hall tiles as he thrilled to his master's return. Absently Clive scratched behind the wolfhound's ears and under the bony neck. 'Now, Lucy,' my husband said at last, 'just what have you been up to?'

I confessed to having whisked away Ethel and the children, ending plaintively, 'I was so scared for them, you see. As I am now for you. First the attempted hanging, then Durrant's murder and the fire at their house; finally your disappearance. It all sprang from Garston and our attempts to find out who had attacked him. I truly believe that only with you killed will the murderer think the danger past, because you are the sole person who can get to the truth of the man's lost memory. That is why we must guard you. Even here we can't be sure you are safe. There has been someone watching the house at night, in the shadow under the high wall opposite.'

So then I told him of what had happened and how the police knew now, so would be keeping a lookout for anyone lurking outside.

Clive was appalled at my having chased the man. 'Even with Cuchulain, it was a terrible risk to take. You must promise never to do anything so foolhardy again.'

'Yes, I know. Sergeant Bradley said the man might have had a knife or a gun, and then I realised Cuchulain could have been injured or even killed in trying to protect me.'

I gave Clive my arm and guided him back to the garden room where Mrs Bowyer had set out a tea table. 'Bring cups for yourself and Mabel,' he said to her. 'We must have a council of war.'

So they gathered, with Petra too, set down on the rug to wave her legs and wriggle on her stomach. He was amazed to find how in a few days she had learned to crawl at speed, wearing through the patched knees of her leggings.

'Under the circumstances,' he said, peering at us as we surrounded him, 'I think I should send you all to Stakerleys. There are staff enough there to keep an eye on you, which clearly I can't as yet.'

'Papa's just left for India,' I told him, 'in the Prince of Wales's party; but Mama's at home. And actually, so is the entire Garston family, lodging at Forge Cottage. Uncle Millson's been looking after them generally, but I think that Patrick needs your personal help.'

It was a lot for him to comprehend in a couple of sentences, and it left him open-mouthed. Had the other two not been there, I'm sure I'd have received a dressing-down for my headstrong actions; but he recovered enough to hold his tongue, at least until we were alone.

Then he explained how one couldn't abduct a patient from his hospital bed without a formal notice, and how I had treated Dr Atkinson with contempt in overriding his authority. 'You cannot interfere in professional matters in this way, Lucy. I don't know what can be done to put this right.'

'You speak as if you too hadn't gone against your surgeon's orders in discharging yourself from the East London Hospital. As for Patrick Garston, he shall not leave the protection of my family until you are well enough to deal with him yourself,' I said defiantly. 'In fact, it would be best if you were to join us all there for your convalescence. There must be ophthalmologists in Aylesbury you could consult, and for the rest, Uncle Millson could oblige.'

'But I am needed at the clinic, Lucy. Besides, doing that would imply that I condone what you've done.'

'And you don't? Not perhaps one little smidgen? My intention was for the best, Clive. I had to protect them, get them somewhere secret, away from London.' By then my cheek was pressed against his, and his arms had found their way round me. Cuchulain, not to be outdone, forced his shaggy nose between us and I felt the wet, coarse touch of his tongue on my chin.

When we drew apart, Clive seemed to be appraising me quizzically, head tilted. He traced my features with the index finger of one hand and seemed to strain to keep my likeness in his mind. 'I was well warned, of course,' he said. 'I knew, even as a young boy, just what I was taking on with you.'

'That's as well,' I said, 'because I'm not going to apologise. Not to you, anyway. To Matron and Dr Atkinson perhaps, to explain why I did what I did. I'll write to them now, and then perhaps we can pack, ready for going down to Stakerleys tomorrow.'

In the event, we didn't leave until mid-afternoon the next day, because Clive insisted on being driven first to the clinic to check on how things stood there, and I, remembering that Isabelle would be expecting a sympathy visit, spent the morning listening to her chapter of complaints at the nursing home, where she was taking the familiar cure.

Her raffish fine-weather friends had abandoned her to it and, unsurprised, I refrained from commenting how louche I'd found them. Nevertheless, she picked up my attitude from my silence on that and was clearly irritated. 'How stuffily middle-class you've become, Lucy,' she accused me. 'So appallingly respectable. I declare you've forgotten how to enjoy yourself – if ever you knew.'

She seemed to have overlooked her own near-imprisonment of the moment. This place was no pleasure-dome. Isabelle had first been brought there from a minor scandal at the Embassy Club, where HRH had been present, as onlooker, with his friend Metcalfe and his cousin Mountbatten. It concerned a wild 'camel race', in which eight young, piggy-backing revellers had careered, whooping, round the dance floor. A drunken Isabelle, skirts about her thighs, had been riding and whipping on the younger son of a Scottish laird some sixteen years her junior. An injury to one shoulder when they'd collapsed against a pillar had been excuse enough for the family to have her put under some kind of medical restraint. For the moment, even she had been sufficiently shamed to lie low until the incident became stale gossip.

Waiting at the clinic to collect Clive on my way home, I sat considering what my natural mother had said. I supposed I did rank as middle-class, having made a professional of myself through my painting; and marrying a medical man confirmed it. Not that I had ever been a genuine aristo, because of my bastardy. I supposed Isabelle had started my descent by taking for a lover that red-haired Lothario of an Irish actor. More mad blood to add to her own. Small wonder some regarded me as eccentric.

Yet class wasn't the same as the irredeemable caste system of the Hindus. Class was subject to change – much more so since the Great War had introduced a new social mobility and less rigid manners. I liked to think I was a true modern, mixing freely, as I did, with whomsoever I found of interest, whereas Isabelle was stuck fast in the remnants of Victorian etiquette, stretching threadbare formality to cover all manner of doubtful behaviour.

When Clive was ready to leave, Dr Atkinson accompanied him to the door, standing there with the wind tugging at his thin, sandy hair and sucking his cheeks in sourly as he regarded me. I wondered if he had the same general distaste for women as Jeremy Owen. Perhaps dealing with the female body was enough to put doctors off the sex for ever. (Not a contagion that had affected my husband, thank God.) I made no verbal apology then, assuming Clive's partner had already opened and read the letter I had written to him the previous night.

As the cab set us down at our gate, I noticed a splendid motorcycle leaning against our porch wall. 'Surely you aren't expecting to ride that now?' I asked, imagining it had been delivered on his earlier orders.

He bent down to peer closely, running a hand over saddle and handlebars. 'This certainly isn't mine,' he said wistfully.

Good. I wasn't sure he would ever be fit enough for that, or even whether it would really be considered *comme il faut* for a rising specialist in psychiatry. (You see, I really was becoming middle-class, with such pretensions to respectability!)

Despite my doubts about its seemliness, this superb machine had advantages for our visitor, the middle-aged and authoritative Sergeant Bradley of Scotland Yard.

He had removed his goggles on entering and these, with a pair of elbow-length leather gauntlets, lay on a salver in the hall. He rose stiffly from perching on a chair edge as we came into the sitting room and asked anxiously after Clive's health. He was clearly put out at his having discharged himself from hospital, particularly since it was easier to keep a guard on him there.

'Do you really think that is necessary?' my husband asked, and was told severely that this was so.

Clive felt for a chair and eased himself into it, still in considerable pain from his injuries. 'We intend leaving London this afternoon,' he explained, 'taking refuge with my wife's family in the country.'

The sergeant considered this and seemed slightly mollified. 'In that case it's even more essential that you tell me now everything that you can recall of your attack and the person responsible.'

'That's difficult. As I told you before: being blindfolded, I never saw the man. And he never spoke. He overtook me from behind, clubbed me, and I was knocked out. Afterwards I was in a room which felt little bigger than a broom cupboard, tied to chains set in the wall and unable to move. I dimly regained consciousness as I was being dumped there, but then I was injected and never quite came round until I found myself in the parked cab. I learned later that I had lost almost an entire day. You were probably told there were marks on my arm from a hypodermic needle.'

'But surely you picked up something about the man: his size, his way of moving? Did he have a discernible smell?'

'He never spoke. He must have been strong enough to lift or drag me, because I never sensed a second person there. In the cab, as he finally went for me with the knife, I remember only his shadowed eyes under a hat pulled down to meet a dark scarf hiding his lower face.'

'Does that mean he was someone you knew, and he feared you might recognise him?' I put in.

As Clive hesitated, Sergeant Bradley shook his head. 'He wasn't disguised for your benefit, because he never intended you to survive. Remember he was in an alley where others might have seen him and later could describe a man who ran away. We think someone approaching disturbed him, and that was why he didn't stay to make sure he had finished you off.'

'Thank God,' I said fervently, feeling quite sick. 'But can't that person be found and made to talk?'

'We are questioning house-to-house and shop-to-shop round that quarter,' the sergeant said. 'Up to the present nobody has admitted being in that alley at that time. Any witness could be someone with reason to fight shy of the police. Or someone who was in that neighbourhood on only that one occasion, and hasn't seen the notices we've posted up. I assure you we are pursuing this matter most strenuously.'

'And you do believe that it's linked with the other incidents I told you of?' I insisted.

He nodded. 'It is a distinct possibility. And if so, we are looking for a very dangerous criminal, who by now must be quite desperate to cover his tracks.'

He turned to Clive again. 'We examined the clothing you were found wearing.'

'Not my own.'

'No. It could have come from some charity bazaar – or even a dustbin. But one significant thing we found was a brushing of fine, whitish powder on the lower sleeves, and several threads of white lint, all one inch long.'

'The powder wasn't cocaine?' I asked, jumping to conclusions.

He smiled. 'Nothing so dramatic. Ordinary household flour. As for the threads, we believe that they came from a length of surgical bandaging; and considering the marking on your wrists, it's most likely that was used to tie you up. Were you by any chance carrying such a roll on your person? I understand that you had recently come from treating a patient at a West End hotel.'

'The patient had a psychiatric condition. She had no physical injuries. I seldom have reason to use bandaging. As for the flour, perhaps that came with the clothes, from a pastry cook or some such.'

'Or from the building you were held in. Did you detect any smell of—'

'Cooking!' The word suddenly exploded from him. 'Yes, some greasy sort of meat. Sausages perhaps, or pork pies. I remember now, almost coming awake, and I was faint with hunger. The smell was tantalising, but at the same time I found myself retching over it.'

'Perhaps that will remind you of something else now to help us.'

Try as he might, though, that was all that came back to him. Sergeant Bradley took his leave, slipping a note with the Stakerleys telephone number into a pocket of his leather jacket. From the front window I watched him straddle his motorcycle and waddle it out through the front gate, which Mabel took care in closing after him.

I was left thankful that Clive had agreed to come away with us. Mrs Bowyer had arranged for the same hire car to transport us and our luggage as we'd used to take Mabel down to her friends at Thorndike Farm. By now that carefree day seemed a lifetime away.

Clive, Petra and I were to travel that day with a few overnight bags. I had assumed that Cuchulain would accompany us, but Clive preferred him to stay on overnight as bodyguard, to come down later with Mrs Bowyer, Mabel and the main luggage on the following day. The motor having arrived just after afternoon tea, we left at a quarter past five, both my darlings soon falling asleep, lulled by the sound of the engine, and leaving me to my heightened suspicions.

I wished I had taken the good sergeant aside and confided to him my new fears of Jeremy Owen. The last detail concerning Clive's wrists and ankles having been tied by surgical bandaging confirmed for me the identity of his attacker. That would account too for why the man had stayed silent and kept Clive's eyes covered. He wouldn't have risked confronting his victim in such vicious treachery.

Nineteen

However secure I might feel now, installed at Stakerleys, I was deadly conscious of the need for caution. One thing I was determined on was to write down my suspicions, just in case anything untoward should prevent me warning the family if Jeremy should unexpectedly turn up. So I made an excuse to Mama of visiting my old studio, the garden folly, and settled to listing the events that had convinced me of who was behind them.

Yet I wasn't utterly sure. I knew this, because I was avoiding the word 'killer' in my mind. I still had this picture of my husband's friend, undersized, monkey-faced, with his lightly mischievous wit, sudden smile and socialist leanings – how could I connect him with what had happened to the Garstons, and to Clive? But weren't there pathological criminals who appeared quite normal for most of the time, revealing themselves only in their hideous crimes, like Jekyll transformed into Hyde?

Durrant's death affected me less than the other attacks because I hadn't known him personally. Now I saw how that meant I was approaching the whole matter too subjectively, seeing Jeremy intending murder in that one case but not in the others. It was essential to get it all down on paper and coolly analyse what I had.

How had he become involved in the first place? I remembered mentioning Garston to Jeremy when we had lunched together at Gianni's after our chance meeting in Knightsbridge. What I hadn't told him then he could have picked up next day when he met Ethel with little Sophie at the clinic. That was surely when he'd learned of the drain-digger, because afterwards he'd sent me that note by Clive: 'Don't overlook the road-worker.' Prompting me to do his research for him?

I had found out from Ethel that she knew the man and where he lived, so I'd tried to speak to him myself, only to be prevented by his being out drinking. Then, diverted by my brother's return from Ireland with news of Robert Grainger's death, I had given up, and actually telephoned Jeremy to tell him of my failure to reach Durrant at the address in Wapping.

Thereafter he'd taken it on himself to track the man down, the second time ostensibly to pay him to remember Garston's return to the house. When Jeremy had reported finding Durrant's body, the police had seen him as a suspect for the murder. A random crime would not have been uncommon in that area, a mere coincidence; but silencing Durrant could have been necessary to anyone guilty of Garston's hanging.

Jeremy's clothing and hands had been bloodied from the corpse – something he'd explained away by an attempt to resuscitate him. Sergeant Bradley was still sceptical of that. How much more so now, after the attack on Clive and the evidence of an injection and bandages being used to tie him up? He'd thought Clive might have carried a sterile roll of it himself, but it would have been much more likely in an aspiring surgeon's pocket.

Later there was something else of significance that had solidified suspicion in my mind, but I couldn't place a finger on it. Clive's mysterious disappearance and learning of his awful injuries had set my brain jangling. I felt dimly that it had been something Ethel had said on our walk up to the big house on my previous visit. She had recalled in detail the day she'd come home and found Patrick hanging from the banisters. It had been a Saturday and the children had gone to a magic-lantern show at the Baptist chapel: something about missionaries.

In my mind I heard an echo of Ethel's voice saying over and over, 'Sat'dy', in that East London accent. ''E'd gorn to the Sat'dy surg'ry down the river.'

Of course! Patrick had meant to get some syrup for Sophie's cough; but he'd never brought any home, because Ethel had searched for the new bottle and couldn't find one. She'd used Friar's Balsam instead. So how had he been diverted into drinking gin in some pub? And who had persuaded him? It

181

seemed most unlikely for a good family man suddenly to change course when his youngest urgently needed medicine.

Perhaps he had actually done as he'd meant to. Suppose he had gone to this Saturday surgery for children. It would have been a charity clinic somewhere in the East End. And wasn't that the sort of work Jeremy was known to undertake in his spare time?

It came back to me then how passionately he'd spoken of the needs of the undernourished poor when we'd lunched together in that expensive Mayfair restaurant. I had been so taken aback by catching sight of Clive there, entertaining the too-enticing Selina, that I had given it scant attention. I didn't doubt that Jeremy actually was the enthusiast he seemed to be, but much of his passion at that moment must have been provoked by the contrasting wasteful splendour of the way he supposed I lived.

It seemed that now I had a possible link between Jeremy and Patrick Garston on the day of the hanging; but instead of it suggesting a motive for killing the man, it was the reverse: the young doctor was dedicated to serving people of his kind.

So what could have happened if Patrick had walked in on a surgery Jeremy was taking? Nothing, surely, if they were strangers. Did it mean, then, that there had previously been some sinister connection between them? Must I search back further into both their lives?

For the present, that seemed beyond me. Discouraged, I returned to my earlier attempt to define and elaborate on motives. Fear, frustrated sex, money and revenge had been in my mind then. I didn't see how any of these could apply to Jeremy Owen. Surely there was nothing fearsome about Patrick Garston. He wasn't in any position of power that could endanger Jeremy's career or social standing. As for sexual frustration, there had never been any mention of Jeremy in an amorous relationship. When I had suggested to Clive that we find a pleasant young woman companion for him, he'd replied that marriage was not on the cards for his friend, which had caused me to think Jeremy had homosexual leanings; and that might well be supported by what I'd seen of the decorative style of his new rooms in Bloomsbury. But it beggared belief that he and Patrick Garston should ever have been conducting an affair.

Yet what did I know of Patrick, apart from what Ethel had told me? I was hardly a woman of the world when it came to experience of single-sex relationships.

So I put that unlikely theory aside for the present and considered the remaining two possible motives: revenge and money. Could Patrick Garston ever have offended Jeremy enough to deserve being killed for it? If so, when and how? Something to do with his employment with the unsavoury Meadows, who was now revealed as a dodgy money-lender? Had Garston been party to some loan-shark activity that had ruined somebody close to Dr Owen?

Even then, I couldn't see attempted murder as the natural outcome. There must have been some legitimate way of setting the balance right – and Garston, as an accountant's clerk, would have been no more than a pawn in such a game. Wouldn't Jeremy have confronted Meadows himself with any offence and had it out in the open?

So much for revenge, which left only greed for money as the motive factor, and I couldn't accept that wealth ranked very high in Jeremy Owen's priorities. Except that for some reason the physician suddenly intended to change to surgery, a more lucrative business; and furnishing his new living quarters must have cost a pretty penny.

I recalled the way Clive, Mabel and I had worked on the rope noose and I regretted I'd never seen Jeremy put pen to paper. So I'd no evidence of his being left-handed. At lunch in Gianni's I would have noticed if he'd reversed his knife and fork, but that was something all parents schooled their children out of, as being socially unacceptable. What a pity we had never played tennis together, a certain way of observing the preferred hand; but then I doubted he'd ever permitted himself the self-indulgence of tennis parties.

It seemed that again I'd merely made circles in my mind and arrived back with no certainties. At that I gave up, locked away my notes in an old chest where I'd kept a spare set of paints, and returned to the house. I found Clive sprawled asleep in a sheltered corner of the rose garden alongside Grandfather's invalid chair. There were still plenty of the tissue-papery kind of blooms that grew there almost up to Christmas, but the bushes were getting straggly and I guessed that Grandfather, always devoted to Stakerleys' gardens, longed to be active again with his pruning knife.

I stood unnoticed a few moments, watching the two of them, saddened that a brilliant young man, so precious to me, should be reduced to immobility like this stroke victim nearing the end of his years. Confronted by these two dear men, I felt the pain of it quite physically then.

Through the archway from the cherry walk came Aunt Mildred, carrying a spare tartan rug, which she wrapped round her father's shoulders after feeling his mittened hands. 'The sun's moved on,' she said, smiling. 'Are you both ready to go indoors? Look, Lucy's here to take your arm, Clive.'

He came awake and sat up stiffly, twisting to see where I stood. Whatever dim shape he picked out, he must have recognised me, because his smile was the special one. We walked slowly alongside as Mildred wheeled the invalid chair, with Grandfather occasionally whispering the name of a rose he was specially fond of. It felt so reassuringly secure there, that the horrors of the past few days seemed impossible.

'This evening,' Clive said suddenly, 'I should like to have a private session with Patrick Garston. I want you to be there, Lucy, to write down everything he says.'

'Must you?' I pleaded. 'You really need to rest.'

'It's essential. I've wasted too much time already.' He sounded determined.

So that was that. I wondered what changes he would find in the sick man after his few days in this peaceful place, restored to his love of horses.

Before dinner the motor arrived from Chelsea with Mrs Bowyer, Mabel and more luggage. From the drawing-room we watched the women alight, Mabel flying straight to the nursery to check on little Petra. Then out leapt Cuchulain, stretched and gave himself a thorough shake.

Instantly a bunch of house dogs burst from the front door and hurled themselves at him: two black Labradors, a Border collie and a springer, barking their challenge. The wolf-hound stood his ground defiantly, hackles raised and growling evilly deep in his throat. The advance on him slowed and the Stakerleys' defenders started to circle more modestly, pretending to snap at his heels, but then the hire car's driver came round and took up his stance beside the new-comer.

He needn't have troubled. Cuchulain was more than capable of defending himself against these country bumpkins. The Labradors, softies at heart, gave in first, grinning as they panted, wriggling forward in obeisance not far short of grov-elling. Then the springer spaniel followed suit with a little more dignity, squatting demurely on the gravel. The collie, Ben, always unpredictable, ran in circles with his tail brushing low, sniffing out imaginary sheep to round up.

Cuchulain stalked stiff-legged past the lot of them like a general inspecting a motley unit of troops, and entered the strange house, looking for his master. He found him in no time and the reunion was touching.

After dinner we drove down to the smithy, since Patrick was more likely to feel relaxed there than in the comparative grandeur of the big house. Aunt Mildred and Dr Millson came with us, primed to ensure that Ethel and the children shouldn't interfere in Clive's plans. While we drank tea at Dan's insistence Uncle Millson gave Patrick an injection. He accepted passively and didn't enquire what it was for. He struck me as the sort of patient who trusts implicitly, handing over his body entirely to the professionals for healing. He spoke only in monosyllables in a low voice, but I could appreciate how his colour had improved since the day he'd left the clinic.

As I watched, he seemed to droop in his chair and his eyes glazed over. Uncle Millson glanced at his fob watch and nodded to me.

'Let's move into the next room, shall we?' I suggested. Clive went ahead, trailing one hand along the waist-high dado, then waiting until I backed him towards a chair. Garston followed, and I made him comfortable on a horsehair sofa under the window. We settled to our task.

'You are very tired,' Clive murmured. 'Your eyelids feel heavy. You are falling asleep.'

The man's reaction was unexpected. He made an attempt to sit bolt upright. 'No,' he said quite loudly, but his voice was slurred. In the silence afterwards I was conscious of the little girls' continuous prattle in the next room.

Clive didn't appear surprised. 'There will be no dreams,' he said quietly. 'There is nothing to fear.'

I had been so sure that the man would co-operate, but he was resisting. Perhaps the narcotic had not yet taken full effect. Or he had suddenly found a streak of obstinacy to save himself from the challenge of self-discovery. I wondered how I would feel if anyone tried to invade my privacy. For the first time I wasn't sure we were doing the right thing.

'Clive?' I appealed.

He looked in my direction. 'Talk to him, Lucy,' he said. 'About anything.'

So I did. I mentioned Sophie and how I hadn't heard her cough a single time since we'd been in the house. The country air was suiting her; and it was time Ethel had a good rest herself after the discomfort of crowding in at her sister's. Dan and Molly were good friends and thoroughly enjoyed putting them up, but in a week or so a cottage would become free; then they could move in and be just a family again. 'You were a countryman yourself once, I believe? Born and bred in Harefield.'

Clive was nodding approval, and Patrick had settled back sleepily again. What else could I say to him? His eyes were closed now, his features tranquil, but Clive wanted me to continue.

'Have you been out with the horses yet?' I asked, remembering the little group standing fascinated by the anvil as Dan hammered at a horseshoe. Patrick had been there with little Sophie in his arms, perhaps familiar with the scene from his days as a Hussar. 'Wouldn't it be good to ride again?'

A low gasp escaped the man and his face screwed in pain. He seemed almost to choke, then broke into spasms of sobbing.

'That's enough,' Clive said tersely. He leaned over and reached for the man's flaccid hand. 'Fall into deep sleep now. Everything is all right. There are no regrets. When you wake up you will feel refreshed and remember nothing of this. Nothing. We will talk again.'

Again? – but they hadn't talked at all. Not he and Patrick. Only my blather, and that had upset him. So had we achieved anything, or perhaps even done harm? I tried to read Clive's face, but it was as blank as my notepad.

186

The driver of the hire car, who was to be given supper, had still been unloading as we drove off for the smithy. He had looked up red-faced and appeared on the point of speaking to me. However, I was concerned with our forthcoming session with Patrick, so had just waved as we passed, knowing that the senior footman would hand over his money for the hire fare.

As we returned, I was surprised to see the motor still drawn up before the portico and Mabel in conversation with the man. They waited until we had alighted, then Mabel said, 'Jenkins would like a word with you, ma'am.' She looked a little put out, so I let Clive go in with the Millsons while I sorted out whatever domestic problem had arisen.

Jenkins stood at attention with his uniform cap under one arm. His maroon uniform was immaculate, his boots and gaiters brilliantly polished, but I read unease on his open, honest face. Some fault with the car then? Is that why their arrival had been so late?

Mabel retreated towards the house, yet stayed possibly within earshot. Jenkins cleared his throat and suddenly I guessed. There was an understanding between them.

I had thought of Mabel as a friend, as a help with my baby, and part of our little family at the Chelsea house, but not really as a woman with feminine needs of her own. A youngish widow, who had lost her only child as a toddler with scarlatina, and I had blindly supposed that that part of her life was over.

Jenkins was having difficulty knowing where to begin. 'You and Mabel are friends – is that it?' I helped out.

Then it all came in a rush. A heartfelt apology – not for that, but because he had caused me such alarm. He had been the man lurking under the wall opposite, whom I'd chased off with Cuchulain. Because of the dog he had taken to his heels, hoping not to be recognised. He'd truly meant no harm, but he was anxious because Mabel hadn't come out to the post-box as she normally did of an evening, and looking along the side of the house he'd seen there'd been no light in her room all evening.

'I know now,' he said, 'that she had been sent down here with a lady and her children. She had expected me to drive them, but that was my free day, so it had been booked to another chauffeur. I can't say how sorry I am, ma'am, that you took me for a burglar, and I beg you not to take it further.'

How much further would he expect me to take it? To his employer? Surely not. After a surge of relief that my fears on that score had been unfounded, my main concern was how much further he and Mabel intended to take their relationship. However, that should rest between her and me. I thanked Jenkins for relieving my mind and for his service on this double trip, smiled to show there was no ill-feeling and went back towards the house.

Then something occurred to me. I went back to him. 'How did you get on with Cuchulain today?' I asked. 'He must have recognised your scent.'

Jenkins looked sheepish. 'He did, madam. I thought at first he was going to eat me alive. Then Mrs Bowyer took my hand and made the dog sniff it again. He's as intelligent a beast as I've ever seen.'

I heard the motor start up some five minutes later and shortly after that Mabel's heels rang out on the hall tiles.

'We may have a minor problem, Clive,' I said cheerfully, joining the others around the fire. 'How should we manage, do you think, if Mabel were to leave us?' I explained what I had just heard, and for the moment at least it lifted his mind off the subject of Patrick Garston.

Twenty

O ver the next two days I was conscious of a change in Clive. It was as though, surrounded by other people, we were losing touch. And yet, when I entered a room or sat watching him, he would sometimes jerk his head in my direction like a stringed puppet, intuitively aware of my presence but withholding contact. We lay side by side in bed at night, but that was all. I thought: *Male pride. Maybe he feels inadequate and is ashamed because of it.* Perhaps I should have made the first move. I had done it once before, but this time was different Something held me back. It seemed as though he was waiting. So I waited too.

He spent a lot of time at the telephone. Unsurprisingly, things were going badly at the clinic. They were understaffed. The two nurses they had taken on couldn't replace Clive. Dr Atkinson was no leader, having been trained to follow orders. There were blunders. Several in-patients were sent home with appointments made for later treatment. Things got overlooked; patients at risk weren't properly watched over. As if this wasn't disaster enough, Tilly Marks managed to kill herself.

I had seen Tilly about the wards, pushing a tea trolley from bed to bed, with her white-scarred wrists hanging from the sleeves of her tatty, blue dressing gown. Her head was always lowered. She liked to help, but more often got in the way. Apparently a nurse had been sharp with her after she had slammed a window shut so hard that the glass shattered.

The glazier who came to mend it had left behind a wedge used for stabilising his ladder. She had hidden it to push under the bathroom door, which, to be safe, should have opened outwards. She had filled the bath with warm water, got in still wearing the blue dressing gown, then reopened both wrists with a shard from the smashed window. When they had broken in, she was lying, staring up white-faced through the crimson water. Quite dead. No explanation; no goodbye note. Simply gone.

Having been absent when needed, Clive felt responsible for this tragedy, as though his own disability could have been avoided, whereas any initial fault must have been mine for pursuing the Garston mystery so doggedly. If I hadn't led Jeremy to Durrant, the man might still be alive. Perhaps then the murderer wouldn't have gone on to attack Clive. Killing, it's said, is easier to attempt the second time.

Still I couldn't bring myself to speak out, plainly accusing Jeremy Owen of meaning to kill his best friend. Was that because Clive would more likely believe him than me? Or because it would be too much for him to bear in his present state? Whichever, I found myself confused and untypically short of confidence.

Tilly's death was a scandal Clive felt he must deal with personally. It was all that Uncle Millson and I could do to prevent his dashing back to London. Our main argument was that the next morning was his first appointment with the ophthalmologist in Aylesbury. He could surely put off his journey until the Metropolitan Police had thoroughly looked into the matter.

By telephone he arranged for the wards to be closed and resident patients transferred to the day clinic. A research student from King's College Hospital was drafted in to help out there, and Dr Atkinson would take a day's leave to visit Clive and discuss the matter.

Forbes, who normally drove Mama, took us to Aylesbury, I sitting with the Millsons in the Daimler's rear. Clive appeared subdued and cut off from the rest of us. When he was ushered into the consulting room he asked me to remain behind with Aunt Mildred. The half-hour they were away seemed a lifetime. I discovered later that I had almost shredded my fine kid gloves in the waiting. The side seams of three fingers were split right open.

Eventually Clive came out independently of Uncle Millson's arm. They both looked less than satisfied, but certainly not downcast. 'There's a definite improvement in the sight,' Clive said. 'I'm hopeful that damage to the optic nerve may only be temporary.' He sounded like the doctor, not the patient.

Thank God for that much hope. I wanted to sweep the dear man into my arms there in public. All we needed now was confirmation from the neurologist that the brain's function was unimpaired.

After lunch, while Clive rested, I drove to the station to meet Dr Atkinson's train. He arrived with a leather grip full of papers containing the latest charts and reports on his patients' progress. 'We have good news on Clive's sight,' I said to cheer him. He gave me a hard stare, then removed his spectacles to polish them on a chamois cloth. Without them he looked defenceless, the eyes weak and tucked close under his beaky nose. The irises were strangely pale, appearing almost silver. The same colour was threaded through his straggling beard.

'You could not please me more,' he responded. 'We are all praying for your husband's rapid recovery – and return.'

The last two words stood apart, and I wondered if he meant them. Perhaps he required time alone to restore matters at the clinic and recover his own reputation.

As we passed Forge Cottage, a little girl in a white pinafore was swinging on the gate: Kate, the Garstons' eldest and boldest. I heard her call out to me as she waved. Then a smaller child came to peep through the bars.

'That child,' Dr Atkinson exclaimed.

'One of the blacksmith's daughters,' I said quickly, not wishing to give away the Garstons' whereabouts, even to him. There was no knowing to whom he might inadvertently pass on the information.

He sat back, apparently satisfied. I hoped he was one of those middle-aged single men to whom all children look rather alike. To my knowledge Sophie had been brought only the once to the clinic, so he couldn't have a very clear recollection of her.

'We're almost there,' I announced, turning into the long drive up to Stakerleys.

Because Clive couldn't see to read I remained with him throughout the interview with his partner, reading aloud the reports which most vitally concerned him. He had certain of them put aside, and when the two of them were through, he asked me to ring for Hadrill's niece to have them copied.

Ever since the old butler's descent into senility the young woman had been living at Stakerleys to help look after him, surrendering her position as a shorthand typist with a solicitor in Uxbridge. She had brought her machine with her and had proved of enormous help with family paperwork.

'Well, you wouldn't wish to leave the originals with me, would you?' Clive asked reasonably, sensing that Atkinson was somewhat taken aback.

The doctor assured him that he was most happy with the arrangement, provided, of course, that Clive didn't overtax his strength. 'Otherwise,' he warned, 'you may delay your fitness to return to work.'

I poured tea for them both and later suggested that our visitor might like to make a tour of the house and grounds while the typing was being completed. This offer seemed to lift him from the sombre mood he'd been plunged in, and soon he was chatting agreeably enough with Mama, eager for details of family history and visiting the various buildings that made up the estate. He appeared to be quite knowledgeable on early tapestries and wines, having spent childhood holidays in Touraine with an aunt married to a French vintner. So we showed him the gallery where our best tapestries were hung, and then we descended to the cellars.

I let Forbes drive him back to the station, being needed by Clive to reread the copied reports and make notes on them.

He must have been exhausted by the time he retired that night. I know that I was. All the same, I had trouble getting to sleep and awoke abruptly at a little before four, not remembering what I'd dreamt, but full of awful foreboding. Clive stirred beside me and sat up, turning on the bedside lamp. 'Lucy, what is it?'

'I don't know,' I whispered. 'Perhaps a goose walked over my grave.' Then I knew what I was most afraid of. 'Clive,' I begged, 'promise me something.'

'If it's within my power,' he said lightly.

'If . . .' I began. 'Just suppose . . . if something were to happen to me, you would take care of little Petra?'

'Of course. I love her like my own. But what do you suppose is going to happen to you? Nothing bad, while we're all here to look after you. What a strange notion that is.'

I couldn't explain then, and his words barely reassured me. I simply knew there was terrible danger about; and when daylight came – a murky, overcast Saturday with mist rising from the river – I was appalled to be told by Mama that Jeremy Owen had telephoned late the night before. He had been granted a free weekend and would arrive late morning to be with Clive. He was to have the same room he'd been given before. On the same corridor as our own.

I needn't drive to meet his train. This time he would come by road. 'So has Jeremy bought himself a car?' I asked Clive over breakfast. He had no idea, but this answer didn't satisfy me. 'How long has he been able to drive?' I demanded.

My husband gave me a long-suffering glance and didn't trouble to reply.

Of course, most men of Jeremy's age and profession would have learned to handle a car, but I had never been sure of it. It was important to know now, because someone with ability to drive had certainly transported Clive's unconscious body in the taxi to where it was found. This could be yet another pointer confirming the Welshman's guilt.

'Before he comes,' Clive decided, 'I'll see Garston again. His earlier reaction was disturbing, almost as though . . .'

I waited for him to finish his sentence. When he didn't, I prompted him. 'Almost as though . . . what?'

'I had the impression he knew what was expected of him and was afraid.'

'That's why he resisted? Perhaps he'd had an unpleasant experience of something similar before.'

'Not at the clinic. I'd been holding off, building up his confidence, hoping his memory would return of itself. You know I have a horror of a therapist leading the patient's mind in an imposed direction. And his is such a sensitive case. Certainly your mention of horses struck home; but now I think I should push him to reveal what's troubling him at depth. For all our sakes.'

I was sure this was right. *And before Jeremy should arrive.* Then perhaps we would be better warned in advance against any further attack. A new thought struck me: 'Does Jeremy know that I sent the Garstons down here?'

'Yes. He asked me, because it seemed a likely assumption.'

'When was this? He wasn't allowed to visit you in hospital,

and when he came to the house you never mentioned it. I was there and would have known.'

Clive gave me a curious glance. 'I've spoken to him since by telephone. He was one of the most assiduous enquirers after my health.'

Yes, he would be. I didn't think it augured well. I hoped fervently that Garston might identify him as his attacker before he was able to wreak any more harm; and in any case, Saturday or not, I was determined to ring Sergeant Bradley myself, so that he knew of the possible risk.

A message was sent to Forge Cottage that we would visit Patrick after breakfast while both Clive and he were freshly rested. This time only Uncle Millson was with us, Dan arranging to take Ethel and the little girls off to Aylesbury in the wagon. They were loading up as we arrived, and I was interested to see that Patrick seemed quite happy trusting them to horse transport.

This time no injection was given, but Uncle Millson produced a flask of some amber liquid which he poured for Garston. I rightly assumed this would take longer to make its effect felt, and in the meantime we discussed the cottage which was being made ready for the family and what kind of work Patrick could hope to take up when his cure was completed. Taciturn at first, he began to show interest and eventually even ventured to suppose he might obtain some kind of clerical position locally.

He was wearing a silver fob watch on a chain and, on Clive's showing interest in the chasing of the case, offered to remove it and hand it across for examination. Clive sat quietly swinging it and droning on until the man's eyes seemed to glaze over.

It was a repetition of what I'd seen him do with the other patient at the clinic; the same invitation to go back in time. Clive spoke of the ship that took him with his regiment to Egypt. 'It is very hot,' he murmured. 'None of you is used to a climate like this. You are perspiring, longing for the cool of evening.'

'Swimming,' Patrick offered dumbly, as if in a dream. 'Running into the waves. Naked as the day we were born. Shouting, wading, splashing. Young men's bodies, still white.

Innocent and beautiful; sent to be slaughtered. Wet flesh glistening in the sun. Salt water's running down my face, stinging my eyes. I knuckle it out and he's there beside me. First time I've seen him, but he knows who I am.'

Clive had been almost holding his breath. 'He speaks to you? Another soldier?'

'Not one of ours. Arthur. He's older than me – been in Egypt three months already. Brown like a gyppo. Tall. Sort of commanding. Like an officer.'

'How does he know your name?'

Patrick hesitated, thrown off track by the question, but he bent to Clive's will. 'He's seen me with the horses. He says Cherry's a fine little mare, just right for my weight.'

'He's seen her? She's all right then? Not down with sea flu like the others?'

'She's fine, now she's found her land legs. We were all wobbly, coming off the ship. So long at sea. Arthur helps get rid of the carcasses. The ones dead at sea went overboard, but some're still not likely to pull round. The vet's marking the sick ones. They have to be shot.'

'Not Cherry, though.'

'Cherry's fine.' This time he was defiant, a trifle apprehensive. I sensed a change in him.

'So Arthur is helping you?' Clive prompted.

'He takes them to the incinerator. Only sometimes . . .' Patrick looked strained. He was openly worried now, shaking his head, eyes tight shut.

'Sometimes . . .' Clive prompted him.

'There are too many.'

'Too many horses?'

'Too many sick. He says he knows horses. He can tell when they'll break into a sweat, get the shakes. He knows before it happens. And then he says Cherry . . . Only it's after Captain Williams says she's clear.'

He fell silent. Clive had to remind him where he'd reached. 'Captain Williams says she's clear.'

'And he's the vet, see? He'd know.'

'So what happened?'

'I'm not well. Keep bringing everything up. Going for tests to the hospital at Alex. Arthur's promised he'll look after her,

195

my Cherry. She'll be all right with him, and the captain says there's nothing wrong. Shan't be away long.'

He stopped at that point. Clive led him forward to the day he was discharged from hospital.

Patrick looked stricken. 'They won't believe me. I swore I took nothing, but they've found something in my fatigues' pocket. The major says . . . he says I got myself ill, to be sent back to Blighty. Because of the horses.'

His distress was terrible to watch. For a moment he was unable to speak, his eyes screwed shut in agony. Then: 'I'm to go out with the next ship to Suvla. At the front there's no court martial. He means I'll be killed and that's punishment enough. Only I never did it. I never did none of it!'

'They've accused you of drug-taking?'

'That first. Then the other. With the horses. Making them sick. Selling them to the gyppos . . . for meat.' His voice broke and his whole frame shuddered. 'I swear I never did. I couldn't do that to my Cherry.'

So his mare had been butchered, along with others. No; I knew he couldn't have done that.

'Then you went out with the next batch, as a foot soldier?' Clive said quietly. 'Did you see Arthur before you left?'

'I'm in jankers.' (He meant military confinement.) 'Arthur's at the opening up by the bars. Can't see his face against the sunlight, but it's his voice. He's scared I'll tell on him. He threatens me. He says . . .'

Garston covered his face and moaned with anguish.

'He threatens . . .' Clive suggested in a whisper.

'When I get killed he'll write . . . to Ethel. He'll say . . . untruths! His filthy mind!'

'He'll tell her about the horses and blame you?'

'More. Much more. About Denny. Only it's all lies. And what is she to believe? I'll not be there to tell her the truth.'

'Denny? What about Denny, Patrick?'

'He was so young. Made out he was of age. To get the uniform. He volunteered and they let him through. He was scared half to death of the Bedouins' knives. They keep coming to the waterholes after we've redug them. They slit the throats of the sentries, then away before the alarm's given. He's not

196

a coward, Denny. A country lad, brought up respectful and decent. He shouldn't be out here.'

'And what lies is Arthur telling about Denny?'

Oh, don't press him, I thought. *You must guess what it was, just as I do.* But Clive, grim-faced, persisted, going deeper into the man's distress, squeezing out the last drop of misery and dishonour.

'Him and me,' Patrick said hoarsely. 'Buggery, that's what. He couldn't swim, see, and the waves carried him out. I brought him out on my back and others saw me, dirty-minded men who believed what Arthur said. When the lad was scared I comforted him at night. We'd say a prayer together, only nobody would think it was that.'

He appeared exhausted.

'Clive,' I said, 'for pity's sake that's enough.' Enough for all of us. I wished I hadn't been so keen on getting the story out of him.

All this anguish for nothing, because it hadn't done my theory any good at all. There was no place for Jeremy in all this recollection of wartime agonies. When he arrived later in the day, I should have nothing to back my suspicions of him. So I still couldn't warn Clive that his friend had meant to kill him.

Twenty-One

I left them together and went out into the smithy yard where Uncle Millson followed me a few minutes later. He put his arms protectively round me, and I let him – I, the unsentimental madcap who preferred to stand on her own feet; but nowadays everything was changed. Now I had so much to lose in my life that I knew myself vulnerable.

'How can a man be so vile?' I demanded.

'War is vile,' he said. 'Faced by sudden, brutal death men will do almost anything to survive. Maybe, under his villainy, this Arthur was a very frightened man. He would have been the one behind the swindle, selling fit army horses for meat. The idea of making money could have made him feel safer, in control and so less a victim of fate.'

'An ordinary man turned rogue by circumstances? Oh, you never think badly of anyone, do you? Well, I do. I've known evil. People can choose it.' I thought of Julian, even now waiting in jail to be tried for murder, and for throwing me into the sea off Rockanore Point. Every day brought him nearer to his hanging – because they must find him guilty; and I must face giving evidence that would make it certain. So the evil would touch me again, bringing added guilt.

We stayed silent a while, and from the open window I could hear Clive's voice murmuring on gently, persuasively, settling Patrick Garston to refreshing sleep, using up his own fragile energy which he should be conserving. 'Clive must rest more,' I said brusquely.

'I'll see to it, Lucy.'

'Will you drive him back? I need to walk. And think.'

So it happened that my husband wasn't there with me when later I looked through the morning-room window to see Jeremy

Owen arrive on his motorcycle. I went out at once, as though he was a welcome guest.

'Clive's mentally and physically exhausted,' I told him. 'Please don't discuss his work with him. He needs a complete break from it.'

He still sat straddling the bike, a lighter, more modest one than Sergeant Bradley's. He made some ceremony of removing his leather gauntlets, which had small, red-glass reflectors on their backs. 'Good day to you,' he said eventually, putting me firmly in the wrong.

'I'm sorry,' I said. 'Forgive my manners,' and then remembered that with Jeremy I was constantly doing this. 'But you know how uncouth I am; and I am extremely worried about my husband.'

He looked at me with something like sympathy in his eyes. I would have been fooled if he hadn't been my prime suspect. Yet since Garston's pouring out of what had happened at Alexandria, I had begun to think there must be an alternative villain, to whom we had no lead at all.

'He's been working on Patrick Garston,' Jeremy said, and it wasn't a question.

I shrugged. Let him think I hadn't been there when it happened – knew nothing. 'Where's your luggage?' I covered up.

Jeremy removed a small bag from behind the saddle and nodded to the bemused stable-lad who'd come round to lead the bike away. 'I'm not burdened with much.'

He followed me into the hall where Foster, Hadrill's replacement, led him off to the same room he'd been given for the wedding. Nobody else was about: Mama out riding; Grandfather dozing in the conservatory; servants busy before lunch. I waited a few minutes, then went upstairs to where Cuchulain lay guarding our bedroom door. I thought I heard movements from within, so knocked and put my head round the door.

Clive, in his dressing gown, was standing at the window looking out. He turned, holding out a hand to me. 'Let me tell you what I can see,' he said, and drew me close. 'A gardener brushing up fallen leaves, and another clipping the yew hedge.'

'That's good. But the one with the shears is Mildred. What else?'

'Sheep grazing on the hill above the river.'

I looked where he pointed. Clive's sheep were irregular out-croppings of limestone, but I couldn't tell him that. 'Jeremy's here,' I said. 'He came on a motorbike. Is that where you got the idea of buying one?' Then I could have bitten my tongue out for the gaffe I'd made. Clive didn't need reminding that that was beyond him now.

'I actually managed to think of it for myself,' Clive teased. He seemed in a much lighter mood.

'What did you make of Patrick Garston's story?' I dared to ask.

He frowned into the distant view – distant *half*-view. 'It was better brought out than left in to fester. Its repression is certainly enough to provoke a lot of his trouble.'

'Although it happened so long ago? Five or more years?'

'Time makes no difference once the damage is there in the psyche. What interests me is why it should surface suddenly to distress him now. There has to have been a trigger. I think it's possible he has met up again with someone from that past and so the trauma is recalled.'

'Someone from his regiment? This Arthur who tormented him? Or the boy Denny?'

'Or the veterinary officer, Captain Williams. Or the unnamed major who sent him as an infantryman to Suvla.'

'What chance have we of tracing who that might be? Will you delve into Patrick's memory again for this?'

'Eventually we shall have to work forward and reach into the day of the hanging, but I dare not rush things. Better perhaps to enquire into regimental records. We know Patrick had no court martial, but at least we may find the exact date at which he was shipped out of Alexandria; and who else was named as being there at the same time. I might approach it through the Army Medical Corps, as relevant to my present researches. Garston told us he'd been a patient at the hospital at Alexandria.'

'I wish you could leave it to someone else, Clive.'

He didn't answer, interrupted by Uncle Millson knocking at the door to come in and remove some of his thigh stitches.

I forced myself to watch and winced for him. At the completion, 'Mama insists you take lunch in your room and rest afterwards,' I lied.

He said there was no need for special treatment, but gave way. I settled him on a comfortable sofa and went down to order a tray to be sent up and to repel all other interruption.

I didn't dare let Jeremy out of my sight, trailing after him when he left for a cigarette in the vegetable garden. He had this landlady-dominated belief that one shouldn't smoke indoors. I prattled away, desperately seeking some interest in common that wasn't my husband.

'You're very tense,' he said after a longish period of silence.

'I am?' It came out offended, whereas I was only startled.

'It's quite natural, you know.' He even managed to sound kind, then spoiled it by turning medical. 'Survivor guilt. You think you should have been attacked, instead of Clive.'

'Because I was the one sticking my nose in where it didn't belong?'

'Initiating.'

'But of course. After all, I'm a manipulator, aren't I?'

He faced me directly for the first time, recognised the hostility. 'Lucy, we don't have to fight, surely.'

What could I say? There was no alternative to fighting if I wanted to defend Clive. I needed to drive the man away. Hadn't he done enough harm, with my husband so badly injured, left half-blind, and his work at the clinic disrupted? I realised then just what Clive had created at that little spot of organised sanity where the mentally wounded came for asylum – real asylum, not the mockery of a prison-like institution. It had offered family warmth under the medical mask, providing a tender concern I hadn't seen in the cold corridors of real hospitals before. For the men and women who came there it had meant hope: in some cases a slender thread, but Clive had been at the other end, making a lifeline of it.

We watched Grandfather's valet push his wheelchair through the flint archway and position it opposite the turned-up soil of a prepared earth bed. He would sit there, perhaps for half an hour, planning in his mind a future of artichokes or asparagus. Perhaps reflecting on this, Jeremy murmured, 'One makes of life what one can.' It sounded personal. Was he considering his own intended switch of career or whatever had suddenly made of him a deadly enemy to his one-time closest friend? He was too complex for me to know exactly what was in his mind then.

I sensed impatience. It was Clive he had come to see, not to waste time with my irritating chatter. As our tour of the gardens took us round the corner of the house, he looked up at my husband's window. I was reminded how he knew the layout of Stakerleys and I was glad I'd set Cuchulain to guard the bedroom door. I'd be sure to leave him there overnight, because the greatest danger could come in the hours of darkness.

The first luncheon gong sounded and we went indoors, Mama and the Millsons could now share the burden of entertaining our guest. I excused myself to check that the kitchen had sent up something suitable for Clive and then came back to join the others. I suggested that the grass had dried out since the most recent rain, so Jeremy might care to play tennis after lunch, but already he had arranged with Mama to spend the afternoon with Clive; and I, she told me, was to accompany her to the cottage which had been set aside for the Garstons, and give her my views on the new decoration. So I wasn't to be allowed to monopolise our guest's company, nor to be included in any conversation he had with my husband.

On our return, Foster told us that he had taken an urgent phone call for Mama, and she was asked to return it as soon as she should be free. It made me more than curious, because its very urgency implied that it was news of Papa still on his way to India. If the Colonial Office had needed to ring Stakerleys, it might concern some mishap to him.

'Who was the caller?' I demanded, quite out of order.

'It's all right, Lucy,' Mama said coolly, indicating the note Foster had passed to her. 'Simply a local matter.'

Therefore personal. There was no reason why she should share it with me. Nevertheless, with Jeremy in the offing, I was generally apprehensive and watched her through the glass-panelled door of the conservatory as she made the call from the drawing-room. She was obliged to wait a while after her first few words. I assumed someone was being sought or the call was being transferred to another line. Then her manner changed, became tense; she held the mouthpiece in both hands; shook her head over it. She appeared to give some measured opinion, frowning, waited for a response, nodded slowly, looked again at the sheet of paper from the Stakerleys telephone pad. She nodded, murmured a few more words and replaced the receiver. Before she turned to come back she stood, drooping rather, then straightened to her full, imposing height and came back to me. This had to be bad news.

I hadn't expected it would concern me. All my anxiety was for her and Papa. She rang for a tray of tea, seated herself and waited until it arrived. As soon as she started to pour I found the comfortable familiarity of the ritual unbearable. 'Something has happened, hasn't it? What has gone wrong now?'

'That was a friend of yours who called. Yours and Clive's, my dear. A Dr Barrow.'

'Iggy,' I said. 'What did he want? Why was it you he asked for?'

'He asked for Papa. Since he's away I was next in line, and he didn't wish to disturb Clive's recovery.'

How typical of the man not to contact me directly, a mere woman. Expecting Papa, he would have required some courage to ask an unknown Viscountess Crowthorne to pass a message to me. 'He's socially clumsy,' I excused him, 'and not very good with women.'

'He appeared to be concerned for you, and sounded most sincere.'

'He's a trusted friend; but for heaven's sake, what is all the concern about, Mama? You're hedging.'

'He wishes you to ring him for the full story, since he gave me only the bare bones of it.'

She paused. I knew she was about to break bad news. But from *Iggy*? He wasn't directly involved in assessing Clive's medical condition, so what else had he learned that I might find upsetting?

'I'm afraid it concerns Julian.'

My bigamist almost-husband. This was unexpected; I'd managed temporarily to push him to the back of my mind. 'They're bringing the case forward then. Is that it?'

'No.'

I couldn't see what business it was of Iggy's anyway. What he had been helping me on was another matter altogether, less personal: Garston's would-be killer.

'The case will not be brought to court, Lucy. Julian has taken it into his own hands.'

For a brief instant I didn't understand.

'He was found dead in his cell this morning. It seems that he had hanged himself.'

Twenty-Two

It took me a few moments to understand fully. First there came relief because my private humiliations hadn't any more to be argued over in public. I felt saved. The wretched past was truly dead. It had gone with Julian; and what he'd done was merely to bring forward the inevitable, taking on his own end instead of leaving it to the public hangman. Then I felt shame at not being appalled by the hideous physical fact.

The ugliness of the image that stamped itself on my mind suddenly struck every sense. Saved in time from jail myself, nevertheless I'd known the harsh, dank frightfulness of a police cell, of high, barred windows, the echo of clanging steel doors, the clank of keys on my gaoler's chain. The same nausea came back, the same ineradicable smell of old urine, stale food and disinfectant. Then, this time, the rope, the slumped body. Julian lifeless. One moment an awful climactic act of will, then nothing ever any more.

I tried to see him objectively. It could have been how Uncle Millson had described the unknown Arthur: a man feeling himself at risk, desperate for some control over life – or, in this case, death. Just so was Julian. Whatever some might think about mortal sin, he had saved himself the obscene ritual of the condemned man's final breakfast, the procession to the execution chamber, the official witnesses, the chaplain's awful last words.

He had preferred the privacy of unimaginable loneliness to that hideous pageant; and while, whether intentionally or not, he excused me further public humiliation, I was to be left for ever unsure of his mind at the last: whether he felt remorse, or bitterness against me for having brought him to justice. Or simply horror.

'This friend, Dr Barrow,' Mama reminded me gently. 'He said he was present soon after.'

'He's a prison doctor.' But Iggy worked at Pentonville, not the Scrubs, where Julian had been held. I would need to ask him about that. Would he find it gross of me to demand every detail? I should have to picture it, suffer it all visually before I could hope to come to terms with it. Imagination would torment me with a dozen different scenarios. Better to know for certain the single one that was the truth.

'Do you have his number? I'm afraid I've forgotten it.'

'If you feel ready to speak to him.' She handed me the note Foster had made. For the moment, I felt numbly calm. The full shock would come later.

Iggy – Dr Barrow – had been waiting for my call and picked up the telephone instantly. 'It's Lucy,' I said. 'Mama has told me you were there.'

He explained simply: because of his professional interest in prison suicides he had been informed immediately by the prison's governor. He had actually visited Julian the previous week and found him ominously withdrawn. 'Contemptuous of all and everyone,' he added, as if it was a recognisable symptom. 'I meant to go again, but he made up his mind too quickly.'

Did Iggy mean he foresaw the outcome, and would have tried to talk Julian out of it? 'A terrible thing to do,' I said. 'How was he allowed access to the rope?'

Iggy stayed silent.

'I'm sorry,' I said, 'but I have to know everything. Then there will be no more questions for me to ask myself. This will have to be decently buried, like so much else of my life with that man.'

Iggy hummed between his teeth. 'Yes, perhaps you are right, if you feel you can deal with it all. The *Gestalt*,' he said as if to himself, and I remembered the German term from psychology books of Clive's that I had looked through, uncomprehending.

'It wasn't a rope,' he said. Then he explained that Julian had ripped the cover off the horsehair mattress in his cell, torn it into strips which he had tied together to form his noose. Wearing it, he had climbed to tie the other end round a window bar and then jumped down. It had been a matter of only seconds, because the hyoid bone had snapped and the blood supply been instantly cut.

I fought against a rise of nausea. 'Thank you, Iggy,' I said. 'Do you know if he left a note?'

'There was one. But not for you.'

No, it would have been for Edith, his legal wife, still awaiting trial as his accomplice, although there could be little proof of her involvement. Perhaps there was enough in his final message to exonerate her. I hoped so. She had certainly not taken part in the final attack on me.

'Iggy, what exactly is your specialism?' I asked.

'Psychopathy and Persistent Criminality. Does that help you?'

'Some day it may. When I know more. Did you hear about poor Tilly at the clinic? She killed herself too – only yesterday. It seems like a madness abroad just now.'

'I'm informed of most suicides,' he said sadly, 'since it's a part of my study. Living where I do, there's a chance sometimes of preventing a small number. There is a deal of despair among prisoners, as you may imagine.'

'But for Tilly? The clinic's no prison.'

'She might suddenly have felt it was, with Clive absent. We can't always hear the conversations people hold in their minds.'

He fell silent again. 'May I talk about this with you again some time?' I asked him. 'And do you think I should tell Clive what's happened? I thought that today he seemed less downcast.'

'If you feel safe doing it. He will recognise your strength and be relieved.'

I thanked him again and went back to Mama. The tea had gone cold. At risk of her thinking that I took a leaf out of Isabelle's book, I refused a fresh pot in favour of something stronger.

'I think I'll join you,' she said, leading the way to the dining-room's decanters. 'I've never known exactly where the yard-arm is, but I'm quite sure the sun is well over it by now. Already it seems a long day.'

Reinforced, I went off to find Clive in the library. Jeremy was still with him and they seemed to have reached a hiatus in their conversation. Both men rose as I came in. 'Mama is pouring tea in the drawing-room,' I told our guest, and he moved obediently towards the door, turned and waited for Clive.

'We'll follow in a moment,' I told him firmly, then led my husband to a leather-covered bench in one window. 'Darling, there's news of Julian,' I told him. In much the words Mama had used, I explained what had happened.

I felt his grip tighten on my wrist, then loosen. 'So he's gone.' It was impossible to interpret how he felt.

'And there will be no trial.'

'We can thank God for that much.'

'Shall we blame God then, for a mortal sin?'

'Don't be clever, Lucy.' He spoke almost harshly. 'There are so many ways to face this. It's enough for the moment to let it sink in. Poor devil.'

Yes, he had been a devil, and it was right to pity him. Clive was more charitable than I. 'Iggy said I should tell you, but I wasn't sure at first. So much has happened lately. And then, after the shock of Tilly . . .'

Clive closed his arms around me. 'Thank you for not keeping it from me. You're more truthful than I deserve.'

'What on earth do you mean?'

His mouth tightened. 'I lied to you this morning, standing at the window. I wasn't clearly seeing the world outside. I heard the sweeping of the leaves and a snipping sound. Then the scent of bruised yew reached me through the open casement. I threw in the sheep for good measure. I so wanted to cheer you with belief in my progress. Oh Lucy, it's so grindingly *slow*. I couldn't bear you to lose heart.'

We swayed together, locked in each other's arms, and my spirits soared that he had been open with me. The recent distance between us had disappeared.

'It doesn't matter how long it takes,' I promised. 'I know you will recover your sight eventually, and you will continue your work. Even if you were to stay a while in a sort of twilight, I know you will succeed, because you are so determined. We both are, together. Why, already you are using your other senses more. Perhaps in the end, when you can see clearly again, you will have enhanced your skills because of it.'

I was fiercely glad that he knew how much I needed him. That way it would be easier to accept that he badly needed me right now.

We joined the others. Mrs Bowyer was present as a guest, and I smiled my thanks to Mama. She gave an almost sardonic glance in return, dispensing the English panacea. Where would we be without the teapot?

Then I thought: we'd be at even more of a loss without the telephone. I drank my tea quickly and excused myself to go and check on Petra, but hurried back to the library instrument and had the operator ring Whitehall 1212.

Sergeant Bradley was not in his office, so I dictated a message that Jeremy Owen was at Stakerleys and nobody appeared aware of any danger except myself. I asked in the strongest terms for the good sergeant to return my call with his advice – and a report of any progress made, I added. Short of pouring out my suspicions to Clive, that was all I could do for the present.

A steady drizzle had turned into quite heavy rain, and this restricted our activities for the rest of the afternoon. I agreed to play the piano, though badly out of practice, and hunted out the sheet music for Schumann's 'Songs without Words' and Beethoven's 'Bagatelles'. I accompanied Mama's sweet alto until Jeremy took over in duet with Clive for some hearty student songs. I hadn't known he was so musical, but of course he was Welsh, with a fine singing voice.

We could have been a small Edwardian house party keeping up our spirits before some expected disaster. All the same, time dragged. The only interruption was the arrival of a telegram from Geoffrey at Dover. He was on his way back from a second visit to Provence, and disappointed at the news of Isabelle still being in the nursing home.

Sergeant Bradley's call came late, just as our company was about to retire. I managed to speak with him privately while still keeping an eye through the drawing-room's open doorway on the nightcaps being served there. If I had seen Jeremy hover near either Clive's or my glass, I would have broken off short and made sure the drinks remained untouched. He was to be here only this one night, so if he was to make any move against us, it must be now or in the hours of darkness. Thank heaven we had Cuchulain with us. I shouldn't risk leaving him on the landing, with Jeremy having access to all manner of drugs. Clive's wolfhound should share our room tonight, at the foot of our bed.

With my mind racing over such plans I barely took in what Bradley was saying. He wanted Clive back in London, to go over the ground with him and sniff out the building where he had been held. It struck me as unlikely to succeed, since most eating places in that area produced roughly the same unimaginative kinds of cheap food. It was only in the West End that chefs produced individual menus. At least to me, all fried fish and beef stews smelled much the same unless accompanied by special sauces.

As for any threat from Jeremy, Bradley seemed less keen on the idea than previously, having checked with him where he had been at the crucial times. He was still the only suspect for Durrant's killing, but had been dealing with an emergency at UCH when Clive had been snatched. Although he claimed to have been at home next day for the two hours during which my husband had been transferred to the abandoned taxicab, he had no witness to the fact.

'I believe it was Jeremy who tried to kill Garston,' I insisted. 'Can you find out if he was at the charity clinic that Saturday morning, the one where Garston went for little Sophie's cough linctus?'

The sergeant knew nothing of this, so I explained what Ethel had told me. 'Was an unopened linctus bottle found at the house?' he asked.

'No, but Jeremy would have removed it. Otherwise it could have led us to him.'

'He's a small man,' Sergeant Bradley said thoughtfully after a slight pause. 'He would have difficulty manhandling a man's inert body upstairs to push it over the banister rail.'

'But he didn't need to. He hauled it up on the rope from the downstairs passage. That's why the hyoid bone didn't fracture, but instead there was slow strangulation.' It seemed clear to me now, since that awful image of Julian having performed the act in the more efficient way.

'Yes,' the sergeant agreed. 'I was forgetting the pathologist's report. But even then it would take a deal of effort, which was why we were able to eliminate the wife as a suspect. She's too frail.'

This in itself was a shock to me: that poor Ethel should for a moment have been thought capable of wanting her Patrick dead. I began to lose faith in my policeman. He sounded weary, having doubtless spent a long day investigating crimes in no way connected with our problems. 'I will tell my husband you would like to see him in London,' I said finally. 'He will telephone you at Scotland Yard.' Then I wished him goodnight and rang off.

Over the last moments my attention had been distracted from what was happening in the drawing-room. The Millsons had left, Mildred squeezing my arm as they passed by on their way to the stairs. I went back to the others. Mama now kissed me goodnight, leaving Clive and Jeremy talking together over by the curtained window. My cognac stood isolated and apparently untouched where it had been poured. As I lifted it, Jeremy turned and gave me a hard stare.

I felt a terrible chill go through me. It wasn't difficult to make my stumble seem genuine. Perhaps it was. In any case, the drink spilled. 'Lucy,' Clive called, alarmed by the little scuffling sound.

'It's all right, darling,' I said. 'Just me being clumsy. I've spilt my brandy.'

'Let me get you another,' Jeremy offered. I watched as he did so, using the decanter from which his own had been poured. There was no harm in accepting it. I could have done with a second refill, but warned myself that I needed to stay alert, possibly all night.

Clive raised an eyebrow at Cuchulain's being introduced into our bedroom. 'There's a fiendish draught whistling along the gallery,' I exaggerated. He cautioned me against turning the dog into a milksop. 'Unless perhaps you mean him to protect you against me?' he teased.

I hadn't considered that, or the animal's likely reaction when we began our love-making. It wasn't possible to explain that I was fearful for Cuchulain, without confiding my fears about Jeremy. So, it being too late that night for lengthy explanations, I gave in and again installed the wolfhound on a rug outside our door.

Tired as I was, sleep took its time coming. Clive's breathing was steady and deep, broken now and again by little gasps of pain as he moved on some still tender injury. It was a low growling that brought me back to the rim of sleep. Cuchulain was disturbed.

I flung on a robe and slippers, but by the time I had silently opened our door the gallery was empty. I heard the soft pad-pad of paws descending the stairway, then a grey shadow moved over a slanting patch of moonlight on the hall floor. I caught the click of his nails as he crossed the tiles.

Over by the hearth one of the house dogs raised its head to listen, but the growl was Cuchulain's. The Labrador half-made to rise but thought better of it, sighed and sank low again, the dying embers of the logs limning his back in crimson outline.

Cuchulain froze into stillness, nose pointing, like a gundog's, towards the closed dining-room door. I moved past him, laid a cautionary hand on his collar and leaned my head against the mahogany panels. Someone inside was moving about and muttering – not a real conversation, but a broken monologue. Or else a second person, if there was one, spoke so low that the sound never reached me.

If there were two of them, it would be folly to throw the door open and barge in. Cuchulain might show killer instincts in such circumstances and I wouldn't risk his later being put down for savaging. I could feel his throat vibrate under my fingers and I whispered, 'Quiet.'

Now there were other sounds: a soft clinking of metal objects being moved about. *The silverware*, I thought. *It's not Jeremy – just burglars breaking in to take what they can lay their hands on.*

For a moment it seemed best to leave them to it, then bring down the servants by striking the dinner gong in the hall; but if I was rather scared, wouldn't the intruders be more so, caught out when they thought they were safe? 'Steady,' I warned Cuchulain, and opened the door.

The room was pitch-dark, the heavy brocade and velvet curtains closed against the outer moonlight. The sounds went on uninterrupted. It was unreal. I moved forward, blundered against a chair and it screeched against the polished wood-block floor. I could feel someone near me, heard breathing, but

212

still could see nothing. Then Cuchulain lunged past, there was a sudden cry, not so much startled as feeble, and a body fell at my feet, the wolfhound's pulsating ribs hard against my leg.

I reached out for the lights, found a switch and wall sconces came dimly on. The first thing I saw was the tray of objects on the table. Silver, yes, but china too, cutlery and napkins. Someone had been setting out a meal.

Then, beyond the dog's quivering flanks, I saw the bundle of pale-striped flannelette into the sleeve of which his teeth were sunk. 'Who on earth?' I called out.

At that point someone came in behind me and more lights came on. It was Thomas, an under-footman. 'Oh Lord, Miss Lucy, I'm sorry. He's at it again. This is the third time he's done it. He oughta be put away, so he did.'

'Hadrill?' And it was. He appeared to have struck his head in falling and was more than half-unconscious. 'Call Dr Millson,' I told the man. 'He'll know what to do.'

I drew off the dog, fetched warm rugs from the garden room and made the old man as comfortable as possible with least movement. When Uncle Millson came, he checked Hadrill's pulse, pulled each eye open in turn and shone a little torch in.

'Sleepwalking,' he explained. 'There's nothing much wrong that a plaster won't mend. Then we'll get him to bed. By morning he'll probably know nothing about it.'

'Thomas says he's done it before. Look at the table.'

The footman looked embarrassed. 'Miss Hadrill asked us not to let on. He has these dreams about training up the staff. Then he comes down and goes through it with them. Only there ain't nobody there to train. He's gone potty, see?'

Uncle Millson sighed gently. 'He's old, that's all. A devoted servant so many years. He finds it hard to stop. Even asleep.' He turned to me. 'Better get back to your warm bed, my dear. We'll manage now. Just get rid of all those dogs.'

By now the house dogs had decided to join the company, standing around like curious spectators at a street accident, the springer on three legs, the other vigorously scratching at its belly. I saw now why it was only Cuchulain that Hadrill's stealthy movements had disturbed. To him the old man was a stranger, familiar enough to the others. 'Come on, boy,' I encouraged him and led him off again upstairs.

Back in our bedroom Clive slept on. I pulled back a curtain and looked out at the night, half-clouded, half-moonlit, uneasy still at the little tragicomedy acted out downstairs. I held up my watch to catch the glimmer and saw it was almost two in the morning. As I turned to go, a distant movement caught my eye. Something crossing the far end of the drive, down near the lodge gates; a creature smaller than a pony, taller than a fox. There was a prowler after all, but not near the house.

Too tired by now to make anything of it, I climbed back into bed and curled into the warmth of my sleeping husband.

Twenty-Three

It could have been only a matter of minutes before I started fully awake again, disturbed by a dream. Yet not really a dream because I had been only on the rim of falling asleep. My mind had started wandering, fantasising on its own. Sending a warning, surely. With conscious thoughts switched off, the subconscious had nudged me back to real danger. I'd seemed to be standing at the window again, yet a different, immensely tall window heavily hung with black velvet. Suddenly I'd been able to see right through to a road outside. It was like the one where the Garstons had lived in Bermondsey, with its rows of smoky-bricked, cramped houses; but at the far end was the Stakerleys' lodge where I'd lately glimpsed a figure cross the drive. He was still no more than a black shadow, unrecognisable at that distance, but gradually coming closer, closer, so that the perspective was making him huge. Yet his legs never moved. It was as though he travelled on some invisible trolley or was seen through an adjusting camera lens. He reached out claw-like hands towards me and they were stickily red.

He was coming towards the house. Jeremy *returning*, having stolen out while the servants were asleep? – having committed some unimaginable outrage against poor Garston? Was that the warning of my instincts?

A half-wakeful fantasy, I reminded myself. But it was too vivid to leave me unmoved, and it contained an obvious truth: while I had been so concerned about safeguarding Clive against attack, the real victim could be Garston. Clive would already have told Jeremy that he was resuming his treatment here. Any of the servants could have supplied the information of where the family was lodging. I had left them unprotected against a man who hadn't thought twice about

215

stuffing paraffin-soaked rags through their letter box to set their old house alight.

My jodhpurs had been laid out ready for the morning ride. I seized them, my boots and a thick sweater, and ran again downstairs. Nothing stirred. Hadrill must have been led back to bed. Tom and Uncle Millson had disappeared. The house dogs were dozing again before the logs' dying embers. Nothing was left of the sad farce of the old man's wanderings.

I rang through on the direct line to Forge Cottage. It took an age for anyone to answer, and by then I was roughly dressed and ready to leave. Eventually, as I almost despaired of rousing them, Dan answered in his low, heavy brogue. 'Forge Cottage. Who's calling at this time o' night?'

'Lucy Sedgwick,' I snapped. 'Is everything all right with you? I thought I saw someone down the drive, maybe an intruder.'

'Could've bin it was him here. The dogs set up a helluva row. Pardon me, Miss Lucy. I jes' bin out with me shotgun to look around. Seems all safe and secure now. Dogs've gone quiet again, so I've shut 'em in the barn. Probably some tramp looking for a bale of hay to sleep in, but he's gone on elsewhere by now.'

Or lying low until the lights should go out again? 'Dan, I'd like you to stay up and wait for me. I'm coming down.'

He started to argue. 'I'm on my way,' I said and hung up.

I knew where the kitchen-maid's bicycle was kept, under a tarpaulin in the vegetable store. It wasn't locked and the bike offered an almost silent approach over the grass verges, though I couldn't risk using the headlamp. Light continued to come and go as tatters of cloud spasmodically shuttered the moon. I pedalled madly, left the Stakerleys grounds and turned into the village road. It was the silent time of the early hours when owls had completed their night-time forays and the blackbirds still slept tight before breaking into their dawn chorus. Far away I heard the cry of a dog fox and wondered who had lost a hen or a lamb.

Of course I was being stupid, rushing off so. Dan would never accuse me of that in so many words, but his attitude would be graphically over-patient. As I steered into the fore-court of the smithy, the place was in total darkness. I couldn't believe he would have ignored what I'd said and gone back to bed. 'Dan?' I called softly and at once he emerged from a shadowed doorway, his twelve-bore sloped under one arm.

'Are the Garstons safe indoors?' I asked.

'Where else?' He sounded mulish, robbed of the sleep that was essential to his physically demanding life.

'You think I'm making an unnecessary fuss, don't you? If you knew how often Patrick's life has been put in danger, you would know why I worry. It was no accident that their house burned down. It was a deliberate attempt to wipe them out.'

'I know, lass,' he granted. 'Ethel's made it plain. There's them that don't want her man talking. Though him, poor soul – he don't know what it is that he should be saying. So that's what your good husband is trying to find out.'

'I'm glad that you understand. There are risks in them being here with you. I should have explained it more fully at first, Dan. I'm sorry.'

'No need to be. And they're safe enough here, with me and the lad to take care of 'em.'

'But I'd be happier if the dogs were let out again. Then if the stranger comes back, you'll know. He may be just a tramp, as you said, but you don't want him breaking into the forge and stealing your tools.'

Dan guffawed. 'Like he'd make off with me anvil? I'd like to see it, so I would. Still, since you ask so nicely, Miss Lucy, for old times' sake I'll do as you say.'

His voice had returned to normal level and now he strode across to the stone barn and lifted the bar that slotted the entrance shut. 'Come, Jock; come, Willow,' he called as the heavy door swung open. In the ensuing silence no answering rustle came from the straw bales inside. 'Come now,' he ordered more sternly.

'Is there a light?' I asked.

'Jest a lantern.' He went forward, reached out to his left and there followed a slight clank of metal, then the flare of a match being struck. I watched his big face poring over the light, going golden as the wick was adjusted. He held the lamp high and turned towards the interior.

Then I saw the first dog stretched out dead on the straw, its tan-and-white coat streaked with blood. From somewhere farther in came the merest whisper of a whine. I moved towards it, but Dan's arm snaked out to hold me back. He moved on ahead, called, 'Willow, girl. Where are ye?'

I watched him search about by his feet a few yards farther in, then bend swiftly, and his breath was expelled in a fearsome whoosh. 'The black devil! Whoever killed my dogs . . .'

I tried to call out to warn him, standing there lit up like on a West End stage, but he'd no chance. There was a brief flutter of sound and he pitched backwards, the shotgun in his hands arcing up and discharging one barrel. In the shocked silence after the shot I smelled harsh cordite and ran to where he had fallen. He gave a single groan, and as I reached him, the rolling lantern threw out a track of fire across the spilled straw. My boots crackled on broken glass as I stamped out the flames. Then all was dark again. Somewhere, hidden ahead among the straw bales, the killer was waiting. He'd hidden here before being shut in with the dogs, killed them as silently as he'd downed the smith himself.

How seriously hurt was he? I groped about, found the body and my hands slid wetly over his chest to the haft of a knife. The attacker, invisible in the dark, had thrown it with accuracy. What kind of man was this – a circus man, a foreigner? Had I been wrong, then, about Jeremy?

I felt for Dan's pulse, which was rapid but weak. I could hear his laboured breathing. Dear God, don't let it have pierced a lung. I knew better than to remove the knife and cause the blood to flow freely. He must be got away with all speed, no matter what state his attacker was left in. It seemed impossible that the shotgun could have found him in the dark. It was an involuntary discharge as Dan was struck by the knife. The shot had streaked up towards the roof.

Then I heard a rustle of dry straw almost over my head and somebody sneezed at the dusty chaff. He was in the hayloft. I reached out blindly to remove the ladder, but it was fixed fast. At any time the man up there could climb down and finish us off.

I threw the shotgun a few feet behind me, then tried to drag Dan's deadweight after me as I crawled back towards the doors. The heavy timbers had swung closed after we'd come through, cutting off any outside light. I might be going in the wrong direction.

Dan was so heavy, a big frame, well fleshed and heavily clothed. I gritted my teeth, seized him under the armpits and pulled, praying I'd do him no further damage. I made slow progress on my knees and at last one of my boots struck against the butt of his gun. As I paused for breath, two things happened: someone swung over the edge of the loft opening; the rungs of the ladder creaked eerily as he came down. At the same time I caught the muffled throb of a petrol engine in the yard outside. A motorcycle. It could be Jeremy – but if so, who was this in here with me? His hired assassin? Had he sent this man to kill Garston? And were they to meet up later to dispose of the body? I rose to my feet and blindly levelled the gun, then kicked out behind, where I thought the door to be.

My boot struck the heavy doorpost and sent needles of pain up my leg, but then I shouldered past and leaned on the timbers with all my puny weight. The door shuddered and began to swing open. I turned. The moon slid out from behind black cloud and left me cruelly exposed, as the newcomer swung off his bike and came towards me.

Everything was happening at a snail's pace. I had time to think how I'd only the one cartridge left and there were two men to shoot down, one ahead and one invisible behind me.

Facing outwards, 'Stop or I'll fire,' I shouted. I knew it was Jeremy because of his size, although his face was in shadow. Then a great weight landed on my shoulders. I crumpled and again the gun discharged to no purpose. My face struck the concrete surface of the smithy yard and it felt as if my nose was broken.

Someone ran past, and I was dimly aware of another figure kneeling over me. *So this is how it all ends*, I thought regretfully, and braced myself. But instead I must have fainted.

Usually, I believe, when unconscious people come round, they say, 'Where am I?' Clive told me I didn't. I kept on repeating, 'Find Dan. He's stabbed.' But I didn't remember that, too doped down by an injection.

I felt outraged that Jeremy was there with Clive. He should have been under lock and key. 'What are you doing here?' I managed to get out. Clive squeezed my hand. 'He's staying with us at Stakerleys. Have you forgotten?'

'She tried to fight me off,' Jeremy said. 'She took me for the opposition.'

'Dan,' I said. 'How is he?'

'None the better for taking on hand-to-hand fighting,' the little man said. 'His attacker left the knife in him, which was fortunate, as it took a while to get him to an operating table. In fact we used the scrubbed kitchen one at the smithy.'

'Jeremy saved his life,' Clive told me. 'As he probably did yours. I was quite useless, still asleep in bed.'

'Dan wasn't stabbed,' I protested. 'The man threw the knife. You'd think he came from a fairground.'

I looked around and discovered that I was in the morning-room at Stakerleys, covered in a rug and lying on a sofa. My nostrils and upper lip were caked with blood, which Clive was gently washing away with warm water and cotton wool. Mama was there too, the only one of them properly dressed in day clothes. Seeing my confusion, she explained how Tom, rechecking on doors and windows after the Hadrill incident, had seen me leave on Doris's bike. I'd gone off at such a desperate pace that he thought to advise Dr Millson who, in turn, had knocked on Jeremy's door and begged him to go after me on his machine with himself riding pillion.

Clive had slept on throughout, having taken a sleeping draught once he'd thought I had dropped off. After Uncle Millson had rung through to Stakerleys with news of the out-come at the smithy, Mildred had driven down to collect me.

'I never faint,' I grumbled. 'How feeble of me.'

'You didn't,' Clive said tightly. 'You were knocked out by a blow to a pressure point. Your uncle found marks left on your neck by the attacker's fingers. Your fairground knife-thrower was either lucky or had some knowledge of anatomy.'

'So who is he?' I demanded at last. 'Don't say we all let him get away!'

The silence that this outburst met was answer enough. 'Sad to say,' Jeremy confessed, pulling a droll face, 'he made off while we were busy with the casualties. And even sadder, as far as I'm concerned, he took my motorbike.'

I found it hard to believe. The man trapped behind me in

the barn had managed to elude them, and even made off with Jeremy's bike? Had he contrived this – given it to him rather than risk the man revealing to the police Jeremy's own involvement?

'It's galling, isn't it? After all you'd risked in chasing down there and Dan's being knifed – that we let him slip through our fingers.' He made himself sound genuinely contrite and frustrated.

'How is Dan?' They hadn't properly answered me. I still had that image of him implanted in my mind, lying at my feet, the haft of the knife sticking out of his chest.

'It was a deep wound,' Uncle Millson answered from the shadows, 'but he was fortunate that it was so high, missing anything vital. The collarbone's chipped, I'm afraid, so he's been driven over to the hospital at Aylesbury. Molly's with him.'

I sat bolt upright, making the room swim for a moment. 'But that leaves the Garstons unprotected!'

'Not at all. Your Mama sent young Tom down and one of the gardeners. Besides, Dan has good friends in the village. They'll rally round to protect his home and family.'

I turned to Clive, who was looking more grim than I had ever imagined he could. If I gave him half a chance, he would be forbidding me to have anything more to do with the Patrick Garston affair. 'Darling, I'm feeling quite well now, but shouldn't we all be getting back to bed?'

'Especially your Uncle Millson,' Jeremy chipped in with his twisted smile, 'since his wild career as my pillion passenger. He tells me his preference is still for a pony and trap.'

I stared at him, still uncertain if he was friend or foe; but this wasn't the moment for open accusation. 'You've all been wonderful,' I told them. 'Goodness knows what would have become of Dan and me if you hadn't turned up in time.' All my life I should never forget the horror of that last shot being discharged and knowing myself helpless against a proved killer.

Clive put an insistent hand on my shoulder and I rose to go with him. When we were alone again in our room, he took both my hands. 'Never,' he said, '*never* do that to me again. I want you to promise.'

It might have seemed the desperate measure of a scheming woman when I burst into tears, but it was the real thing. So much had happened without my feelings catching up that suddenly the dam burst. 'Not now,' I pleaded between sobs. 'Don't be horrid to me, please. I can't stand it.'

So for the time being, I was let off – to plague him again.

Twenty-Four

C live was determined to return to London because the clinic was a shambles and he must make some effort to reassure its financial supporters. So it was my duty to go with him, however intuitively I felt the need to stay near Patrick Garston. He was the one the killer had been after the previous night, and obviously the family's whereabouts were no longer a secret.

Mama offered to move them into Stakerleys where the servants would be able to shadow and protect their every move, but I wouldn't allow the danger any nearer her than it already had been. So it was decided that Patrick, Ethel and the children should move at once into the cottage being prepared for them, together with four able-bodied men from Stakerleys' indoor and outdoor staff, two of whom would be on full-time duty there at any time. The two older girls were to be accompanied to and from the village school, where the teachers were warned to allow no strangers near.

Bishop Malcolm had telephoned twice since our arrival, and during his second call had announced that his offer of a motor car for Clive was now a necessity. I agreed, and promised to advertise for a chauffeur as soon as we returned to Chelsea, where Forbes was to deliver Clive, me and Cuchulain on the Tuesday. Mrs Bowyer, who was by then visiting her sister in Old Windsor, would return first to the house to put everything in order.

It was hard to leave my little one behind, even for a few days, but there was much to arrange back in London, and one detail should, if my plans worked out, provide an eventual outcome pleasurable to all of us.

On the journey Clive was plunged in thought, absently scratching at the wolfhound's head, and rather than interrupt any problem-solving about the clinic, I stayed mainly silent too. I had picked up on Aunt Mildred's interest in the government's intention to remove their ban on wireless telegraphy, making it available to the general public. She had ordered the necessary apparatus and was to apply to the Post Office for a receiving licence when they were issued in December. The broadcasts would enrich Grandfather's restricted life with occasional concerts, items of news and lectures. Until now Mama had been obliged to hire small local orchestras to supplement what the family and her guests could provide in music. Since Clive was at present unable to read, this was something I too should look into, to offer a change from the gramophone. I had already made a habit of reading him the daily edition of *The Times*, cover to cover.

We found our house warmed by banked fires and fresh with cut flowers. Mrs Bowyer had prepared a light luncheon for as soon as I had read aloud the accumulated postbag. I insisted that she and Forbes should eat with us in the dining-room that day, since this was a family home free of rigid protocol. They bore with me, but I think they would have preferred to take their meal privately in the kitchen.

Clive made a number of telephone calls in the afternoon, before we departed to the clinic, and while he was busy I left explicit instructions with Mrs B. concerning arrangements for Mabel's return with Petra. I also set up an appointment with a recommended builder concerning part-demolition of the garden wall and construction of a brick garage.

We found the clinic strangely quiet. I went through to the empty men's ward to review my mural while Clive was closeted with Dr Atkinson and Matron, but I was soon called in to take notes. Individual case records were discussed and a number of outpatients selected to be re-offered beds. These didn't include Patrick Garston, although Dr Atkinson suggested it.

I was conscious of Clive's new injection of confidence. Even unable to appreciate facial expressions, he was sure he could fully tackle diagnosis and therapy. 'In fact,' he said with a smile, 'I have frequently found that if I close my eyes, I can better hear the message behind the words.'

Nevertheless, I saw him tiring. Physically, he wasn't fully

recovered. Sir Digby had wanted him to stay a further four days in hospital; and that evening he was to meet, alone, with the clinic's board to discuss the circumstances of Tilly Marks's suicide and how he intended to run the wards without additional staffing and finance.

Afterwards he returned home by taxi, looking drained of energy but triumphant. By nine fifty he was in bed. I lay on the coverlet a while beside him, holding his hand until he was soundly asleep. Then I returned to the kitchen to discover what progress Mrs B. had made with my own plans. The builder had already called and taken measurements. If I agreed, the work could start within a week. That should give me time enough to insinuate the notion into Clive's mind for approval. As for Mabel's return, my good housekeeper had requested, and been granted, the same car and driver as had taken us down to Stakerleys.

She eyed me with a sort of half-amused suspicion. 'May I ask, madam, what exactly you have in mind?'

'You know me too well by now, Mrs Bowyer,' I acknowledged. 'Since Mabel and Jenkins are good friends, the journey will give them an opportunity to talk in private. If he proves to be the sort of man I take him for, we shall find his references qualify him for a post I intend advertising. A decision on his suitability, resident or otherwise, shall rest with you as much as with me. How does that strike you? No, don't answer now. You shall have ample time to make up your mind about him.'

'Oh, I already have,' she said, smiling. 'I know that, like Mabel, he is recently widowed, and has a small boy of three years old. It wouldn't surprise me if they were to come to some arrangement between them.'

'In which case,' I speculated, 'Mabel would wish to set up home elsewhere?'

'I'm no fortune-teller, madam,' she warned.

The small boy was a complication I'd not envisaged. Much would depend on whether he would make a tolerable addition to our little family. The Chelsea house had rooms enough if I surrendered some of the top, studio floor, but I hoped I wasn't biting off more than I could chew.

Until Clive's return from the board meeting I had settled down to catch up with my neglected correspondence, which included arrangements for a show of my abstracts and land-scapes at the Marylebone gallery, and a note to Sergeant Bradley informing him of our return to London. He had already telephoned me at Stakerleys after I wrote fully about the night-time incident at the forge, and he had explained that he was in touch with the War Office and the present Commanding Officer of the Yeomanry, trying to identify the character known to us only as 'Arthur'.

At home I had expected to be measuring doorways and the height of steps for alterations to accommodate a wheelchair, but almost at once Clive consigned the contraption to the cellar. He resorted only to a cane for walking, tapping his way round the house and murmuring the number of paces between one doorway and another. On the stairs, which he took painfully slowly as yet, he ran a hand along the dado rail and scorned to gaze down at his feet. It reassured me that he was now so positive about dealing with his impaired sight.

Next morning Iggy was to visit, and my presence would not be required. For that I was thankful, guessing that Clive and he would be taken up with business arising from Julian's suicide. I took the opportunity to call on Isabelle in her nursing home.

Surrounded by flowers, chocolates and the latest romantic fiction, she complained of being bored out of her mind. I priggishly reminded her that the logical French used a reflexive verb for the condition, and she promptly burst into floods of tears. *Of course* she was bored with herself; she hated herself, despised herself, didn't know how any of us could bear her. It was right that she should be put away like a leper or a madwoman – and so on, for embarrassing ages. Accustomed as I was to her histrionics, I felt there was a measure of real emotion behind them this time.

I tried not to feel responsible for the distance between us, reminding myself that it was she who had repudiated me at birth and so I'd naturally found a real mother in Eugenie. Anyway, her low spirits must be mainly due to the break in her addiction to cocaine as well as to alcohol. I knew little about the long-term effects of the drug – only that Freud had personally experimented with it in his early days, ostensibly for a scientific purpose, although he must have been as capable of self-deception as any of his 'hysterical' patients. Whatever the excuse, the outcome had been found unsatisfactory, compounding existing problems.

I comforted Isabelle as well as I could and elicited a promise that she would at least agree to see Geoffrey next time he visited. He was a kind, patient man and their marriage had been the only stable structure in her recent years.

Returning home I found the luncheon table laid for four, as Sergeant Bradley had called early to take Clive 'sniffing round' the Holborn area and had been persuaded to join in his discussions of the case with Iggy Barrow. I watched them closely as they talked over our meal and was aware what a strong team they made, the psychologist, the prison doctor and the policeman. Yet the weeks were going by without any glimmer of light on who was the criminal behind this violence.

'With your knowledge of the mind,' the sergeant said, between chewing steadily, 'can you say with any certainty what kind of mentality we're looking for?'

Clive was gazing unseeingly into the table's central arrangement of hothouse flowers. 'A man of average intelligence and some education for a start, or he wouldn't have acted against us with such self-confidence; but also one becoming increasingly nervous. He is taking ever greater risks of exposure. I thought at first he might have used an accomplice, but I think by now that he is alone, desperate, and will take on any vicious attack himself. It could be that, after a considerable period of inaction, he has returned to some violent pattern of behaviour from his past – which is why I see him as having seen active service in the war, a source experience for his present pathological condition.'

'Do you mean,' Bradley demanded, leaning forward and pointing with his fork at Clive, 'that in layman's terms the man's mad?'

'I mean that he's detached from reality when the need to protect himself recurs. He is ruled by some interior prompting – fantasies perhaps, an obsession, an overriding need to go further in what he has begun. The man is a danger to anyone who blocks his path in this. He could appear for most of the time to be quite normal, possibly withdrawn and subdued, but at a given trigger will become a demon driven by obsessive emotion.'

'In this case both victim and killer suffering from the trauma of war? That's ironic,' I broke in.

'Something I come across quite often.' Iggy took up the theme. 'Make a man into a killing machine and he'll not wipe the experience totally from his mind. Some, naturally brutal or desensitised, may thrive on it, continue to use it for their own ends.' He raised his hands hopelessly. 'War is civilisation's suicide.'

I shivered at the word. We were back to what I dreaded confronting. I saw again in my mind Julian's body swinging from the makeshift noose, against the cold stones of his cell wall, and I had to stumble from the room.

Poor Iggy must have been appalled, surely having forgotten I was present. Clive came through with his abject apologies as the company broke up. He and Bradley had a police car standing by and would drop Iggy off on their search for the eating-house smells remembered from his captivity.

I was left to puzzle over who, if not Jeremy Owen, could have discovered where the Garstons were lodged, and how he had travelled to Forge Cottage, since all his other attacks had been carried out in London.

In Jeremy's case, he would have learned all he needed from Clive, and conveniently he was there at Stakerleys, by invitation, arriving on his motorbike. I thought he remained the most likely attacker, except that, while Dan and I had stalked the intruder, he had been found in bed by Uncle Millson and roused to race him down to the scene. The two of them had looked after Dan until the ambulance arrived; and it had been Jeremy who'd rushed towards me as I ran from the barn, when I'd thought myself caught between two attackers. If I was wrong there, had I been wrong all along about him? Or would it have gone very differently for me if Uncle Millson hadn't been there as a witness?

How was Jeremy to recover his bike? And how far could it be ridden before needing to be refuelled? If a search was made, would it be discovered hidden near Great Missenden station? In which case, would the booking clerk there remember a stranger who had bought a ticket early on Sunday morning? Or, having already come down by train, did the killer have a return half, hiding until the moment of the train's departure?

With so many questions unanswered, I needed to telephone Mama and find out what had turned up.

So far the Buckinghamshire police had made little progress beyond discovering that the knife removed from under Dan's collarbone was most likely the one previously used on the dogs. The poor beasts had now been buried and the little Garston girls were inconsolable. Molly expected Dan to be home from hospital in a couple of days but forbidden to work. A young apprentice was being sent down from Olney to help out in the smithy.

As for the villain of the piece, there had been neither sight nor sound of him elsewhere that night, which wasn't surprising, since village folk are hardworking, retire early and sleep soundly. The missing motorcycle had not turned up but, following reports of a car being driven away noisily at a little before 3 a.m. from the Barley Mow, nearby Black Pond was to be dragged in the hope of recovering the bike.

Little progress, then. I sent my love to the family and hoped that Mabel would enjoy the return journey tomorrow.

Towards five o'clock a visitor was announced. 'I had expected Clive to be back by now,' Jeremy said awkwardly, uncertain whether he was welcome. He stood, dangling his headgear from his fingers, and with a sudden pang I was back in the war: my lover photographed in his flying suit with the same goggles and leather helmet

I ordered tea by the sitting-room fire and cautiously tried to make up for my earlier coolness towards him. 'There's possibly good news of your motorbike,' I told him. 'But it may have had a soaking. Have you heard?'

He hadn't, and seemed quite relieved. 'At present I've borrowed a machine from a mechanic friend. I'd bought my own only five days before,' he said dolefully, 'and it almost cleared out my savings account.'

'Since you'd just launched out on your elegant new apartment.'

'Oh that! It's not mine, just rented. It belongs to a colleague who lets me have it at a special rate.' His face took on its mischievous monkey look. 'I understand that his lady friend found a more generous protector. The rooms came free at the right time for my new position.' Which accounted for the almost meretricious style of décor. And the colleague, I was instantly certain, would be Sir Digby himself. How demeaning that his mistress should pass him over for someone superior. Who could that be? – surely a cabinet minister at least! Even a royal?

The snippet of gossip made Jeremy seem immediately more approachable. I found myself confiding that Iggy and Sergeant Bradley had been there that morning, comparing notes with Clive over the Garston case.

'That's what I needed to see him about myself,' he said sombrely. 'There are suspicions I want to put to him, because at last I think I may be on the right track.'

'You must have seen the man running past when you came to help me,' I said. 'Did you recognise him then?'

'It was still dark across the yard,' he said, 'although you were picked out in bright moonlight, a perfect target for him as he came up behind. I had the impression of someone quite tall, moving fast, but not like a young man runs.'

'He was hiding in the hayloft, so must be agile enough to climb up there and jump down. And he seems to make a habit of attack from the rear. That's how Clive was surprised. You examined Durrant's body. Was that the same?'

'That was true of the initial blow. He's a sneaky fellow, right enough.'

That struck me as a mild epithet for a murderer, but I didn't miss the contempt with which it was uttered. Jeremy was sure he knew the man's identity. Would it be one of my suspects?

'Did you ever meet an accountant called Meadows?' I asked him.

He appeared surprised. 'No. Should I have?'

'Or a Baptist minister by the name of Ieuan Roberts?'

Again a negative. I was running out of names. 'Are you going to tell me who it is you've settled on?'

He stood up, nibbling for a moment on the knuckles of one hand. 'I think not. It would be incautious. Mrs Malcolm, do you have any idea where your husband could be at this moment?'

I felt a stab of fear, as much at the suddenness of the question as at the formality of the address. Wasn't I Lucy to him? Why the abrupt change of distance between us? Admitted hostility? And where *was* Clive? Still with the good sergeant, I imagined.

I darted a glance at the clock. They'd been a long while gone. In his present tired state he should have come home by now. 'I don't know,' I stammered. 'Something must have come up to delay him.'

A flash of unease crossed the little man's face. 'I think I'll take a look for him.'

As protection, or to do some further harm? All my doubts about him came flooding back. I couldn't trust him to go alone. 'I'm coming too.'

'Indeed you're not!' His reply snapped out. He was whipcord-taut, no longer the little prancing monkey. I remembered Clive's words describing the likely killer: a man who most of the time can pass for quite normal, but in an instant becomes a demon driven by an obsession, without feeling for what anyone may be made to suffer.

Jeremy had reached the outer door. Mrs Bowyer failed to materialise to let him out and I recalled then that, as she had brought in the tea, she had asked permission to slip out to the Royal Hospital. There was some occasion she was helping the Chelsea Pensioners' committee with. Jeremy, too, would have heard her ask. He knew we were alone in the house.

I stepped back, and in that instant he had seized the key from the front door, slid out and whipped it shut behind him. I heard the mortise lock turned on me. At least shut away I was safe from him here, but would Clive be? I had to get out and go after him.

It would take some minutes to leave the house by the rear and follow. But follow him where?

Clive had to have parted with Sergeant Bradley by now. I must try to recall whether he'd mentioned plans to go on somewhere afterwards. If I couldn't, the only thing left was to ring round to everyone I could think of, and find out where he was.

Twenty-Five

Sergeant Bradley walked Clive along the alley with a guiding hand under his elbow. It was dark and there was débris stacked on the pavement, spilling over into the gutter: wooden crates of empty bottles, paper sacks of evil-smelling refuse, greasy cardboard cartons. Distant sounds of traffic and raised voices reached them from the brightly lit Kingsway, an alien world.

Clive lifted his head and sniffed the local air. 'Any of these buildings,' he said wearily.

'You can't eliminate any?'

'Not really. I think I was in a cellar. I heard footsteps passing now and again above head level. There'd be a grating or something giving on to the outside.'

'You noticed nothing apart from the smells of cooking?'

Clive paused. 'Yes. I remember now. Just once, someone was smoking quite near. I heard the strike of a match, then the scent of a Turkish cigarette. I couldn't call out. My throat wouldn't work. And anyway he might have been the enemy.'

'He wasn't necessarily your abductor; but Turkish tobacco might point us towards the right doorway.'

'In the whole of central London? Why have you picked on this spot, anyway?'

He's tiring, Bradley thought. *I ought to have taken him back home an hour ago. We're getting nowhere.* But he'd had hopes of this alley. It was somewhere here that his man had lost the suspect he was shadowing, a suspect Clive Malcolm had no inkling of because there wasn't enough on him yet to be certain. Just a matter of Bradley's having a nose for the game, and because of a coincidence. Or half-coincidence. When the War Office eventually came up

232

with the information he'd requested, it would be clear one way or the other.

The ex-subaltern he'd managed to trace, now invalided in wretched circumstances in Peckham, had been vague enough, remembering the men of his troop only by nicknames; and they'd been of the routine kind: 'Dusty' Miller, 'Nobby' Clarke, 'Tommy' Atkins. But he'd been able to give thumbnail sketches. His recall of Garston fitted well with the known facts as already supplied by this young doctor. It hadn't accorded with the accusations that had him sent off in disgrace to fight at Suvla. Garston had come over straight as a die, concerned for the horses, and trusted by the regimental vet. Someone must have had confidence in him. Otherwise there'd have been a court martial.

Still, something had to be done about a scandal like the theft of army horses, so the major, whatever his doubts, had acted first and thought later. Who had actually been behind the swindle? The subaltern didn't like to say. There were several theories aired at the time, after Garston had been disposed of.

Had he been aware of any close friends of Garston? Bradley had asked. One by the name of Denny, and another Arthur?

He'd then been reminded stiffly that officers didn't mix socially with the ranks, so how would he know their first names?

'But you'd have noticed how your men associated,' Bradley insisted, himself well aware of relations between the constables under him. 'Was there someone putting undue pressure on rankers like Garston?'

The subaltern had appeared uneasy. 'Bullying, you mean?' He hedged. 'In wartime you value a man who can get the others moving. It's essential.'

'So you turn a blind eye on his peccadilloes, because such a man gets results? I think you had more than an inkling of who was responsible for the crimes Garston was accused of.'

'Look, this is all water under the bridge by now. It was officially dealt with. Garston was removed from the scene and there was no repetition.'

'All the same, someone had made a considerable amount

of money out of the deal. He'd be throwing it around, buying favours, gambling perhaps. You observed this.'

The ex-subaltern turned his palms up. 'All right. There was someone. Not one of the Yeomanry, but he visited our sergeants' mess. Very full of himself. A lot of the Quartermaster's staff were like that, buying their way in with a packet of tea. In civvy life he'd been some kind of actor on the halls. You know the sort, flashy, a show-off, overbearing. None of the others got a look in when he was around. He hung about the veterinary picket at one point. That's when he could have met up with Garston. Eventually I got to thinking he'd set the whole thing up.'

This could be our man, Garston's 'Arthur', Bradley noted. The sergeant had framed him, leaving him with a crippling sense of guilt – for being absent when Cherry and other fit horses were slaughtered for meat – and he'd driven it home harder by accusations over Garston's protective fondness for young Denny.

'Where did this sergeant go after Alexandria?' Bradley had demanded, but it seemed the man had disappeared into the restructuring of land forces at that point, which had been as immeasurable as the shifting Saharan sands. So the subaltern, himself sent to Suvla Bay within a week or so, had never come across the man again.

'Where did the stolen horsemeat end up?' Bradley asked as an afterthought.

'Simply vanished, like the Bedouins used to. One moment there's live horses; next, they're gone. Frankly there wasn't enough evidence to justify any serious inquiry.'

'Who would buy the horsemeat?' Bradley persisted. 'Surely not the Bedouins; they'd steal what they wanted. Egyptian officials? The Army Catering Corps?'

'Possibly.' The ex-subaltern looked uncomfortable. 'Who knows? It was a long time ago.' He paused. 'There were some questions raised about a serious outbreak of food poisoning at the base hospital. Meat past its best, they said, left exposed to the heat. There could have been a connection. But Egypt, in summertime – what would you expect? It happened regularly. Just a lot more Europeans to feed than usual. Gyppy tummy, we used to call it.'

All vague, but suggestive nevertheless. Sergeant Bradley decided to pack it in his pipe and smoke it. Point: a quartermaster sergeant and the hospital at Alexandria. Interesting link, especially since Garston had been sent there sick and later accused of substance abuse; and there were medical implications in the present case.

Bradley hummed to himself. He hadn't let on to Dr Malcolm yet – nor to his own top brass – that someone could fit the bill. Material evidence was still lacking; and no specific connection had yet been found between his suspect and this unsavoury alley they were in at present, which was why he hadn't yet applied for a warrant to search the premises they stood outside.

'Thanks for your time, Dr Malcolm,' he said. 'My driver'll drop me off at the Underground and then take you home.'

'I'm sorry I haven't helped at all. You've been very patient with me.' Stiffly Clive stretched out his injured leg in the rear of the car and closed his eyes. He was barely aware of Bradley getting out at Piccadilly Circus. The car moved off in thinning traffic. Suddenly he came fully awake and leaned forward to rap on the driver's glass screen. When it slid open, he asked for the clinic, giving explicit directions to find it. He sank back gratefully. There were things there he should see to while the place was still empty. Just half an hour, and then he would ring for a car to take him back to Chelsea.

Jeremy Owen, goggled and gauntleted, sped along Sloane Street on the borrowed motorcycle, threading through traffic and cursing the occasional pedestrian who lurched into the roadway in party gear. It was possible that Clive was still roaming central London with the inexhaustible Sergeant Bradley, but the wretched man should surely have seen that the after-effects of his injuries were taking a serious toll of the young doctor's constitution. Clive would be vulnerable to a fresh attack in his present state.

There was just a chance that they had parted company and Clive had stopped off at the clinic to pick up something. However, as Jeremy saw, roaring the bike to a standstill in the small forecourt, there were no lights on. He had never seen it so deserted. Even outside, the almost denuded plane trees stood solitary, with fallen, dried leaves ticking as the wind sent them bowling along on their points.

He straddled the borrowed machine back on to the road, intent on seeing if Clive had tried to contact him at his Bloomsbury rooms or UCH. With the subdued local lighting he failed to notice the dark car drawn up in the shadows of the clinic's rear. The roar of his engine had barely died away from the building when lights began to go on inside.

Had Clive been more alert he might have recognised the crouching figure on the speeding bike that approached and passed the police car; but then, in helmet and goggles, it could have been any young person tearing irresponsibly through the night.

'Are you sure, sir?' the driver said doubtfully, querying the new orders contrary to Sergeant Bradley's.

'I'll manage very well now, thank you. I can ring for a cab to get me home. There are just one or two things I have to sort out while I'm here.'

So no more was said. Clive was duly deposited before the clinic's front door, where he opted not to struggle blindly with a key but rang the bell. The driver saw the door open, a moment's pause, and then Dr Malcolm disappearing inside.

'I'm surprised to find you here,' Clive said. 'How have you been managing?'

'Well enough,' said the other, 'but more to the point, how are you? Specifically, what progress with the eyesight?'

'It's slow. I need an amanuensis, but I'm becoming more mobile.'

'You're looking tired, Dr Malcolm. Very tired. Here, let's use Matron's office where the chairs are more comfortable. I'm going to make you a pot of tea. No, I insist. Sit you down now. I'll be only a wee minute.'

He was fussing, and Clive wished he wouldn't. You'd have thought the man was past middle age, but he knew from his records that he was little more than thirty-seven or so, a bumbling, fidgety man, but well-meaning enough. Not the ideal person to be dealing with the mentally unstable, but perhaps they accepted him as precarious, like themselves. Although Atkinson was qualified only in general medicine, Clive had seen an advantage in taking him on. He preferred to train his staff to his own ways. The newly founded institute had yet to make its name and qualified clinical psychologists could be prickly to work with, confrontational and too keen to branch out in new therapies as yet untried. It had become the pattern ever since Freud had opened up the science. Even now a Kleinian establishment had been set up at the Tavistock Clinic, opposed to the Freudian Institute of Psychoanalysis. Clive's preferred system was based on a rather different discipline: to remove the hysterical symptoms by exposing the cause, but rigorously to avoid any change to the sufferer's personality or attitude to life. To do so was a dangerous practice. Better to go cautiously for empiricism, which Freudian theory notably lacked.

Clive shook his head, aware that his mind was wandering. He wasn't far off sleep. He hoped the tea would arrive before he dropped off completely.

Here the man was again, pulling up a chair opposite and handing over the cup and saucer. 'No milk, I'm afraid. It's gone off, so I've left it black.'

'That will do nicely, thank you.' It tasted horrible, rank and bitter. Clive waited a moment for it to cool and then sipped at it.

'How far did you get with untangling Patrick Garston?' his assistant asked.

'He's retrieved some of his wartime experiences, but from that point onward I'm conscious of being blocked. There's no chance of starting deep therapy yet. It's as though he knows what to expect of me and is wary. I wonder if he has already been the subject of narco-hypnosis elsewhere – whether, in fact, he is still under hypnotic instruction and that is at the base of his amnesia. Certainly the suicide scene was staged, and I suspect now that he was drugged rather than drunk when discovered. It would have been easy to drench his clothes with gin, so that the police looked no further. And by the time we saw him here he had been cleaned up.'

Clive put a hand to his head, which appeared to be moving round of itself. Or else the room was. He was talking too much, almost febrile, and he really needed to rest. To . . . lie . . . down . . . somewhere . . . quiet.

Dr Atkinson watched the man's figure slump, then slowly

237

crumple to the floor. He knelt to pull down a lower eyelid, and examined the pupil. Then he returned to Dr Macolm's office, where he had been sorting papers ready for removal.

I saw the lights go on in Clive's room as I paid off the cab. Thank God I had caught up with him. There was no sign of Jeremy or his motorbike. I ran up the three shallow steps to the front door and rapped on one of the glass panels. Nobody answered, but after a moment I felt I was being watched from inside, turned to the nearest unlit window and waved.

The door was being unlocked. Dr Atkinson stood there, drooping and bumbling as ever, fiddling to put his spectacles back on his nose. 'Ah, Mrs Malcolm. What are you doing here so late at night?'

'I've called for my husband, Dr Atkinson. It's more than time he gave up working and came home. He's still in a very weak state.' It came out like a rebuke.

'Indeed, Mrs Malcolm. I would agree.' He gave me a slithery sort of smile. Tonight there seemed something of the reptile about him.

'He's just left. I fear you must have crossed with him on the way here.'

'But I just saw his lights go on.'

He considered me for a moment. 'That would be when I took some reports in. I have a duplicate key, you know. But come in and satisfy yourself he's not here. I'll be off home myself in a few minutes.'

That sounded like 'come in' and 'stay away' at the same time. I wondered what he had been up to in Clive's room, so I walked in and looked around. Apart from the desk's drawers being open and a wad of papers left on the top, there was nothing unusual. So perhaps I had indeed missed Clive on the way here. He must have been very tired to leave the office so untidy. Yet something else made me uneasy. It was to do with the doctor himself. Why should I think he was lying?

I reached for the day book, which lay open on the desk. Clive hadn't signed in since the day he'd gone missing. 'How long was he here?' I asked.

'Barely five minutes.'

As I turned to leave, he seemed to edge towards me, ensuring

I didn't go farther along the corridor. On an impulse I stepped past him, making for the lights in Matron's office. What had he been doing there, and why was the man in the building at all when there were no patients to look after?

The door was slightly ajar. I pushed it and stepped in, almost on to an outstretched hand. Clive was lying there, half on his face. 'Here, help me to turn him,' I cried.

'Don't touch him. It's a seizure,' the doctor snapped at me. 'I was about to treat him when you called me to the door.'

And wasted time talking, to send me away? I turned on him in anger.

He took a step closer, fiddled with the chain of his pince-nez and removed his glasses. I remembered seeing his eyes uncovered once before. They were a strange sort of pale silver, almost white, with pinpoint black centres. As he came closer, these seemed to grow larger. He was speaking in a whisper now and I had to concentrate to make out the words.

'You will sit down. Over there.' His eyes were enormous, compelling. The drone of his voice came from far away. I felt his arm guiding me and I had to go with him, stepping over the inert figure on the floor.

Something stopped me. I looked down. Was that Clive? Why was he sleeping here on the floor? He should be at home. I tried to cry out to wake him, but the man's fingers were hard on my arm.

I was seated now, with him facing me, leaning close. 'It will soon be over,' he promised gently, and his grey-streaked, sandy beard opened to show a gash of red mouth with distorted, yellowish teeth. I had never known him smile so before. It was fearsome, but I was powerless to move away.

Then I felt a prick on my bare arm, saw the tiny red puncture there between his finger and thumb and, unaccountably, my jacket discarded on the floor, which seemed to be miles away. I was floating higher, floating free.

Momentarily we were back in Dan's barn and I gripped desperately hard on his gun with the single shot left. There was a rustle in the straw above me and the man stepped from the hayloft on to the ladder. I heard the rungs take his weight, thud, thud, thud, like the beat of my heart. It was the same man.

Dimly I seemed to hear a motorcycle roaring into the yard.

Jeremy running towards me. Now I was between the two of them, with only one shot to save me.

I felt the great weight land on my back. As I crumpled, the gun went off in my hands.

No hope left. Nothing.

Twenty-Six

O ur roles were reversed. This time it was Clive hovering
anxiously over my bed and me opening my eyes, unaware
what had happened. Then abruptly the terrifying scene swept
back.

'I'm not dead then?' I managed to croak out.

'Thanks to your knight in shining armour,' Clive said
with heartfelt relief. 'Though that's certainly what Atkinson
intended. It was a lethal dose he started giving you, but Jeremy
got to you in time.'

I could barely follow what he said. 'Jeremy?' Jeremy my
rescuer? At Dan's barn perhaps. So had I only dreamed what
had happened since?

'I'm not thinking straight,' I said. 'I thought I was at
the clinic.'

'You were,' he said, 'but never mind now. Go back to sleep.
There'll be time enough later for explanations.'

I made a desperate effort to clear my mind. 'Are you all
right?' I asked him. 'I saw you in Matron's room, on the
floor. You were hurt. Then I heard Jeremy's motorbike. But
I couldn't have. It's in Black Pond, isn't it?'

'You were passing out. What you heard was Sergeant
Bradley arriving by car, with his bell clanging full blast. And
then the clinic door being broken down.'

Clive assured me he'd never felt better in his life, and despite
his appearance I must have believed him, because I almost
instantly fell asleep and didn't reawaken until next day.

Then it was that they told me, he and Jeremy taking turns
with the story. Clive had been dropped off at the clinic after
his outing with the sergeant. Working on the medical angle,
Jeremy had already decided that Dr Stanley Atkinson was
showing too much interest in where the Garston family were

hiding; and perhaps there had been something familiar about the dim figure escaping from Dan's barn – which was why he'd locked me in at home, adamant that I shouldn't run any further risks while he checked whether Clive had returned to the clinic.

When he'd found the building in darkness, he had gone on to Scotland Yard, crossing with Clive on the way. Sergeant Bradley had been on the point of leaving, having just received by special messenger the report he'd expected from the War Office. He assured Jeremy that Clive had been driven home. However, just then his driver returned to explain that Dr Malcolm had insisted on being dropped off at the clinic, had rung at the door and been let in.

The chances were that the only person there at the time was Dr Atkinson, since Matron had gone on two days' leave to her elderly mother in Cambridge; and he was the suspect both were now sure was the man behind the attacks.

Bradley had ordered them all out to the car. They had roared off like cavalry to the rescue, with the police bell clanging, and arrived in time to resuscitate Clive from the morphine dose in his tea.

'Your condition was more serious,' Clive said sombrely. 'The injection had been meant to kill. By then Atkinson was getting desperate, and a second unconscious body on his hands would have been more difficult to deal with than a corpse neatly dropped in the Thames.'

'He'd had more than enough of my interference,' I guessed.

'This is all my fault, dragging you into these dangers,' Clive groaned. 'I'd meant to give you real security after the dreadful experiences you'd been through.'

I remembered then how Bishop Malcolm had cautioned me about expecting much the same. 'But marriage should be an adventure,' I couldn't help repeating. 'And it is. I'm glad. I just wish I'd worked out the mystery as Jeremy and Sergeant Bradley did. I had much the same facts to go on. So how did they reach their conclusions?'

It was a long story, putting together all the loose ends. Just in time the information on 'Tommy' (actually Arthur) Atkins had arrived from the War Office. An NCO with the quartermaster's stores at the time of the regiment's arrival in

Egypt, he had remained at Alexandria for almost a year after Garston's departure. Then he had contracted a fever, later diagnosed as encephalitis, from which he had barely survived. Eventually he had been returned to England and demobilised, physically a much frailer man.

'It was during his stay in the hospital at Alexandria that he must have encountered a Dr Stanley Atkinson of the Royal Army Medical Corps,' Jeremy said, 'and when the doctor was killed in a motoring accident outside Cairo, it seemed to him providential. Perhaps the similarity of the two surnames suggested it, but shortly after Arthur Atkins returned to Blighty, our 'Dr Atkinson' appeared in London with a full set of credentials stolen from the dead man's effects.'

'So he wasn't a doctor at all?' I asked, amazed.

'He wasn't by any means a stupid man. He used his time as a patient to study how the medicos behaved, and he'd always had confidence as a conjuror. Once he'd availed himself of the necessary documents he was free to bluff his way.'

'Small wonder he preferred following instructions instead of taking the initiative,' Clive put in wryly. 'I was fooled, believing it was only psychology he was new to. My patients were terribly at risk.'

'In fact,' Jeremy explained, 'as Sergeant Bradley discovered from an ex-officer of Garston's, Atkins had earlier worked the music halls, as an illusionist and knife-throwing artiste, until he seriously injured his female assistant; but he'd also some reputation as a stage hypnotist, which is probably why he took such an interest in Clive's line of business. He hoped eventually to set up as a doctor for mentally disturbed patients, but beginning by picking up the elements of general practice in charity work. Then, out of the blue, Patrick Garston happened along to an East End clinic and the deception was at risk of being exposed.'

'At the Saturday children's surgery,' I whispered.

'That was all he could get at first, until he'd worked himself into the part, learning from his own mistakes and secondhand books on anatomy and phyisiology,' Jeremy explained. 'Once I started to see him as a suspect, I asked questions of colleagues at the centre, who'd found his work unimpressive.'

'And did Patrick Garston recognise him?' I asked.

243

'Apparently not,' Clive said. 'Encephalitis can completely change a person's body and personality; and besides losing weight he had grown a beard. Yet the fear of being discovered grew on him, became an obsession overriding all reason. He used hypnosis on Garston to ensure a blacking-out of memories of their wartime association in Egypt, but it didn't quite work. Other repressed memories were provoked and the sense of guilt returned. Patrick began to show symptoms of mental disturbance, and that was when he was first brought to my notice. You can imagine Atkinson's horror when he found I was treating him as an out-patient, hoping to uncover the traumatic past. That was when he decided Garston must be eliminated. He couldn't risk losing his new profitable career.'

Now they had reached a part of the story where I'd done more than just get in the way. I had been right about the killer's part in the apparent suicide attempt. I could see now how Atkinson had used a combination of drugs and hypnosis to overcome his will and deaden resistance. But how wrong I'd been in picking poor Jeremy as villain of the piece. Dr Stanley Atkinson had been so negative that I'd never considered him at all.

'He'd prepared the noose in advance,' Clive said.

'The left-handed noose,' I remembered.

'Yes. I'd never observed that Atkinson was left-handed, because as a stage illusionist and conjuror he was almost ambidextrous; but Sergeant Bradley caught him out at the police station by throwing an enamel mug at his face. It was totally unexpected and Atkinson shot out his left hand to catch it.

'The sergeant explained what we'd found out about the noose and that was when he knew the game was up. He started raving and had to be restrained. It was more boasting than confession, but everything began to come out: how when Garston had been admitted to the men's ward he still used his sinister influence to strengthen the man's amnesia and resistance to therapy. Also how he'd followed Jeremy out to Durrant's lodgings on the second occasion, having overheard our discussion at the clinic about a witness from outside Garston's house. He'd known the man had seen him drive away, a patient at one of the East End surgeries, who might have recognised his car.'

'And did he admit he had tried to kill you, Clive?'

'Was furious that I'd survived. It must have driven him finally over the edge of reason. You were right, Lucy, when you saw the killer as pressed for time. He'd known I was heading for the prison that evening because I rang the clinic from a restaurant on my way. As soon as he came off duty he drove there and waited for me to come out, chose a dark point for his attack and struck me down from behind. We still don't know exactly where I was kept overnight, but he worked through next day normally as a sort of alibi, intending to finish me off during his two-hour supper break.'

'And that was him in Dan's barn, after he'd knifed the two dogs?'

'He was frantic by then to finish Garston off, and didn't care what risks he took.'

'But Patrick's safe now. He'll be all right, won't he?'

'We'll have one or two more talks together. Guilt is a complex thing and takes some unwinding. There's the Hardwick and Meadows factor too: he bitterly regrets being a party, however small a pawn, in their cruel money-lending operations – which was why he took the less well paid post at the soap factory. He's a good man, Lucy, and never deserved all that's happened to him.'

'Until now. Everything's going to be better in future.'

'We'll see that it is.' He lifted my hand and kissed it. 'You must rest again now, Lucy. Tomorrow I'll come and take you home.'

I watched him tap his way to the door with his white stick, and tears oozed out under my eyelids until they grew heavy with sleep.

For all that I was tired I stayed awake a while, thinking of all the intricate deceptions of the man we'd known as Stanley Atkinson, once the rapacious, bullying sergeant who'd made a small fortune, and almost ruined Garston's life, over the horses swindle. He'd become this meek, rather creepy character I'd met, outwardly kindly, blinking nervously behind clumsy spectacles, and ready to kill rather than have his false identity revealed. So in a way I had been right that the criminal's motive was to protect his public face. That and greed, of course.

But he'd failed, and now must pay for the one murder he'd succeeded in, the bludgeoning to death of Alan Durrant, the witness whose testimony might have prevented the later attacks on Clive and Dan and me.

By that point I heard myself grunt, and knew I was asleep.

Over the next few days, having returned home, I was obliged to take life slowly and had time to consider the helter-skelter activity of the previous few weeks. Jeremy came to call and somehow we had made a new start, as friends. It was sealed when I ventured to ask him why Clive had required his help with the mystery patient at Claridge's.

'It needn't bother you,' he said perceptively. 'It was a drugs overdose, but he managed it alone in the end. The young woman was a private patient he was treating for depression, so he was anxious.'

'I see.' I thought I'd gathered more than he had actually said.

'And as you've guessed, she was known to you, which accounted for the discretion.'

I nodded: Selina, of course. And it had been a semi-professional meeting at Gianni's – not a lovers' tryst.

'You saw them,' I accused him, 'in the mirror, and you pretended you hadn't.'

He said nothing, but gave me his monkey-face grin.

In my mind I apologised to the others, besides Jeremy, whom I'd thought of as suspects. Ruefully, I was yet to make up to them in part. There remained the portrait that I must paint of Meadows, the pompous and unscrupulous accountant. I was resolved he wouldn't care for the finished effort.

Then there was Mr Miles of the soap factory: must I perhaps seek a second interview with him and try to get Garston's job back? I hoped not. If Ethel found the country as appealing as the little girls and Patrick did, then it shouldn't be hard to find permanent employment for him locally. Helping out Dan perhaps, for a start, handling the horses. Eventually, when Garston was quite cured, there would be vacancies at

Stakerleys' stables, because however many motors Papa had he would always keep hunters and carriages too.

So at least one good thing had resulted from the sorry story; and then there was Mabel's future to consider. I hoped Jenkins would accept the position of chauffeur-handyman which I meant to offer him. Having another man about the house would be a distinct advantage, since Clive's practice had proved such a dangerous one – which reminded me that I hadn't explained why at any moment Clive would discover that part of the garden wall had been breached. I had yet to sell him the idea of having our own car. I hoped I'd be as persuasive a manipulator over that as Jeremy thought me.

This brought me again to consider my husband's little friend, and mine too by now. When Clive arrived to bring me home from hospital, I admitted how badly I felt about my misjudgement of Jeremy. 'Twice he saved my life – my knight errant, as you said. But there's always been such an awkwardness between us, and that's my fault entirely. I was stand-offish and really drove him to dislike me.'

'An awkwardness,' Clive had repeated ruefully. 'There's perhaps a reason for that which you don't realise. He wouldn't have me tell you, but I think I must, to put you straight. You see, Lucy, he confessed to me from the start that he was strongly attracted to you. Because he was my friend and his position was impossible, he was forced on the defensive, avoiding contact. But it means the world to him to have been of service to you. I know you will be discreet about this and treat him kindly.'

I found it hard to believe, and yet it explained so much. I knew now why Clive had opposed my foisting a suitable partner on him; and yet eventually why not? Since he was susceptible to women, there must somewhere be one who could some day fit his requirements.

In the event, the new garage announced itself to Clive before I took the plunge, and a visit from the bishop was accompanied by his gift of a splendid little blue Morris Cowley with a folding rainproof roof. At that point I dared to put forward my suggestion about Mabel's chauffeur friend. My husband, already worked upon by the others, was sufficiently impressed to interview the man himself and offer him the post.

So it was that on a foggy mid-November morning Clive and I set off in state on a short and belated honeymoon, bound for a delightful suite, with sea view and balcony, at the Grand Hotel, Torquay. Jenkins was to return next day to Chelsea to transport Mrs Bowyer, Mabel, Petra, himself and all the baby impedimenta to a cosy boarding house just a few minutes' away.

As the porter unstrapped our luggage for the maid to unpack, Clive reached in and produced a small, roughly wrapped package. 'For Petra,' he said, 'from Iggy.'

I pulled the tissue paper off and exposed a mechanical giraffe. A tin one! I pictured her soft little gums closing on the sharp protrusions.

'It took his eye on a street-market stall,' said Clive ruefully.

'I shouldn't care for Petra to handle it,' I said. 'We'll find a high shelf in the nursery to leave it on show. It was so kind of him to think of her, Clive.'

He grinned. 'Well-intentioned. That's Iggy to a T.'

Along the south coast the weather turned unseasonably mild and sunny. Utter bliss. At last things seemed to be settling favourably for us. Clive enjoyed taking walks unaided along the sands and promenade. Every day his sight was improving. In ten days' time, when we should return to our London routine, there would be a new, qualified resident to assist him at the clinic.

I wondered, though, just how uneventful life would be in future. When stones are upturned, strange creatures can be found lurking there. It's much the same, I was learning, when anyone dares to plumb the human mind.